# The Makeover

# The Makeover

by

## Marcia Biederman

ACADEMY
CHICAGO

Published in 1986 by
Academy Chicago Publishers
425 North Michigan Avenue
Chicago, IL 60611

Copyright © 1984 by Marcia Biederman

Printed and bound in the USA

ISBN 0-89733-226-1

# One

Muriel hurried down the staircase toward the checkpoint, uncomfortably aware that inside the bag on her shoulder were several malodorous, sickly white sheets of paper—the kind of copies produced by an ersatz Xerox machine. The Foundation had told her over the phone that she would have to take photocopies: her testimony would have to be substantiated by documents. They said she had better get herself a big purse to carry them in.

So she had gone out and bought this big straw handbag at Cost Plus; the open weave kind that could be worn on the shoulder even though the handle was rather short. It wasn't stylish—not that Muriel really dressed in style. But with the aid of this airy purse, she hoped that her evidence would do all those things they told her it had to do: it would "Hold Water, Carry Weight, Have Bearing."

It probably would help, too, if she had been able to use a better copy machine. The copies would be clearer, and probably a good machine would make less noise. The top of this one moved as it ran, emitting loud squeaks which could be heard throughout the entire International Division. And its light was like a flashbulb popping in the operator's guilty face.

Muriel and three other secretaries neared the penultimate checkpoint in the dark corridor where the Lovell Munitions security guard stood at his post. The guard should have been intimidating, but the Lovell Company had little sense of theatre: he was a friendly man in an ill-fitting polyester uniform which bagged at the knees. Muriel, a movie buff, thought of the dreaded Germans in *Alexander Nevsky:* this guard should have been wearing a metal helmet with a sculpted human hand on its crest. True, he was carrying a gun, but Americans are used to guns. In fact, the three secretaries walking with Muriel did not pay any attention to him until he called out, "Have a good weekend, girls, and behave yourselves." Since this Friday was special for him, he added, 'I won't be seeing you for a couple of weeks. I'm off for a little fishing trip up north." The secretaries, intent on beginning their own weekends, chorused "Have a good time," and hurried on to the company-owned street and parking lot.

Muriel wondered if the guard's substitute would take his job seriously and stop her at the checkpoint on Monday. Would her large handbag arouse his suspicions? But no—to the Lovell guards all the secretaries seemed to be simply a blur of skirts and gabardine pantsuits that made swishing noises. Muriel had been asked for her blue plastic ID card only on her first day of work, six months ago, and never again since. A handbag search? Never. Handbags were part of the female anatomy.

At the door Muriel paused. She felt a sudden need to be brave and reckless, to call attention to herself. She cried out to the guard in a cheery Greer Garson voice, "Well! I won't be seeing you for quite a while then. My own vacation starts week after next." A loud pulsebeat later, she added, "Have a wonderful time."

"You too, sweetheart," he called back to her, whoever she was (one of the sweethearts). Muriel waved and pushed the glass door open. A gust of cool air flattened her dress against her thin thighs. She buttoned her coat and went on; she had fallen behind the others. It was obviously true what they had said at the Foundation for Investigative Reporting—nobody's going to suspect a secretary. They had said that at the Foundation, and also at COCOA, Contra Costa Office Activists. The COCOAS had listened to her vague anxious tale over the phone—she had said it was something that was happening to a friend of hers—and advised her that if her "friend" worked in South San Francisco she could call the San Francisco office workers group. Then they had asked her if she had time to come over and stuff some envelopes.

At the gate she yelled farewells to Francine and Sharon, who were heading toward the north parking lot. Their responses were lost in the wind. Muriel clutched the straw handbag against her body and hurried onward on her damned high heels to the last checkpoint, the one for pedestrians only. (The parking lots had their own garrisons.) The bored guards were listening to the radio in their little kiosk; they hardly looked at her as she passed them. The streams of production workers had gone hours before and few office workers came this way to take the bus.

The sound of the radio faded behind her, and was replaced by the pleasant bell-like pinging of wire against concrete: the sound made by coils of barbed wire blowing intermittently against hastily constructed walls. The Lovell Munitions Company had made this neighborhood into a South San Francisco Berlin: Lovell Street was private and city traffic was routed around it. Children wore themselves out, forced to circle the complex on their bicycles in order to visit their friends on the other side. Lunch counters and sundry shops, their customers cut off, had rapidly lost business and were now boarded up.

The mayor had given the road to the Company in order to buy them off when they had threatened to move out of the city. Now Management had explained that the factory had to be isolated so that necessary repairs and improvements could be made to the antiquated buildings. But several months had passed, and Muriel had seen no changes made in the offices or the factories. Everything looked the same.

Lovell stood barricaded against invasion from without, but it had been attacked from within. A few months before this breezy Friday, Federal investigators had turned up in the offices of International Sales to ask a few questions. That was when Mr. Baziotis had told Muriel to start taking his files on South Africa down to the paper shredder.

*   *   *

The bus to the BART station churned the passengers on their taped-up seats. Outside the filthy windows the sun appeared to be shining. The bus passed doughnut shops and dime stores, their signs painted in squat gothic typefaces with widely spaced letters, like the chapter headings of old math books. People with Midwestern faces were pinching fruit outside small grocery stores or waiting on seats in the windows of laundromats for the spin lights to go off. Her brother Bernie called them dustbowl people. He was a man who felt alienated from others—possibly the result of growing up Jewish in Los Angeles. Muriel imagined Bernie standing before his bathroom mirror, wishing he had that dustbowl look.

At the BART station, Muriel stood aside from the crush of passengers, searching in the straw bag for her electronic ticket. She found a strip, tore one off, and poked the rest back into the bag. Muriel was an orderly young woman and this search for the ticket did not disarrange the photocopies, which were neatly arranged around her wallet and hairbrush.

The BART, working well today, hurtled Muriel quickly to Walnut Creek where she lived on the ground floor of a small house on a street of lawns and silent neighbors, a fifteen minute walk from the station. The top floor of the house she lived in was rented to some computer programmers—men of regular habits. The only difficulty with them was their quantity—the house seemed to overflow with them. Muriel's roommate Dennis said that they had been hired by a Lafayette electronics firm to fill in for employees who were on strike. Muriel had no opinion about that. The programmers were no bother except when they all decided to walk around upstairs at the same time. But since Muriel had trouble sleeping even when it was quiet, she didn't think much about them.

Dennis's cat Pennsy was curled on the concrete stoop, asleep at the edge of a sunbeam. It was almost six o'clock, but the sun was shining on this side of the Bay much more brightly than in the city. The weather was one of Muriel's main justifications for living in dull Walnut Creek. She had told Bernie that there was wild animal life there. And she had heard that several deer had been killed by the BART trains, although she had never seen a deer herself.

"I'm home," she called, hastening to the bathroom. Dennis did not answer. She could hear his model trains running behind his closed door. Proceeding to her bedroom, she kicked off her high heels, yanked off her dress and bra and slipped into an old cotton. Off with the office clothes. She thrust her feet into rubber thong sandals. They were cheap and not very comfortable but Muriel spent most of her meagre salary on a "correct" wardrobe for work and had to improvise loungewear.

Sitting on her bed, she pulled the papers out of her bag. Damn. They had come out really light today. Bernie had said something about making copies of copies—something about legal protection to prevent the company from proving that she had been using their equipment without permission. These looked too faint to reproduce a second time. Anxiously she fanned the papers out over her green chenille bedspread, trying to evaluate them as evidence.

Of the nine documents, only one looked promising. In retrospect it had obviously not been worth the risk to copy the others while Randrup's secretary was in the same room shredding the contents of an entire file cabinet. Muriel had stood there watching the photocopier's dream-like sliding action, and listening to the paper shredder whir, efficiently destroying evidence that the Lovell Company was promoting "shoots" in South Africa with illegally exported U.S. guns. The shredder contents were emptied into plastic bags and left in a utility room for any employee who wanted to stuff a rag doll or a bean-bag chair.

The only worthwhile copy seemed to be a memo from one of her bosses, Jules Baziotis, to his superior the Vice President of Sales, requesting approval for a trip to Johannesburg. Object: "to meet with the local agent re sales development."

Muriel glanced at the clock. Six-thirty. Bernie would be home now, between office and date. She picked up the photocopies and padded into the kitchen, where the sticky linoleum tried to pull her sandals off. Why didn't Dennis ever clean anything? He had plenty of free time. She dialed

Bernie's number and stretched the curly cord of the wall phone closer to the window where the light was better.

"Hi, Bernie. It's me. Now do you really think it's safe to discuss this case over the telephone?"

"Listen, Muriel, I told you nobody cares about this. You've been watching too many James Bond movies. Your phone is not being tapped over something this inconsequential."

Muriel was incensed. "What do you mean, too many James Bond movies? This is your sister Muriel, dear, remember? I'm not one of your rich hip drug clients."

She was used to Bernie's patronizing attitude. He was her older brother and he always belittled everything she did. But to use movies to insult her was going too far. She and he had shared a love of movies as far back as she could remember. They had watched *Yankee Doodle Dandy* together forty-seven times on television. They disliked all American films produced since 1960. There were a few exceptions, but the James Bond movies were not among them.

"Okay, okay," Bernie said. "Now what is this call about, Muriel? I haven't got much time."

He was sounding more lawyerly by the second. Maybe his guest was already in his apartment, puttering around in the kitchen, knocking together a salad. What did Dennis call them? Singing swingles.

"Well," Muriel began, "today is Friday—"

"Yeah, yeah, it's Friday. That I know. Thank God it's Friday, thank God, thank God. So?"

"So next week is my last week before my vacation. So, Bernie," she began to speak with more confidence, "I have spent yesterday and today xeroxing incriminating evidence from the Lovell Munitions Company files, as requested by the Foundation for Investigative Reporting. You remember me now, don't you? Your little sister Muriel, the one who is going to get a big check any day now from this well-known foundation, directed by the likes of Jack Anderson?"

Which reminded her. The mail was on the kitchen table and the check hadn't come yet.

"Oh, God," Bernie said. "I haven't picked up my jacket from the cleaners yet and she's giving me a scene from *The Front Page.*" He dialed loudly in her ear and sank his voice into a hard-boiled growl. "'Hello, sweetheart, give me rewrite.' So what did you come up with in the way of xeroxes?" he asked, in normal tones.

She told him about the memo. As usual his reaction was skeptical and professional. "But you have no evidence that this request to go to South Africa was granted. Correct?"

"No, Bernie, but see, this memo gives me a date. I can look for follow-up correspondence. Or maybe evidence in Accounts Payable somewhere."

Muriel did not know much about how the Company worked, outside of her immediate department. This had been the case in all her jobs in the five years that she had been doing office work. At Lovell she had taken little interest in the complete picture until the Federal investigators had turned up and an atmosphere of panic had filtered through the plant. In a couple of lunchtime conversations Muriel had learned what the more experienced employees had known for years: the International Sales Department sold arms to an agent in Johannesburg.

Everyone at every level of responsibility knew this, and they knew it was illegal. They knew also that this illegal traffic helped pay their frequent raises and provide pleasant working conditions for them. Frances and Sharon and the woman with frosted hair from Customer Service and the secretary to the Asian Sales Manager who wore her glasses around her neck on a cord . . . these women did not know much about South Africa, but they knew there was a law against selling arms there. That was something Muriel had not known; she was surprised to hear it. Bernie did not know anything about it, either, and he had no time to research it. He sent Muriel to the Boalt Hall Library, where the indexes confused her. Finally she called Washington, D.C., long-distance and the State Department told her the law was 22 USC 2776. She went back to the Library, found the U.S. Code and photocopied 22/2276.

That was the first of many photocopies. Francine and Sharon and some of the others were worried; they confided in Muriel over lunch and coffee. They confided in her because they thought she was their friend. Little did they know she was running back to her desk afterward to write it all down on a steno pad. "Take contemporaneous notes," Bernie had said. It was simple for him: he didn't have to face these people whose lives were on the line, who had implicated themselves for the sake of a ten percent raise. And now even this meaty travel expense memo wasn't enough for him. He wanted proof that it had been approved.

Muriel drifted back to the kitchen table, relaxing the strain on the telephone cord. She wet a fingertip and began to pick up cornflakes from the table top: souvenirs of Dennis's breakfast. "I think maybe this memo is good enough to show that the salesman went to Joburg," she said. "I know there are a lot of other things to prove, but . . . the Foundation told me that this isn't really like a legal case. The Feds are in Lovell already. What I have to do is publicize the whole story, show how many people were involved, how elaborate the scheme was. This will help put public pressure on the grand jury to hand in an indictment instead of sweeping it all under the rug."

"Now don't get defensive just because I'm pointing out

that there are holes in your argument. If you're going to do something, do it right." Bernie was playing patriarch now. "I don't know if I agree with your Foundation about everything they say, but at least they finally persuaded you to stop farting around and start carrying evidence out of the plant. You did put all the originals back where you found them, didn't you?"

"Of course," she snapped, distracted from her cornflake picking. "I'm not suicidal."

"All right," Bernie said. "Now back to the travel memo. You're sure your boss actually went there?"

"One of my two bosses went there. The Manager of Sales to Africa. The other guy I work for handles Latin American Sales. He's the Argentinian I told you about. He took care of the trans-shipment plan. See, they sent the guns to somewhere in Mexico first. That was supposed to be their ultimate destination. You know about export licenses, right?"

"No, I honestly don't. That's not my field, Muriel. What are these licenses again?" His tone was bored. He had been forgetting everything she told him ever since she had retained him as free-legal-counsel-cum-wet-blanket. It was surprising that Bernie knew nothing about international law— not even things that she herself had picked up at Lovell.

"Don't you have to know stuff about drug shipments coming to the U.S.? Isn't that the kind of thing your rich clients are involved in?"

"That's imports, not exports. Anyway, Sanford takes care of that kind of thing when it comes up. I'm strictly into criminal. Listen, the other day one of my clients asked me something about taxes. I had to put him on hold and run into the law clerk's office to look it up in a little book called *Tax in a Nutshell*. I swear to God."

"Well, the State Department has to issue export licenses

before things are shipped out of the country. Maybe it only applies to guns. The Commerce Department comes in somewhere . . ." She stopped, uncertain. Bernie remained silent. "Anyway, there's this space on the export license application where you have to write in 'destination of goods'. That means final destination. So the export license clerks write in 'Mexico' for all these guns that are really going to end up in South Africa. I told you, this has been going on for five years."

"But the guns did actually go to Mexico, right?"

"Yes, but only so they could be converted there from sporting arms to military rifles. Then they were packed right up again and sent to South Africa. To a dealer named Tyson. A woman."

"And she's the one that your boss went to see, supposedly. What year was that?"

Muriel glanced at the memo. "The trip was taken last December. Bernie, I know he really went. He talked about South Africa all the time; he said he wanted to move there, but his wife wouldn't hear of it. Boy, he'd love to have a whole fleet of black servants to push around. It would be his idea of paradise."

Bernie ignored this. "But you still haven't found any records of the sales to South Africa for that year?"

"That's what's stumping me. The Foundation is really pushing me to get those figures. It's no problem to get your hands on one of those sales charts—they're all over the place. But the sales to Mexico add up to peanuts. Just a few thousand dollars worth of hunting equipment."

"Those illegal sales wouldn't show up in the African Manager's charts?"

"Naturally not. The only sales to South Africa shown are a few hundred dollars' worth of kiln gun sales; they use them to set off explosions in furnaces or something. So it's legal to sell them there. But Mexican sales don't show up at all—I don't even know how they were paid for."

"You've got a problem." Bernie was beginning to lose interest. "So what else did you turn up?"

"Well, yesterday I realized about the warranty cards. You know those cards you send in when you buy a watch or a toaster? Well, I think they left them in the packing boxes even after the guns were converted in Mexico. Although . . ." her voice faded. Why was she always uncovering evidence that worked against her case? "I don't know why individuals would be buying converted guns. They would be military or paramilitary . . . Anyhow, when the South Africans bought these Lovell guns, they actually sent in the warranty cards, and filled in their addresses."

"That's great!" Bernie sounded excited. "You mean you have warranty cards with 'Jan van Vloop-de-Vloop' written on them? That proves they have the guns."

"Yeah? You really think so? I copied the warranty cards just to show that all the executives had seen evidence that the guns were in South Africa. See, the consumers send in these cards to our general mailing address . . . Bernie, are you still there?"

Bernie replied that the drycleaners were going to close before he could pick up his jacket. On the following Friday he would pick her up at Lovell and they would see a movie and maybe go out afterward for a drink. "We'll find some nice place to unwind from the work week," he said.

Muriel hung up and stared blankly at the papers on the table before her. Working on the investigation at home was like never leaving the office. The privacy of her kitchen was invaded by the Sales Division, by her two bosses: Pagano, the small-boned, gentle Argentinian with the Italian name, and Baziotis, the buffoon. And the damn Foundation had promised her five hundred lousy dollars to pay for all this work.

She shuffled back into her bedroom and jammed the copies into her bureau drawer. On her way to the kitchen to fix herself a drink, she heard Dennis's trains rolling to a stop. The door burst open and he hailed her, smiling. He was wearing his glasses, to give his eyes a rest from his contact lenses. How could someone with coke-bottle glasses construct miniatures with such amazing accuracy?

"So what did your brother say? I came out to pee and heard part of your conversation. What's this about a travel memo?"

"Oh, I'd just as soon not go over it again, Dennis. It's nothing spectacular, I guess. Naturally Bernie pooh-poohed everything I had to say. Also, the check didn't arrive from Washington."

"So I noticed." Dennis followed her into the kitchen. Muriel mixed two drinks and they settled down under the ugly fluorescent kitchen light. Relaxing in the company of her best friend, she began to feel hungry. "Do we have anything for dinner?"

Dennis opened the refrigerator door and hung on it for a while. Muriel noted the passage of time. "Take something out or close the door, Dennis. Our PG&E bill is high enough already."

This meant very little to Dennis; his days stretched out lazily before him with nothing in them but model railroading. Muriel felt cross; she was tired of taking over for him.

"Okay," he announced. "It's going to be some soup left over from last weekend, and scrambled eggs. I didn't make it to the Safeway."

Dennis rarely left the house. He had dropped out of an engineering program at Cal and was trying to decide whether he should re-enter. Meanwhile modest dividends from stocks, gifts given to him over the years by prosperous relatives, kept him supplied with money for railroad track and accessories.

Muriel stared at him wearily over her bourbon glass. "You look all fuzzy," she said. "You're not real."

Who had said that? The woman with eczema talking to the minister, her ex-lover, who had rejected her in *Winter Light*. A Bergmann film. This wasn't a very good way to start the evening.

"I'm going to buy a Mexican engine from the hobby shop," Dennis said. The eggs sputtered angrily in the frying pan. He had the gas turned up too high. "What it is, exactly, is a standard locomotive, but I've been researching the paint job and the markings. I'm going to paint it like a Mexican Railways engine." Muriel started. Had she told Dennis about her plans, projected far into the future, to travel to Mexico when the trans-shipment point was finally discovered? After a moment of panic she relaxed. Dennis had Mexico on the brain because of his recent obsession with Karl, an old lover of his who was studying medicine in Guadalajara.

"They're really neat trains—you've ridden on them, haven't you? I would love to go visit Karl, just for the train ride. You can still get sleeping berths for practically nothing. Is that how you went? But maybe he doesn't even remember me. He's probably too busy to show me around, but I could just go and come back . . . Standard gauge, that's what I'm interested in. Do they have model railroad clubs down there, do you think?

He began to ladle out the overcooked eggs.

"You know I don't pay attention to stuff like that, Dennis. Anyway, I really don't remember much about Mexico. It was long ago and far away."

It was too bad that she couldn't be frank with Dennis. But it was bad enough that he knew she was going to Salinas next week. If someone called and asked for her, would he remember to lie? Because she had told everyone at work that she was going to L.A. to visit her parents. When time came for the big trip to Mexico, she would tell no one. That's what the people at the Foundation had said. Always helpful with suggestions.

"This Farcreels de Mexico paint job is really exciting," Dennis said. He had already said it several times over dinner; Muriel finally felt she had to correct him. "Not Farcreels, Dennis, Fer-ro-car-ril-es."

"Okay, whatever it is." He had great news: browsing at the hobby shop, he had met one of the computer programmers who lived upstairs and they were going to play trains together. Muriel, preoccupied with free-floating anxiety, felt dimly pleased that Dennis was happy.

After dinner she looked in vain for some paper so that she could make her list. Finally in a fit of bad temper, she tore a film program off the bulletin board, stubbing her toe in the process. Pouring out more bourbon as an anesthetic, she took her glass and the film program into the bedroom and sat with a lap board—her desk—on the bed. On the blank back of the program she made a list of what still remained to be proven:

   —that the guns really went to South Africa;
   —that the salesmen, and possibly also the Advertising Manager, really went there too;
   —that Lovell subcontracted a plant in Salinas to ship cattle prods and truncheons along with munitions;
   —that somebody paid for these guns and for the conversions;
   —that the State Department knew all about it.

She went to bed early. In the next room Dennis was running his trains again, ignoring the unwashed dishes in the sink. When he bought his *Ferrocarriles de Mexico* loco-

motive, it would whir around the tracks just as his Union
Pacific engine was doing now. Dennis did a good job on his
model trains. They rarely derailed; he could keep them running on the tracks for hours—which he did for much of the
night. The sound they made had the soothing quality of rain
on the windows. Muriel began to doze off, her mind's eye
moving in a slow pan over the familiar scene in the next
room. The figures and buildings which Dennis had set up interested her more than the trains. Tiny laborers, hand-
painted in Germany, loaded H-O bundles onto miniscule
trucks, or swept sidewalks with Lilliputian brooms. A little
woman in a violet dress ran from the station, intent on
reaching the tracks. Muriel admired her. She admired her
sense of purpose.

# Two

"Did you bellow for me, sir?"

The secretary to the Manager of European Sales picked up her steno pad and walked slowly into her boss's office. She was an attractive woman who moved as though she were under water. She was said to indulge in valium, as well as in the affections of the Manager of European Sales.

A buzzer drew Muriel's attention back to the telex machine. She clamped her message to Chile onto the metal cylinder, and when it began to spin, leaned back in her chair to wait for the next buzz. She watched all the secretaries working at their desks for their bosses who were hidden away behind the doors lining the walls. The arrangement reminded her of the Mission district railroad flat where she had lived when she had first moved here from Los Angeles. It was kind of funny to see the layout of the cheapest and most uncomfortable apartments in the city echoed in the executive offices of a Fortune 500 company. The officers talked a lot about moving; they said that the South San Francisco location was an embarrassment to the stockholders. Muriel wondered whether the Annual Report for 1976 would carry photographs of Lovell's new battlement image. How would they explain the concrete walls and the guardposts?

The mechanical drum of the telex revolved languidly, spinning Pagano's message into the wires. The telex was an office dinosaur left over from the days before the aborted installation of electronic communications equipment. It was also a bottle-neck. Already the woman with frosted hair from Customer Service had passed by at least three times to see whether Muriel was finished. Muriel's mind was crammed with arms trans-shipment data; she could never remember Frost Hair's name. Anyway, whatever her name, Frost Hair was a real company woman, always trying to trample over everyone else to get her boss's work out first.

It was really surprising that she could maintain this blind loyalty in the face of the Federal investigation. Everyone else in Customer Service was a nervous wreck: every petty clerk there had signed those false export documents at one time or another. As a sort of reward, discipline was lax in the International Division. Nobody said anything when non-managerials from International lingered in the cafeteria for an extra twenty minutes. This attitude caused resentment in the tightly run Domestic end, but it was obviously Company policy. Baziotis had actually been castigated by a higher up once in front of Muriel for fussing about everyone clearing out early on Fridays.

Frost Hair of course never cleared out early. And now she was back again, impatiently looming.

"Have you got much left to send?" She leaned over and fanned through the telex forms at Muriel's elbow.

"You can have this as soon as this one is done," Muriel said, with determined geniality. "I can send my others later."

She wondered whether her friendly behavior would make

Frost Hair suspicious. Most people reacted to her with irritation.

The operator buzzed and the drum rolled. Frost Hair struck a pose of exaggerated patience. The telex whirred and the typewritten message became a dark blur riding the wires to San Francisco, and on to Chile—something like the tigers turning into butter in *Little Black Sambo.*

Another buzz. Muriel unfastened the message from the stilled drum and hastily relinquished her seat. At her desk she scrawled "sent" on the corner of the paper. Now she had to file the telexes: that would give her another opportunity to look through the files.

Baziotis walked by quickly on his way back to his office from the conference room where he had been closeted with the Vice President of Sales. He would probably have another shredding assignment for her from the African files. He was now shredding orders from Chad and the Upper Volta—places that had nothing to do with South Africa. Soon there would be nothing left. For some reason the Feds had not even asked for the African files, but Baziotis apparently was taking no chances. A real Virgo, as Gerardina would say.

He ignored Muriel until his hand was on the doorknob of his office. Then he jerked around to face her and barked, "Get that call through to Libya?"

"No. The operator said she would try. But that was at nine o'clock."

Baziotis tried to check his watch, an L.E.D. type that would not show the time unless a button was pressed on its side. A stickler for neatness, he had rigged his door with a "Clever Door Closer", a cheap spring device that pulled it shut even if some slob left it ajar. Now he caught the door in motion with the toe of his Florsheim and got a reading on his watch.

"It's eleven now. Tell her to keep trying."

He backed into his office and the door slammed after him, closing him up like a Jack-in-the-Box. Soon enough he would come popping out again barking more orders.

Baziotis had spoken and she had to snap to it. Still holding the unfiled telexes, she went to her desk and, standing, dialed the international operator.

The familiar voice answered. "Operator 34, please."

"You'll never in your life guess who this is," Muriel said. "Mr Baziotis from Lovell Munitions once again, trying to get through to—surprise, surprise!—Libya! Now don't tell me. Let me guess."

"All lines to Libya are closed due to fierce fighting within the country." The chill on the usually cordial voice of Operator 34 could only mean that her supervisor was listening in. Muriel rapped out a business-like "Thank you; we'll try again later."

She went back to the file cabinets. There was less than an hour before lunch, and only four more days until her vacation. It was a race against time and the paper shredder.

As she was pulling out drawer Fl-Gr, Frost Hair walked up. "Telex is free now, dear," she said. She paused to receive Muriel's expressions of gratitude and then suddenly cried, "Oh, my God!"

Muriel's heart leapt in her chest. The woman was staring with popping eyes at the file cabinets and pointing a trembling finger.

"Never," she said, "never never *never* leave two file drawers open at the same time. That is *very* dangerous, dear, don't you know that?" She slammed one of the drawers shut and swished away, static crackling between her nylon stockings and her straight skirt.

When her pulse returned to normal, Muriel finished filing and went back to the telex with her last message, another one to Santiago.

While the telex whirred Muriel thought about the file drawer hazard—she should not give such a frantic impression as she undoubtedly did, pulling out several drawers at once—and the civil wars in North Africa. "Fierce fighting" had become a cliche in International Sales. Now the telephone company was using it too. Baziotis and Pagano used it as a catchall explanation, like "due to circumstances beyond our control." Sales are down in Mozambique because of fierce fighting. It had little reality; it was an expression less threatening than the idea of banging into an open file drawer.

Someone tapped Muriel's shoulder. Without turning she said amiably, "My, this process is slow, isn't it? We really need some new equipment to speed it up."

"Yeah," the tapper responded. "We're going to unscrew the telephone mouthpieces and cram the telexes in."

It was not Frost Hair; it was Francine, her favorite co-worker, her voice cynical, her blonde hair falling out of its bun.

"I'll meet you down in the caf for lunch in twenty minutes," Francine said. She jerked her head toward the two closed doors. "Quiet over here, huh? Where's Pagano?"

"He won't be in till after lunch. Maybe."

"Oh ho! Having a meeting with What's-His-Face in Public Relations, hey?"

"No," Muriel said. She wondered why Francine thought Pagano would be talking to Public Relations. "He called in, his wife's sick. He has to stay home with her part of the day."

"I see. Typical newlyweds. She's a lucky lady, that's all I can say."

On the subject of Pagano Francine was not cynical.

"So how's Advertising today?" Muriel asked. "How's Randrup? As bad as ever?"

"No, he's okay. Only because he's out of town. Off on one of his meetings. Thank God they happen pretty often. Today it's just boring, not aggravating. I've been sitting and staring at my tube all morning."

Francine was learning typesetting and word processing on a computerized system. "How's Baziotis? On the rag again?" Francine gestured toward his closed door. "I heard him slamming around in there when I came down the hall."

"Same as ever. You know Baziotis."

This was true. Francine knew Baziotis much better than Muriel did: she had held Muriel's job for seven years before her promotion to Advertising. Muriel was careful to temper her hostility toward Baziotis when she spoke to Francine, who was protective of him: she said he was just a pain in the neck and his bark was worse than his bite.

Muriel suggested they leave the telex station before they got another visit from Frost Hair. Francine followed her back to her desk, where Muriel put the transmitted telex on her blotter. There would be time to file it later when Francine had gone. At the moment Francine showed no signs of leaving.

"What's this?" She turned the telex toward her. "'El vahpur Imperial sell par-ah Santiago el trays day ab-rill.' What's it mean? Something about a ship and Santiago, right?"

"Yes, good. You're improving. It's funny, they still call their ships *vapores*, steamships, even though there aren't any steamships any more."

"There aren't?" Francine said, surprised.

Oh God, girl, Muriel thought, learn to hide your ignorance. Like almost all the Lovell secretaries—Muriel excluded, of course—Francine had gone to work fulltime right from high school. She had started at Lovell after a short stint as a waitress at the Copper Penny. Her secretarial skills had been polished at night school, but she knew no Spanish. For seven years she had typed the letters that Pagano wrote out for her in longhand; she had no idea what they were about. As for French, the language of many countries in Baziotis's territory, neither Muriel nor Francine knew one word. Nor did Baziotis. If his African clients didn't understand him, he shouted into the phone. When they committed the colossal error of writing to him in French, the letters were routed down to Gerardina, a Dutch secretary in Data Base Administration, who translated them, complaining because this service had not been included in her job description. Gerardina also composed the form letter in French which said that all future correspondence with the African Sales Manager would have to be in English.

"How's the byoob tube these days?" Muriel asked genially. This was a reference to Pagano's accent. He confused "oo" and "yu" sounds and had once called the video display terminal in advertising a "byoob tube." The joke was dying a hard death; Muriel maintained a fixed smile while Francine registered her amusement. But then she sighed, and said, "It's really hard to think about anything funny these days. I don't know why they have to lay all this new stuff on me in the middle of everything that's going on here."

Muriel was surprised. Francine always avoided talking about the Federal investigation; now suddenly she had brought it up. But Muriel did not want to talk about it at that point. She wanted to talk about it in relaxed, informal surroundings: nonchalantly, between bites of a sandwich and sips of milk.

There was a long pause. Francine remained standing at Muriel's desk.

"Don't be depressed," Muriel said finally. She had to say

something. "After all, you didn't sign any export licenses. You never worked with that end of things." Or had she?

"That's not the point," Francine said. "It's what this thing is doing to Arno and Baziotis." She picked up the telex and threw it down again in disgust. "Look at that. A shipment to Chile. Strictly nickel and dime. Before all this stuff happened Arno wouldn't even have come to the phone to take a call from this clown. Sales to Chile! This lousy hunting stuff doesn't bring in more than a few thousand bucks a year. And what's Baziotis up to?"

Muriel looked over her shoulder and lowered her voice. This conversation was not making her happy. "Mostly he's calling Libya," she said, "only all the lines are down and he can't get through. Other than that, he meets with the V.P., locks himself in his office, worries. The usual."

She wanted to add, "He gets his list of what to shred from the Feds and then he shreds it." She remembered how her contact at the Foundation had laughed when she had asked timidly why the Federal investigation was so slipshod. Would the Department of Justice go after the State Department? Not on your life, kid.

"Everybody's asleep at the switch here," Francine said. "Where's Westfeldt?"

Muriel shrugged. "He called Sharon in for dictation about an hour ago and the door's been closed ever since."

Standard office gossip. Safe territory.

"That's exactly what I'm saying," Francine said. "For a while Westfeldt was too busy with European sales to play run-around-the-desk; now he sits around all day with his thumb up his ass, so it's back to Sharon again."

"I think he's scheduled to go to Austria again next month," Muriel said slowly. "To the ski resort. Obergurgl."

Francine shook her head solemnly. "No way. Not till the

Feds blow out of here. Probably never again. And not Randrup either."

Muriel felt that the blood vessels in her face were lighting up like posts in a pinball machine: the curse of the red-headed.

"Oh," she said casually, "did Randrup go there too?"

"You bet he did. I never heard of Obergurgl before I came here and it took me three years to learn to pronounce it but it must be some great place. All the execs are crazy about it. Well, they love Europe, period. Except for France. You know what Randrup calls France? He says it's one big slum, that's what he says. But they all love Austria. Westfeldt used to fly to Obergurgl constantly. And Randrup—he can finagle a trip anywhere he wants, and he did a promotional shoot there a while ago. Alpine hunting. Did you know the Alps were in Austria? Yeah. I suppose you know that. I always thought they were in Switzerland."

"How did the promotional shoot work out?" Muriel asked. "Did they sell a lot of guns to Obergurgl?"

Francine dropped her voice. "Yeah," she said. "They sold a lot of guns there." She looked around and continued in a whisper, leaning over Muriel's desk. "But the guns went somewhere else, later on. *You* know." She straightened up and spoke in a normal tone. "Anyhow, you stop by Advertising some time and see the posters Randrup did of Obergurgl. He's a jerk but he takes good pictures. Oh, I know— when you come in for your lesson on the tube I'll show you the posters."

Muriel was irritated. "Are they still going to make me do that horseshit?"

"You better believe it. They need back-up on the machines in case I'm not here. Anyway that's what they say."

"*I* won't even be here next week. By the time I come back I'll forget everything you showed me."

"Oh, right," Francine said. "Vacation time. L.A.?"

Not L.A. But Muriel nodded. "Right. No big deal, just a visit with Mom and Dad."

"Getting away from this place is always a big deal. They want to keep us busy all the time. They don't really care whether you learn word processing or not. It's just busy work." She looked at the clock at last. "It's nearly twelve. I'll see you downstairs. I've got to go back and get my purse."

She clomped away in her Minnie Mouse shoes; they certainly did not flatter her heavy legs.

Doors were flying open. While Muriel was getting her sweater and her straw bag, Baziotis walked past her.

"Get through to Libya?" he said, without stopping.

"Fierce fighting," she called after him.

As she went down the staircase Muriel's head was buzzing with her conversation with Francine. So the U.S. Department of State had actually approved hundreds of export applications to send guns and ammunition to Obergurgl, Austria. The export licenses read, "Final destination: Obergurgl."

But if that really was their final destination something strange was going on. There must be more guns than people in that remote spa in Central Europe.

# Three

Bernie threw his head back and swallowed. Goddam, anyone who could take pills at a water fountain *deserved* to get well. He brushed a driblet of water off his tattersall shirt and pulled his suit jacket straight. A client was due in fifteen minutes. He shoved the cap back on the non-childproof bottle he had insisted on at the pharmacy and started back to his office. He should have had Willa bring him a glass in the first place; probably his judgment had been affected by the spiteful farewell address he had suffered through from his last secretary. "Menial" tasks, hell! Willa was crazy about him. Every time she buzzed him with a call from a female he could tell she was jealous.

As Bernie approached his office Sanford stuck his head and shoulders out of his own door.

"So what's your old man have to say this morning?"

Sanford got a big kick out of Bernie's father's fly-by-night schemes.

"Oh, God," Bernie said, "another investment plan. Boy Scout calendars, would you believe that?"

"What in hell are those?" Sanford was already in stitches.

His amusement was irritating. After all, he wasn't the one who had to come running with money and legal advice every time one of those schemes went off the rails, which they all did.

"He got the idea from the Avon lady," Bernie said. "You know, one of those things you can't buy in a store."

"Like Electrolux vacuum cleaners," Sanford said.

"Yeah." Bernie didn't know anything about vacuum cleaners, why should he? His ex-wife had bought the one he had and one of his overnight guests usually volunteered to clean with it.

"Only it's not vacuum cleaners," Bernie said. "It's calendars."

He was getting restless; he was bored by these let's-laugh-at-my-father sessions.

"I hope he didn't buy a bunch of last year's models."

"No, it's not that . . . It's the distribution system. He wants the Boy Scouts running around selling door-to-door all over the U.S. *and* Canada. Canada yet. His new jerk partner thinks he has a connection with the International Fucking Council of Boy Scouts."

"Oh, yeah, like Girl Scout cookies. Only cookies at least you can eat."

"*I* can," Bernie said. "*You* can't. Listen, I got a client due in a minute. Catch you later."

Bernie went into his office and sat down in the swivel chair behind the desk. It wasn't nice to poke fun at Sanford's baby fat, but it served the bastard right for making fun of the old man like that. He was an adventurer, he couldn't be pinned down to a nine-to-five job, that was part of it. Of course Sanford's old man had no problem with regular hours. Maybe he wanted more time on the golfcourse instead of in the boardroom.

He checked his watch. The Eddie kid was late again. He

needed a lecture on how valuable a lawyer's time was. Willa should do it at the reception desk. That was more professional. His mouth felt funny; probably those antibiotics were making his breath smell bad. He opened his drawer and took out a plastic dispenser of breath-freshening lozenges. Maybe he should call the urologist and ask him if he could lower the dosage. The discharge was much better. Bad breath. That's all he needed this weekend.

The lozenges reminded him again of his father. The time when Bernie was in high school and the old man had bought over a hundred vending machines placed all over Greater Los Angeles. Half of them were filled with these breath fresheners: they were called Freshen Nuts. Boy, was that embarrassing, running around burning up gas and oil in the Dodge with the old man, and there were about two quarters in each machine. After about a year they dug up some patsy to take over the business, for a fraction of what his father had paid.

That's how Bernie got into law: his father sent him to the UCLA law library to look things up; he was always going to sue his thieving partners or his thieving "help". So a few years later Bernie was back in the library with a briefcase in his hand and a student I.D. in his pocket. At the graduation his parents had been completely dry-eyed. His father was all ready with a suit he wanted Bernie to start against some shyster.

That was why Bernie had vowed never to practice business law. No contracts, no mergers. Just clients like young Eddie, who finally arrived, a bundle of nerves, flicking the hair off his forehead, picking imaginary lint off his pants, punching his fist into his open palm. It was a real pleasure to be in a room with kids like Eddie. Watching them twitch made Bernie feel normal and relaxed. He himself never used drugs.

"We're tightening up your case, kid," Bernie said. He shuffled through his drawer for a legal pad. "These witnesses . . . Benham and the other one . . . Dugan. They're going to come through for us.

He smiled broadly at Eddie, who was biting his nails. It wasn't too often that an innocent client came along. Eddie was actually innocent. He was a nice white kid, from a well-to-do family, busted for passing out angel dust at a party. Only he wasn't the one who did it. One of Eddie's friends had thrown the party at his house in St Francis Wood, while his folks were away in Europe. The cops had busted the party because some neighbor complained about the noise.

St Francis Wood was very swanky; Sanford said it dated from the turn of the century. Of course it was on the wrong side of Twin Peaks, the side where the weather was always lousy. The words "St Francis Wood" were printed on an archway leading to the complex; Bernie had seen the sign looming out of the mist as he sped past.

This kid wasn't going to have a problem. No kid who went with the crowd in St Francis Wood was going to have a problem with the district attorney's office. It was just a matter of copping a plea. It was a matter of having a chat with Haywood Cooke at the D.A.'s office: probably have the kid plead guilty to possession, a minor charge, and that would be that. Eddie couldn't know that, of course. He figured it was going to be like the movies: a trial and all that. And Eddie's parents knew from nothing about the law. They were academic types. They did have enough brains to find Bernie, the hot-shot narcotics lawyer. Eddie would get some fake sentence like "accelerated rehabilitation."

No, wait a minute, uh uh. The kid was really innocent. He was a real rarity. He'd get a *nol pros*; the charges would be dropped. The family would be beside themselves with happiness; they would throw their arms around Bernie. But first they had to sweat it out, so that Bernie could squeeze out the Big Fee.

"We have one obstacle here," Bernie said, and he launched into a bullshit speech about a technicality. Eddie punched his fist into his hand while Bernie told him what papers needed to be filed. He made it sound really complicated. It was too bad all this drama was being wasted. The kid should have brought his parents along. They were in Hawaii . . . or was that someone else's parents? Maybe, with luck, they were too hysterical to leave the house.

Bernie glanced at his watch and, still talking, came from behind his desk, put his arm around Eddie and steered him toward the door. Since adolescents as a rule didn't pick up verbal cues too quickly, it was better to skip the subtleties.

"I'll talk to you soon," he yelled after Eddie. "Try not to worry. You got one thing going for you—a terrific lawyer."

Sanford pulled his door open.

"Kindly stop that shouting," he said, through clenched teeth. "I'm trying to concentrate in here."

Bernie mugged a banjo-eyed look of surprise and Sanford went back in and slammed the door.

A few minutes later Bernie heard Willa's high heels clicking down the hall toward his office. He threw some Freshen Nuts into his mouth and chewed them furiously. He couldn't care less about Willa, but he knew that chewing things was Not Sexy on general principles. The Nuts coagulated into a flat, hard form, like a piece of plastic. The damn things were as hard to chew as they had been to sell.

"Sooo," Willa said pleasantly. "No more clients for today. That's good."

"Actually, Willa," he said, "we don't think that's so good. No clients, no money." She had been working for him for two months now; it was time she found this out. Where in hell did she think her salary was coming from?

She threw a file folder onto his desk. "Here's the dictation you gave me," she said. "How's Mr Nervous Wreck?"

"Who?" Bernie said. He felt offended until he realized she meant Eddie. "Oh, no problem."

He put his head down and studied her typing while he swallowed the nuts with an effort. They went down his throat like a knife.

Willa was hanging around in a special kind of way, so he looked up at her. She was wearing her usual peek-a-boo clothes—a crocheted vest and skirt with some kind of mesh bat wings and a body stocking underneath. Sanford hated her clothes; Bernie thought she looked pretty good.

"I noticed that music you put on the dictaphone for me," she said.

"Oh, you liked that?"

Maybe it had been a mistake to put that music on there.

"See, my 8-track was busted," he said. "It's been at the stereo repair for two weeks. I just wanted to record that tune, and I left it on for you on an impulse. You didn't erase it, did you?"

"Oh, no. It's still right on my desk."

"Good. I'll pick it up on my way out in a few minutes." He picked up the phone and began to dial his friend Marshall. She became aware that she had been dismissed and turned to leave. Her crocheted clothes were so stiff that her outfit turned a few seconds later than she did. While the line was ringing Bernie called after her, "Hey, call Taraval Stereo for me, will you? It's in the book. Ask them when the hell my 8-track's going to be ready."

Marshall was a lawyer too; he and Bernie were considering a subscription to JURIS, an electronic law library. Few offices as small as Bernie's had a subscription: JURIS was very expensive, intended for large firms with varied practices. But Bernie was dying to get in on the gadgetry. Now for the umpteenth time he and Marshall bandied the pros and cons back and forth. It would get them out of the offices earlier, they would have more leisure time. They could do research on judges. They would never need to hire a law clerk again.

No, forget it, the salesman wouldn't come down on the price.

"But, Bernie," Marshall said, "you won't believe this! I was talking to this salesman last night. He kept talking about extra for this module and that attachment, and in between he tells me by the way that this system can play video games."

"You're kidding! Which ones?"

"You name it, you got it. He'll throw it in for free, on one of the floppies."

This was great, but more investigation was called for. Maybe some other people would come in on the deal, now that it was sweetened with games.

Bernie hung up and pulled on his light overcoat. Sanford didn't want the library. He was willing to spend a few thousand every six months on his wife's doll collecting. That was okay. But JURIS was not okay.

On his way out Bernie picked up the tape and asked Willa to call Chuck, the kid he hadn't been able to reach since his arraignment. This kid was a real problem. He had called from jail, pleading with Bernie to take the case. He was some kind of Creole or Italian or something, a good dresser, looked like money. He wasn't white, so how could the fee be any good? He had been dealing quaaludes in some sleazy part of the Mission. The kid lived in a lousy neighborhood out in the Excelsior District. And he didn't want his parents to know about the case. So how come he was driving a Porsche?

It was a five-year-old Porsche convertible, a Targa 911, a

beautiful car. Maybe he could collect the Porsche as his fee? It was a simple case. Quaaludes were no big deal. The kid didn't seem to own anything except the Targa. It would be an outrageous fee for a little case like this, but kids were easily intimidated. They had no sense of proportion.

Bernie climbed into his 1948 pearl gray Packard. That had been payment for a really tough trial case: "in-kind" fees like these made things simpler at tax-time—and that was coming up fast.

He fought through the traffic in mid-city to the clear boulevards of the southern Sunset District. The Packard was an ox; it was hard to drive around Pacific Heights where the population was dense. A sports car would be much better. But Sanford had been really jealous when he got that antique sedan. On the other hand, the sea air was beginning to rust it, and the Van Ness garage was making noises about raising their rates for the weekly hand-wax. God help him if something broke or fell off.

The Packard sailed down the wide boulevards of Garden City, its shiny sides probably reflecting the palmetto trees lining the streets. That would be a pleasant tropical sight, a good shot for the beginning of a '30s movie about Havana. Too bad he wasn't smoking a big cigar. He stopped at a yellow light and rolled down the window to look at the side of the car. There was no reflection; it was too foggy on this side of Twin Peaks. A mass of fog was rolling over Park Merced, the high-rise apartment complex.

Two old women in hats and gloves strolled along the sidewalk. Native San Franciscans, brought up to love hats and hate Los Angeles. They receded down a side street in their pastel cashmere coats. A honk roused him to drive on.

These were the people who really had a handle on things. But the climate was shitty over here. At another light he craned his neck to see St Francis Wood, the scene of Eddie's ill-fated party. As usual the whole place was enveloped in mist like something out of a fairy tale. The neighbors must have had a fit when they heard about the arrests.

Bernie drove toward the shopping center off Holloway, where his health club was. The huge quadrangle made him feel as if he were in a fortress or a corral. He parked, taking up two spaces so that no one would open a car door and dent the Packard, got out and blew into his hand to test his breath. Somewhat reassured, he descended the blue plastic staircase to the gym where he built his body.

# Four

Lourdes Pagano sat at the window of her house in Jackson Street, sipping sherry and watching the sun rise. The softness of her blue velour robe harmonized with the haziness of the San Francisco dawn which she was enjoying, as she enjoyed the *rico* Amontillado in its delicate glass. Lourdes loved the early mornings: things seemed less alien then. Later she would recover her lost sleep in the warm bed a few yards away where her husband now lay. From time to time during the night she had been fingering a dimestore *fotonovela*, a Spanish language story book in photographs which lay on her lap.

Now as the sun entered the bedroom 'she reached up, turned off the lamp and hurled the silly magazine onto the low chair in front of the vanity table. It fell open at a page on which two people were confronting each other with passion in their faces; their words appeared in oval white spaces suspended over their heads. In the next frame on the same page there were no white ovals, just the silhouettes of some buildings and information above them in a rectangle. No one was speaking in that frame.

* * *

Several miles to the northeast, a redhaired young woman was poring over maps of resort towns in the Austrian Alps. It was Muriel Axelrod sitting in her kitchen and racing the clock, trying to organize some information before six a.m. when she could call the Foundation for Investigative Reporting in Washington, D.C., three time zones to the east. Muriel was already dressed for work in a powder blue shirtwaist dress, which she had ordered from the J.C. Penney catalogue. She had ordered this same shirtwaist dress in three different colors. She had worn a different color every day that week. She wondered if anyone thought that was a peculiar thing to do. But it was a perfect dress for the office: conservative, unobtrusive. Not like Gerardina's long skirts and earth shoes.

People would have to notice that Muriel had been having lunch with outlandish-looking Gerardina twice a week in the cafeteria. And the damn woman couldn't seem to keep her voice down—as if she didn't attract enough attention with her clothes and that Dutch accent, to say nothing of the peculiar jargon she used. She said she was helping Muriel because she was bummed out about what the Boers had done in South Africa. It had probably been a mistake to confide in Gerardina. She hadn't really been any help at all so far, although two days ago at lunch she had hinted that some new information had leaked through the data base barriers.

They had a date to meet late tonight at a crowded bar on Clement Street to discuss it. Gerardina had no telephone and she was unwilling for some reason to invite Muriel to her flat in the city, although Muriel had been really blunt about asking. And Gerardina had refused to come to Walnut

Creek; she had even refused to walk with Muriel in the park, or stroll outside the barbed-wire barricades after work. She was willing to meet in the bar because she said she had to go to Clement Street anyway. This was the last chance to get this information—if there really was any information—before Muriel left for her week in Salinas.

Pressing her hands to her temples, Muriel forced herself to concentrate on the map. Time was running out. She had to cut short her date with Bernie in order to meet Gerardina tonight. And last night she had come home late because she had spent a long time looking for a Rand-McNally store in the financial district—the only place she could think of that would sell maps of Austria. And the check from the Foundation for her travel expenses had not yet arrived. A large tear splashed onto the map.

The door of Dennis's room creaked open. She looked up at him with streaming eyes. He stood looking concerned in his Buddy Holly eyeglasses and ratty old bathrobe.

"I don't have enough time for all this," she wept.

"I'll drive you to the BART station," Dennis said. "That'll shave off a little time anyway. I'm sorry I can't do more."

Muriel ran her hands through her hair. "Once it's nine o'clock in Washington I'll be able to get hold of Elba and I'll feel better. Elba will help me straighten things out.

Elba was the administrative assistant at the Foundation. She was a pillar of strength, a sounding board and mentor for Muriel. Dennis placed a comforting hand on Muriel's bony shoulder and they looked at the institutional kitchen clock which Dennis had bought at the Alameda Flea Market. As they watched together the minute hand jumped. Ten minutes to six. In ten minutes Muriel could start the current pulsing between Walnut Creek and the switching station in Oakland to reach across the continent to her telephone friend in the east.

\* \* \*

Down on Jackson Street Lourdes Pagano was thinking of connecting cords, of the umbilical cord which had tied her to her mother, and the one which had tied her mother to her grandmother. The fine glass, in which the sherry sparkled, was an heirloom which had belonged to Lourdes' grandmother in Buenos Aires. It was one of her few possessions in this San Francisco house. *Los demas*, the rest of the furnishings, had been left behind by Arno's first wife.

It was strange that that woman would leave so much behind. Her awful shag rugs and stupid *fotonovelas*. Lourdes had been in San Francisco for five months and only a few crates of her own things had arrived. She wanted to pack up this awful stuff from the other woman. Stuff only a Mexican would buy. In Argentina Lourdes had given such things to the organizations created by Santa Evita for the poor. Here there were places like that too. A woman at the California Historical Society had told her of "Good, Well," something like that. It was hard to make out what people were saying unless they looked straight at you and talked. But it was getting better every day. After all, she had been the best English student at the Normal.

Arno was in trouble with the government. Lourdes knew that, even though he slept soundly without tossing. He didn't even know she wasn't in bed, or else he had grown accustomed to her dawn vigils at the window. Lourdes sipped her Amontillado and gazed at her sleeping husband. She had not noticed before that he was growing bald. Perhaps it was this trouble with the *federales*, it was aging him. Or maybe he was worried about his son Jesus. These pressures come out sometimes in the unconscious. Lourdes had studied *psicologia* for two years. She knew all about it. Yet that *Doctora* at the Historical Society, she had spoken to Lourdes as if she were a child. But when the English came *mas fluido* Lourdes would show her a thing or two.

Oh, yes, Jesus. They called him Chucho. He was missing. Lourdes closed her eyes and lifted her face to the sun which was flooding the room. Things always seemed clearer when sunlight came. Soon she would go back to bed; she was growing sleepy. Then Arno would get up, but he wouldn't go to the office until noon. He spent the mornings calling lawyers about his trouble with the *federales* or trying to find Chucho. Lourdes would have liked to put that young man in a box and stow him away with the rest of his mother's possessions.

Noises came from a room at the end of the hall. Her little dog was stirring. Maybe Arno would wake up soon and take him for a walk in the park; she didn't want to change into her clothes just for a ten minute walk. If she had to, of course she would. The little dog gave her pleasure. It was much nicer to live with the little dog and Arno instead of with the adolescent son who slammed doors and came and went at mysterious hours. Too bad Arno had to keep looking for him.

The lovely little glass was empty; Lourdes put it on the veneer top of the dresser. She looked for a hanger in the crowded closet so that she could hang up her robe and get back between the sheets. Finally at the back of the closet she found one, wrapped in yarn—another strange idea of decoration, another *recuerdo* of the first wife. *Ay,* these Mexicans. What taste. Decorations on the wire hangers, but on the cheap modern dresser, nothing but brushes and combs. They liked to leave the shiny furniture tops empty, gleaming at you.

She lowered her light body into the bed next to Arno. He was snoring softly. How he had changed from those first days when he had begun to court her. She had met him downtown, at her father's office. He had been the elegant salesman from Lovell in the *Estados Unidos*—an Argentinian who *ya* had lived for many years in *la America del Norte,* a real international businessman. Her father, the Lovell agent in Argentina, was very strict, so they had flirted behind his back, meeting secretly as she went from home to the Normal, or to the late afternoon parties held by members of chic Buenos Aires society. Later she found out why her father had frowned when she came to his office in the odd hours that the Lovell salesman just happened to be there: papa had known that Arno was married. But they kept meeting, sometimes in the park where Lourdes took her little dog for a walk, the one that was mother to the year-old puppy now whining plaintively at the end of the hall.

Lourdes shook Arno gently. He woke with a start. She kissed him on the earlobe, yawned delicately, pouted and asked him to hurry and walk the dog. He got unwillingly out of bed and she turned over and closed her eyes, waiting for sleep. Shadows of his hasty motions against the sunlight flickered on her eyelids. The door opened and closed and soon the whining ceased.

This was what she had fought for, while her mother shrieked and cried at the thought of a middle-aged, *divorciado* fiance, while her father protested that he wanted her to live close to her family. She would sleep now until noon or so. Then Arno would leave for his job at Lovell, the cement building complex with the barbed wire. And then she would walk down the street to do volunteer work for the California Historical Society, with Sarah Westfeldt, the wife of one of Arno's business associates.

This was the way they lived, sleeping in alternating shifts, talking in murmurs about trouble with the law, and the missing son. Lourdes drifted off. A sunbeam stretched into the room, lighting up the screaming faces on the page of the *fotonovela* which lay tilted on the seat of the striped chair.

*　*　*

Behind the closed door Dennis was running his model trains slowly so that the noise would not disturb Muriel while she was talking to Elba at the Foundation in Washington.

"No, really," Elba said, "Pete is very interested in what you're doing. He doesn't consider it a low priority at all. That travel memo about the salesman's trip to South Africa —he thought that was terrific."

"Really?" Muriel said. "My brother told me I'd have to find evidence that the trip actually took place."

"Oh, come on, Muriel. We're talking journalism here, not law. Bigger stories have come from flimsier evidence. Don't worry about the trip—worry about the *modifications.*"

Muriel had lined up all her evidence on the kitchen table. There was of course the precious memo from Baziotis asking for expenses for the trip to Johannesburg. There were xeroxes of the South African warranty cards, and Muriel had been very nervous while she was xeroxing them, five at a time. Nobody ever xeroxed warranty cards—why would you need to? Parts and Service could tell the age of a gun by looking at it and they repaired any fairly new gun. It was cheaper to do that than to spend time looking up cards in a hundred different files. She explained this to Elba.

"That's why we need computerization," she said, "like the Domestic Division. Our equipment is obsolete, that's what the D.P. people say—the Data Processing people. They're putting in electronic data retrieval systems, word processing . . ."

"Oh, sure," Elba said smugly. "So they can turn you into more productive workers without paying you more money. I know all about it." Muriel did not like this side of Elba.

"What's wrong with technology?" Muriel said. "Maybe if they hadn't lost money because of all this old-fashioned paper shuffling, they wouldn't have had to sell guns to South Africa."

"That's a lot of horseshit," Elba said. "They're ruthless, that's all—they want to squeeze out profits any way they can. Remember that—and that's why you can't get caught with your hands in the rolodex. These people have no scruples. And you can argue with groups I know who are studying the impact of office technology on workers."

"First of all," Muriel said evenly, "I am not going to get caught because I am careful to cover my tracks. Secondly, I am not going to join the Contra Costa Office Activists Group because I don't know them, and I don't have the time, and so far all they've asked me to do is come over there and stuff envelopes for them. Shit work. And anyway I'm not on their turf."

"What?"

"They said that if you live in Contra Costa but you work in San Francisco you should join the San Francisco group. But the BART closes down after seven o'clock. How would I get home after a meeting?"

"Let's drop all that for the moment. Now tell me what more you expect to be able to come up with."

"Elba, I wrote all that up for you. Remember that typed proposal? That's what was supposed to get me the check for the trip to Salinas."

"Muriel, relax. The check is in the mail. And I did read that proposal. But you've turned up a few more things since you wrote it, and I want to see where you're going."

Muriel glanced at the clock. Even if Dennis gave her a ride to the BART station she would still have to leave the house by 6:50. They were wasting time with these petty arguments. She had to buckle down.

"All right," she said. "I want to show more than that some munitions ended up in South Africa or that one salesman took a trip there. I want to show that Lovell had an elaborate scheme going that involved shipping munitions from South San Francisco to Mexico, where they were converted from sporting goods to war weapons. And I want to show that these guns were paid for by a special system that bypassed the usual accounts receivable procedures. Maybe these payments were never reported to the IRS. Also I'm finding out that before these guns went to Mexico they were trans-shipped to points in Europe—including one in Austria."

This was news to Elba. "What about that?" she said.

"What that means," said Muriel, "is that the State Department approved hundreds of licenses to send thousands of dollars worth of munitions to a little resort in Austria. I mean, shouldn't the State Department have wondered about that, asked a few questions? Doesn't this show they're in it too, up to their necks?"

"Terrific!" Elba said. "Do you have the sales figures for this stuff yet?"

"No," Muriel said uncomfortably. "I saw them when I first started. They were really huge. But by now they could have been shredded. Or they could be locked up in the data base; then only a few departments could get them—like European Sales and Finance. Maybe Marketing."

She had to explain to Elba again what the data base was.

"I'm seeing Gerardina tonight," Muriel said. "She's the secretary to the data base manager. We're going to talk about cracking the code."

"Gerardina," Elba said. "The weirdo, right?"

Muriel had been the source of that impression. She became defensive.

"Oh, she's not so bad. She's very knowledgeable about data processing and she can translate French for my jerk boss Baziotis. Only she says she's going to quit soon; she wants to sail around the world or something. I have to work fast."

"She's not holding out on you, is she?"

"No, no. But she needs to be coaxed. She loses motivation; she's more interested in yoga and natural foods—things like that."

"Well, what *is* her motivation for helping you?"

"She says it's because she's Dutch. She— she's bummed out by what the Boers did in South Africa. Every other word out of her mouth is 'man'. It really gets to be a drag, man."

"And you." Elba's voice sobered. Muriel dreaded the next question. "What's your reason for doing all this—wasting your vacation in Salinas, running risks, putting up with insulting people at the Foundation?"

"You know why I'm doing this, Elba. I hate apartheid, I told you that."

"But you also don't like the Contra Costa Office Activists. You don't see the connections."

"Listen, Elba, it's getting late. I've got to get going. Look. You want me to be a particular kind of person which I'm not. I don't need to work with anyone, I can do this myself. You said yourself other people risk secrecy. You bawled me out for talking about this with Gerardina."

"Yeah, you've told too many people already. Your roommate—okay, I can see that. Then your brother. All he does is give you worthless advice and depress you. And this Gerardina, who is she? Someone people notice, she calls attention to herself. Why talk to her?"

"I'll tell you why. She's the only other secretary at Lovell who reads books and has gone to college besides me. I was attracted to her because I'm a fucking elitist, that's why. You've got all these fancy ideas about workers, let me tell you something. That girl Francine is nice, but she doesn't know South Africa from South Dakota."

"Neither did you until you made friends with a foreign exchange student. You told me that yourself."

"That was when I was eighteen," Muriel said angrily. "These people in the office are adults. They work with guns every day, they send them to police squads in Brazil and all that kind of stuff. And they couldn't care less. They knew it wasn't legal to send those guns to South Africa; there are Federal memos about it all over the place. But all they think about are their raises."

Elba murmured something.

"Don't tell me they don't have any other options!" Muriel said. "What kind of options do I have? I'm not working as a secretary because I enjoy slumming. When I get blacklisted for this I don't know how I'm going to make a living. A college degree plus a quarter will buy you a cup of coffee, especially when the degree is from a city college. You know that damn well. In Mexico I was able to teach school. I can't do that here."

"Why," Elba said, "I thought you had dreams of becoming famous from this."

"Where's my check?" Muriel said.

"I told you," Elba said. "It's on its way. Did you get that letter I sent you? With the address of the UFW man? That is very important information, Muriel, and I went to a lot of trouble to get in touch with him—"

"Are you kidding? I thought you didn't want the whole world to know about this."

"Now just let me finish. The Foundation has had extensive dealings with Guarino. He's perfectly trustworthy. In fact he is a personal friend of one of the people on the Board of Directors here." She dropped her voice respectfully. "Muriel, he's a key union organizer for the United Farm Workers. He knows a lot of people in Salinas, maybe including Pardee employees, and he's brave and knowledgeable and totally dedicated. He's totally dedicated to things like the struggle against apartheid."

"Is he also tall, dark and handsome?" Muriel said. She was only half joking. It would be nice to meet a man on that dreary vacation in Salinas, the salad bowl of the nation. "Oh, no," she added, "of course he wouldn't be tall."

"What do you mean by that?" Elba asked sharply. "That's just a racist stereotype."

"I've got to go, Elba," Muriel said. "Don't start getting La Raza on me."

Elba had been christened Ellen; she was half Puerto-Rican and in search of her roots.

After a minute Elba laughed. "Good luck," she said. "The check is in the mail." She hung up.

"Okay," Muriel called out. "Ready to go!"

Dennis came out of his room, pulling on a heavy sweater.

"Well, that was a long one," he said. "How did you ever get mixed up with those people in the first place?"

"Oh, I saw something in a magazine that said money was available for investigative reporting, and women especially were encouraged to apply. It was in *Family Circle*. You know, that magazine I keep asking you to get at the supermarket, but you always forget?"

"What'd they do—stick it between two casserole recipes?"

"Not quite," Muriel said grimly.

In the car Dennis chattered away about how an article in *Trains* magazine had convinced him that BART was a genuine train system. "It's the wave of the future," he said. "Nostalgia is a dead end. This country is not going to invest in passenger service just to please us railway nuts."

Muriel embarked with Dennis shouting after her, "Why don't you sit all the way in the back? That way you can see the tracks through the window."

She huddled into a seat behind a window. She was busy thinking about her conversation with Elba. Besides, she did not share Dennis's fondness for the Bay Area Rapid Transit. She had rushed to move to Walnut Creek as soon as the tunnel to San Francisco was completed but she had found that the service did not live up to its promises. The trains ran erratically and often stalled. Sometimes when a train halted in the underwater tunnel, passengers panicked, thinking they would be drowned. But all Muriel ever thought was that she would be late and would be fired before her mission could be completed.

Pagano came in later and later every day but of course he was an executive. Possibly he was about to be fired; maybe he was going to be the scapegoat for the Mexican trans-shipments. But Baziotis was more directly implicated because South Africa was his territory. Baziotis always got in on time.

Well, they were all involved. They were all in it together. It suddenly occurred to her that she might be followed. If she took out her compact and pretended to check her make-up, would she see some suspicious character sitting a seat or two behind her? Someone behind her tapped her on the shoulder. The train was rolling smoothly to a stop, but Muriel leaped like a passenger being derailed.

"We're here at MacArthur Station, dear," an old woman

whispered. She was softly overweight, as if filled with kapok.

"Oh, thank you." The old woman walked to the sliding doors, glancing back to make sure Muriel was coming. Was it Miss Froy from *The Lady Vanishes?*

"I know you always get off at MacArthur, dear," the old lady said.

Muriel went down the platform and transferred to the Daly City Line. She had such a rigid schedule that she would obviously be easy to follow. She even wore the same dress every day under her spring coat. "Red hair, can't miss her," she imagined a blue-suited man saying, through the cigar in his mouth, waving the thick mug of coffee in his hand. "This is the dress. You got your three possibilities: blue, pink, green. Why should you be confused because the color changes? What kind of a detective are you, Foley?"

Muriel yawned, waiting for the bus to Lovell Street, the last leg of her long daily journey. She knew that her view of the world came from movies made in the 1940s. Checking the rear in a compact: it was a cheap routine exploited in countless pictures from grades A to D, and parodied in *Shoot the Piano Player.* She was nostalgic for a world shown in movies made before she was born. And Dennis was nostalgic for landmarks built before he was born; he had been wearing a tee shirt that very day that said "Save the Grand Central Terminal". And he had the nerve to say that nostalgia was a dead end. He and she made a depressing pair.

The gray bus pulled up, with goggling headlights. She could look forward to eight hours of struggle to fill her straw bag with incriminating documents. After that, though, she was meeting Bernie to see a musical at the Pacific Theater. He and she were not alike, but they shared this movie mania. He was the perfect movie companion for a musical, delighting in each note of the score, thrilling to the close nasal harmony. Nostalgia, she thought, climbing on the bus. In Spanish it meant also "homesickness." For some reason she thought of the UFW organizer Guarino. Maybe she could induce him to unclench his fist and relax a little.

# Five

Too tight, front and back. The woman from Customer Service with the frosted hair was wearing pants—an unusual occurrence—and patrolling the International Sales corridor like a Beefeater without a palace. Each time she passed she glanced at Muriel. Why don't you pop back to your own department and falsify a few export license applications, Muriel thought. She wanted to reread an interesting photocopy she had just hidden in the tickler file—if that was the name for it. Maybe only Lovell called it that: an accordion file with tabs marked from one to thirty-one. If you opened three—the third of the month—you would find a note to tickle your memory. Or trigger it.

No one else was around: Baziotis was locked up in a conference and Pagano hadn't shown up yet. Muriel thought she might be onto something hot; she wanted to go over it again before it slid into the straw bag.

Ah! The Company Woman was making a fuel stop at the Mr. Coffee station. She seemed engrossed in shaking down little packets of Cremora. Muriel was inserting her finger in the tickler file when Francine appeared, bobbing toward her on thick cork wedgies.

"Don't tell me," she called out before she had even reached the desk. "I know. Arno's not in yet. The man must be in marital heaven."

Muriel thought that he might more likely be in an employment agency, but she said nothing. Francine had not mentioned the Feds, and Muriel did not want to initiate the subject. Francine, unlike Muriel, was bound to Lovell by years of service—years of training, weekly pay envelopes and memories. Muriel saw the years as pages flying off a daily calendar in a strong breeze: January 1, 2, 3, 4 . . . blowing up against the camera lens.

"And Baziotis?" Francine said. She reached down to fuss with one of her nylons, trying unsuccessfully to rotate a run toward the inside of her leg. "Where might he be?"

"At a meeting," Muriel said, yawning. "He's due back soon." She was looking forward to the movie tonight, but afterward she had to meet with Gerardina. She did not look forward to that.

"God, you look more dragged out than I feel," Francine said.

"I'm having trouble sleeping," Muriel said. She paused, wondering if that were a revealing statement. Perhaps she shouldn't have said it. "It always happens before my period," she added.

"Oh, really? I'm just the opposite."

"Well, thank God for Friday." And thank God for these workplace comments. You could fill in with them without thinking.

"How's the morning been going?"

"Oh, it's slow. That hag from Customer Service has been prowling up and down all morning, making sure everyone looks busy."

"Oh, *that* bitch. Who died and left her in charge? Well, don't pay any attention to her. And pretty soon we're going to be very busy. I happen to know that Baziotis is going to lend you to Advertising for some heavy computer training. Not just our usual hour a week. We're really going to hit the keyboard."

Muriel hid her dismay in her best toneless Barbara Stanwyck voice. "Oh, really?" Why were they taking her away from her usual job—and her files? Was someone on to her?

"Umm hmm," Francine said. She checked over her shoulder to see whether the zipper of her skirt was centered properly in back. Francine always checked on these things after she had left the house. She should have a full-length mirror on the back of her bedroom door, Muriel thought. She herself had one. Francine was saying something, with her head screwed around to the back, like an owl's.

"What? I can't hear you."

"Oh, I just said they want a real word processing system set up for all the form letters in International, and all advertising copy. So we'll start our lessons this afternoon."

"Today? Why start today?" She knew the answer. Baziotis the Compulsive was behind this. "I'll forget everything I've learned while I'm on vacation. We'll have to review it all when I come back anyway."

"You know that, and I know that, but Baziotis doesn't know that. He never forgets anything, so he put a bee in Randrup's bonnet about this. You'll see, as soon as he comes back from his meeting you'll be detached to my department. Randrup doesn't know which side is up on the computers. We can fool around all day and he'll never know the difference. He doesn't even know where I am right now."

Foiled again, Muriel thought. But it was soothing to hear that this maddening plan had nothing to do with suspicions about her. Pagano had probably been reduced to part-time, or phased out, and the company wanted to keep her busy doing something else.

Francine seemed to read Muriel's mind. "Get this," she whispered, looking up and down the corridor. "Between you and me, Pagano is going to come in late from here on in. And it isn't because of his wife or because of the trouble with his son, either."

Trouble with his son? Muriel nodded as if she understood, and waited for Francine to finish. But Francine was silent.

"But who'll make those silly calls to Libya?" Muriel asked to fill in the awkward silence. Francine rewarded her with a laugh, an insider's laugh. She was longing for the old days when she had done Muriel's job. Muriel decided to try for more mileage.

"And can you believe it? As of yesterday he's had me trying the wires to Guatemala."

Francine frowned. "Guatemala? Oh, my, then he is really taking over for Pagano. He never touched the Latin American territory before."

"Oh, no," Muriel said. "Pagano comes in every day around three o'clock and leaves me a list of instructions. He's busy the rest of the day with meetings. So Baziotis just sticks his oar in—he's trying to supervise my Latin American work. He looks at my list and so forth. I guess the only thing he could get a handle on was this impossible call to the agent in Guatemala."

She tried to change the subject and picked up a letter of credit to show Francine but Francine's attention had been caught.

"The agent in Guatemala?" she said. "Is that Robles? Have you been trying to phone Robles?"

"Yeah. We can't reach him because there's been an earthquake down there and all the lines are down. I guess Pagano doesn't realize that."

"An earthquake?" Now Francine seemed to be worrying about Robles as well as Pagano. Of course she knew many of the Latin American agents and distributors. She had met them when they came to visit Lovell.

"I'm trying Guatemala a million times a day when I'm not trying Libya," Muriel said. "I think Baziotis enjoys tilting at windmills." She wondered if that expression would mean anything to Francine. Maybe she should have said that Baziotis was after the impossible dream

But Francine wasn't listening anyway. She was fretting over Baziotis's invasion of the Latin American territory and Robles and the earthquake in Guatemala. Finally she retreated to Advertising, dragging her cork soles.

At last Muriel could open the tickler file. Frost Hair was nowhere to be seen. Hungrily Muriel cast her eyes over her booty.

It was a letter from a Piers Vietgrot of Johannesburg to Baziotis, asking if he could send his gun in for repairs. He must be a friend of Baziotis: they were apparently on a first-name basis:

Dear Jules:

Last week I was elephant hunting by myself in Botswana. I was using my Model 63J Cree—970 Lovell Carbine, Serial No. 784122, a gun originally purchased from Florence Tyson in Durban. Just recently the gun had been gone over by Paul Michaels, Michaels Gun Shop, Johannesburg, all of which is by way of saying I had every reason to believe the gun was in very good order.

I started tracking three bull elephants about 0800 hours, and finally came up with them at 1500 hours that afternoon. I selected the largest of the three, and tried for a head shot, which I might add is not my favorite.

With a good sight picture between the elephant's eyes at about 40 yards, I pulled the trigger for which I got a not very satisfying "click." That round was ejected and replaced with one which fired, but by then I was sufficiently rattled to be a bit off to the left in my sight picture, ergo a wounded elephant. I should note I fired three times, all hits, and had no difficulty with my weapon.

I continued after the elephant, slept on the ground in the bloody rain, and finally came up with him at 0800 hours the following morning when I shot him properly. Again, no problems such as described.

He went on to say that on the afternoon following all this the gun had suddenly fired while he was checking the bolt.

Apparently Baziotis had not responded to this letter. There had been no reply stapled to the back of the original. That was not like Baziotis: he was partial to South African and Rhodesian whites and, at least in the old days before the Feds, he had dictated immediate replies to their letters. Maybe the response, filed under South Africa, had been shredded, while the letter itself, misfiled under Botswana, had been overlooked.

Muriel began to wish that she had overlooked it too. It was certainly evidence: here was a South African hunter who would be a fitting candidate to pen the screenplay for a remake of *The Macomber Affair*, and who had bought a Lovell gun from Florence Tyson. That was illegal: U.S. firms and individuals were prohibited from sending munitions of any sort to South Africa. But how could it be proved that Florence Tyson was acting as an agent of Lovell? All the correspondence with her had been shredded. Maybe she was selling second-hand guns, operating a sort of military St. Vincent de Paul's. That was highly unlikely since all those warranty cards had been received from South Africans and used products did not as a rule come with warranty cards.

Nevertheless it had to be proven that Florence Tyson had not originally bought this guy Vietgrot's gun in Europe or in another African country.

The other problem was that the gun was an elephant gun. Nobody was going to get upset if elephant guns were being smuggled to weekend hunters in South Africa. Vietgrot had a sporting life: he was not going to line up a group of blacks against the walls of a squalid ghetto and shoot them in cold blood with his elephant gun. He gave no evidence of being interested in joining a volunteer police force or in fact shooting people of any color.

What would a grand jury think if it were handed evidence like this—elephant-stalking in Botswana?

Muriel sighed. Here was a valuable piece of evidence and it had to be from some guy who had overdosed on Ernest Hemingway.

# Six

Bernie sat in the Packard with Muriel, reading the letter and fiddling with the gold chain around his neck.

"You've got a problem here all right," he said when he finished. "You're right about the grand jury—this won't impress them. But grand juries have no minds of their own anyway. If the prosecutor wants an indictment they'll hand him an indictment."

He flicked the parking lights on. It was getting dark and he was afraid that someone might hit the Packard on this side street where, at Muriel's insistence, he had pulled over to read the letter.

"It's pretty funny, though," he said. "Sleeping all night in the bloody rain. And what the hell else did he do? 'Shot the elephant properly.' It must be funny to hear blacks talking like that."

"Blacks don't talk like that, Bernie," Muriel said impatiently. "They have Zulu accents, accents from African languages." She was in over her head. What had Marilyn, her foreign exchange student friend, told her? High school had been so many years ago; she couldn't remember.

"Okay, okay," Bernie pantomimed surrender. "Don't get mad. What do I know about South Africa? You're the expert."

Muriel accepted the compliment uncomfortably. She didn't deserve it. She hadn't even been reading the newspapers lately. Elba's scolding had shaken her. "You know Marilyn," she said, "that foreign student I was friendly with in high school? The other students really hurt her feelings making fun of her accent. All they ever learned about South Africa was that instead of saying 'beep the horn' there they'd say 'pop the hooter.' Everybody used to ask Marilyn to say that at parties, like she was a myna bird or something."

"So what do you expect from high school? I'll tell you someone else who talks funny."

"Who?"

"Gene Kelly. He lisps. I can't stand it. I hear he sings a solo in this picture. I swear, I'm going to walk out of that theater if he sings."

"You wouldn't do that," Muriel said, smiling.

"Oh, yes I would. I'll walk out of the goddam theater and get in my car and pop the goddam hooter until it's over."

They both laughed, relaxed, as Bernie pulled out into traffic. They thought it would be great to draw up in front of the theater in the grand old car, like stars arriving at a premiere in the thirties, but there was no parking in front, and besides it was the wrong kind of theater. It was constructed of natural woods; its name was outlined discreetly in chrome. Muriel was depressed by its quiet good taste. In the lobby, instead of popcorn, puffed wild rice was for sale, laced with soybean margarine, and there was a lithograph exhibit by a competent, dull artist. In the auditorium, soft lights glowed on the aisles. The moviegoer was thus denied the surreal experience of finding the path back from the restroom by the glow emanating from the actors' heads in close-up.

Muriel and Bernie found seats in the fourth row and tilted their similar chins up expectantly.

*On the Town* was the first Hollywood musical to be filmed on location: in it New York City looked as false and illusory as a Burbank backlot. Gene Kelly, a sailor on twenty-four hour leave, falls in love at first sight with the beauty queen of the subway. Searching for "Miss Turnstiles", he, Frank Sinatra and Jules Munshin, go to all the New York landmarks. In the Museum of Natural History, Ann Miller, a nymphomaniacal archaeology student, dances through the exhibits, singing praises of prehistoric man. It is 1949; fashions of the forties are metamorphosing into fashions of the fifties. As Ann Miller dances, her skirt flies open: its plaid lining matches the trim on her hat, which matches her purse and her gloves. This is as fascinating as the music.

"What are you doing, Muriel, waiting to see who the key grip was?"

The credits were rolling and the house lights had come on full strength. The management of the theatre wasted no time in restoring blinding reality.

"Okay, let's go."

Muriel shrugged into her coat and followed Bernie up the aisle. As she passed the natural food refreshment stand she wondered, as usual, what the Pacific Theatre owners could be thinking of, with their health food, their hardwood floors, their cleanliness? What on earth did all these things have to do with the movies?

Bernie was still complaining about Gene Kelly while they walked back to the car.

"Why couldn't he dance *with* somebody?" he said. "Fred and Ginger worked things out together. And after Ginger,

Fred had the others—Barrie Chase, Leslie Caron, and—what's her name?"

He wrinkled his brow and snapped his fingers.

"Juliet Prowse!" he said. "That's it—Juliet Prowse. Did Fred dance with Juliet Prowse?"

"I don't know," Muriel said. She felt depressed. She didn't remember whether Fred Astaire had ever danced with Juliet Prowse, but she did remember that Juliet Prowse was from South Africa.

"Kelly is a fucking egotist," Bernie said. "He always has to have center stage. Either Vera Ellen—did you ever notice that she looks exactly like a rodent?—is five miles in back of him, or he's scraping and bowing at Cyd Charisse's feet, and she stands there like a statue. Or else he's by himself in a mud puddle."

"While Astaire dances with broomsticks."

"One number with a broomstick, about five hundred with girls."

Bernie stood at the door of the Packard, fumbling through his key ring to find the key to the burglar alarm. He found it, and slid into his seat while Muriel waited at the passenger door. Through the window she could see his mouth moving; he was still arguing. He reached over to open her side and she got in.

"One thing I liked though," he was saying.

"What was that? It couldn't be the whole movie, could it?"

"No, of course not. But Frank Sinatra, it was interesting to see him at that age. Can you believe women went wild over him? I mean, all right, a great voice, granted, but a sex symbol? He was a skinny malink!"

They stopped for a red light, and Bernie looked pensively at his own thin wrists.

"I liked Betty Garrett," Muriel said.

"Who? The lady cab driver? She was all right. But what a voice! It was almost as bad as Gene Kelly's and that's saying a lot. What ever happened to her anyway?"

"I'm not sure," Muriel said. "She was married to Larry Parks, and I know he was blacklisted during the McCarthy era. Maybe she was, too." It occurred to Muriel that she might be blacklisted when she broke the Lovell story. But blacklisted from what? Working as a bilingual secretary?

"Listen," Bernie said, "Larry Parks should have been blacklisted for his performance in *The Jolson Story*. And Evelyn Keyes, my God! Playing Ruby Keeler. I hope she got blacklisted too."

"I don't know what you're complaining about," Muriel said. "That was a great picture."

"Oh, sure, but not because of those two . . . "

They were a block away from the Clement Street bar. "Now don't forget what we talked about, Bernie," Muriel said.

"I think you think you're in a suspense flick," Bernie said. "There's an FBI agent hiding behind the picture on the wall above the bar. I've seen transcripts of the hearings on it—"

"Please be serious, Bernie. This secretary I'm meeting—if she shows up—has been trying to crash the data base, and she might have information I need, about the Mexican agent. She might have his address. I need to find out where those guns are being converted, Bernie. This story has got to be about more than elephant guns; otherwise it'll fall flat on its face."

"Listen, is this girl a computer whiz? I'd like to talk to her. I'm thinking of buying a computer system; it's like a law library on a TV screen. Hey, does she know anything about floppy disks?" Bernie was getting excited.

"I don't think she's a computer whiz; I think she's just

friendly with some of the computer repairmen. *I* can tell you about floppy disks; I'm starting to work with them.''

"You are? Really?" Bernie was hitting the curb, trying to park in his agitation.

"I'll talk to you about it tomorrow," Muriel said. She was going to spend the night at Bernie's; the BART didn't run late at night.

Bernie had forgotten about this. He frowned; what if he met someone tonight? What woman would ride home with him with his kid sister sitting in the back seat? No woman, that's who. The idea was out. He glanced at Muriel as they walked together down the street. Why was she wearing those suburban junior league clothes? Didn't she own a pair of jeans? And all this talk about intrigue and investigations—she was going off the deep end. In a shirtwaist dress and pearl-button earrings.

The bar, called Marshall Pétain's, was new, but Muriel and Bernie had been there before. Tonight was two-for-one night, so the place was full. Bernie established himself at the bar; Muriel wanted a drink too, but she spotted Gerardina sitting on a window seat squeezed in with three other people. Did she know them? Muriel had asked her to come alone.

Gerardina was wearing a long paisley skirt and tennis shoes. Her flat face, with small features crowded into its center, was impassive as usual. She looked like some kind of insect; Muriel half-expected antennae to bobble into sight as Gerardina turned her head toward her and said, "How you doing, man? So where's your brother?" She was talking even louder than usual over the noise of the crowd and the jukebox.

"He's over there," Muriel replied tensely, "in the brown leather jacket with the zippers all over it."

Gerardina squinted across the room.

"He doesn't look much like you," she said. "He's got brown hair."

Muriel still wanted a drink and Gerardina wasn't holding one, but the mob at the bar was ten deep. "Look," Muriel said, "why don't we take a walk? Just for a few minutes?"

Gerardina pulled her shawl around her and nodded assent. She left without a glance at the people on the window seat; apparently she did not know them.

They walked for five blocks while Gerardina talked about the data base. A software malfunction had caused a listing for Accounts Payable to flash across her screen; she had seen a large order for guns to be sent to Austria and billed to Rollins Memorial.

"But that's the name of a blood bank," Muriel said. "Rollins Memorial Blood Bank."

"I know, man. I used to wait for the bus near the blood bank when I worked at Sears. But on the tube it didn't say 'blood bank'. Uh uh. It said 'Rollins Memorial'. I think so anyway. Maybe it was my imagination."

"Your imagination?" Muriel asked, alarmed. "What do you mean?"

"Man, I only saw it for a second. That information is supposed to be read-protected. I'll never catch it again. Maybe it was in my mind; maybe I was thinking about how I used to stand in the rain on that corner freezing my ass off." She pulled her shawl around her shoulders. "It can get to you, eye fatigue, you know? I mean, like maybe my eyes got tired and I saw visions, man."

"What was the name of the city in Austria?" Muriel asked. She was determined to be very business-like about this; she refused to be put off by Gerardina's wigged-out behavior. She had said there was hot news from the data base center and she had seen something on the screen about Austria.

It was better not to think about whether she would be willing to testify about this later . . . and if she did testify, what kind of witness would she be?

"They don't use the names of cities in those lists," Gerardina said. "It was a Marketing list."

"I was wondering," Muriel said slowly, trying to sound off-hand, "I've noticed lately that an awful lot of carbines had been sent to a place in Austria called Obergurgl. I mean, that's kind of funny when you think about it, isn't it, a lot of guns going to this small town. You've traveled a lot," she went on effusively. "Do you know anything about that?"

"Austria isn't my kind of space. Maybe they go hunting there, those Austrian assholes like to hunt. You want a joint, man?"

She extracted a crumbling roach from her antique beaded bag.

"No, thanks," Muriel said politely. Gerardina occupied herself with lighting the roach. "I don't actually think there can be that much hunting in this little Austrian town, Gerardina. I mean, not *that* much. I mean I gather there have been tremendous sales to this place for years. Westfeldt has gone there several times . . . "

Gerardina choked on the inhale. "Westfeldt," she said. "That asshole." She pronounced the word with a broad "a". "So what if he went there? His sales territory is Europe. Maybe he went to visit some whore in Austria."

She raged on about Westfeldt and Baziotis and all the other tongue-tied monolingual executives at Lovell who did not appreciate her polylingual powers. She stood under the streetlight, smoking dope, gesticulating and swearing.

Muriel was miserable. At any moment a policeman could come up. She had forgotten to put on her underarm shields; they lay uselessly in her bag next to her useless elephant hunting letter.

" . . . and that's why I want to go sailing around the world, man," Gerardina was saying. "I could never live in Austria or any place like that. I got to be near the ocean."

"Are you still planning to sail around the world?" Muriel asked. "With that couple from Sausalito? I thought you didn't think they would take you because you didn't have enough experience."

"They got it down to three candidates, man," Gerardina said. "I go sailing with them every Saturday. They're trying me on, to see how we all relate to each other, you know? We're going to share everything—food, money, sex."

She leered at Muriel, who was horrified at the possibility that Gerardina might be on the high seas when the grand jury was empanelled.

They began to walk back to the bar. Muriel asked whether there was any more information about the Mexican agent. Had anything come to light about his address, besides the post office box in Mexico City?

"Maybe we're sitting on his address in our living rooms," Gerardina said. This was the tired old Lovell underground joke about the mountains of shredded files which had supposedly been stuffed into chair cushions. This woman thought about nothing but rear ends.

"Or maybe it's in your friend Francine's head," Gerardina said. "She worked for Pagano for years. Why won't she tell you the address?"

"Well, how am I supposed to handle that? Can I admit to her that I'm snooping around? What if she's mentioned in the indictment? You know as well as I do that all the underpaid clerks and secretaries were involved in this thing."

It occurred to Muriel that she had had this same conversation before, with Elba. Only now she was taking Elba's side.

"If they were involved, let them go to jail, man. You fucking Americans don't care about apartheid or imperialism or anything." Muriel had heard Gerardina's speech before: the Dutch resistance and the risks they took, the admirable Provos. Listening to Gerardina Muriel always felt that she would have hated those people. Gerardina's voice took on extra venom as they entered the bar.

"And how about this asshole bar, man? Look at the name of it: Marshall Pétain's. Look at his fucking picture over there."

Gerardina's shawl slipped off her shoulder as she pointed to the large framed portrait of a bewhiskered military man that hung over the bar. The bartender stared at her for a minute. Muriel thought the name rang a bell, but she couldn't remember who Marshall Pétain was.

"He was a fucking French fascist, man," Gerardina said. "You Americans think the whole thing was a joke."

Gerardina twirled around on her tennis shoes and left the bar, padding away toward the bus stop.

Bernie was at the end of the bar, fishing in his pockets for change. There were two drinks in front of him. Muriel fought her way through the crowd and tapped him on the shoulder.

"Bernie," she said, "Remember that French movie we saw at the Lumiere? It was about three years ago. The one about Vichy France?"

"Yeah, yeah," Bernie said. He forgot about the girl who was waiting for him impatiently at a table. "That sentimental one about the Jewish kid they sent to the country. And the grandfather was a vegetarian? The father raised rabbits, right?"

"Right. And he listened to the BBC. The grandfather. The French resistance fighters were talking in code . . . "

"Yeah, yeah," Bernie said, frowning. "What was that code

phrase they used, the one about their fighting position? Something about food. 'The apples are red.' No, wait a minute, that's not it. 'The potatoes are done'?"

"Yeah, well, but it was Marshall Pétain I meant," Muriel said.

"This place?" Bernie said. "It was in the movie?"

"No, the guy." She gestured toward the portrait. There he was on Clement Street: Marshall Pétain, collaborator, Nazi puppet.

The girl at the table attracted Bernie's attention. Muriel sipped her drink and looked at the stern mustachioed face on the wall. The grandfather had loved the Jewish child. Nevertheless he supported Pétain. He didn't get the connection. Apparently neither did the people who had named this bar and hung that portrait.

Much later in Bernie's guestroom Muriel lay exhausted. She had just phoned Dennis who told her that the check had finally arrived from the foundation. On Sunday she would take the bus to Salinas. After several experiments, she had discovered that if she lay on her side with her legs bent slightly, the waterbed would stop sloshing.

There was a knock at the door.

"The carrots are cooked, the carrots are cooked," Bernie called from the hall. He made a noise like static on an old radio.

"I just remembered," he said, over Muriel's laughter.

# Seven

Muriel sat at the glass and chrome table and watched in fascination as Bernie made crepes for breakfast. She had never seen batter cooked on the outside of a pan. A non-electric espresso-maker emitted vicious sounds as it forced boiling water over the coffee grounds. Bernie, wearing a dish towel over one shoulder, concentrated on the performance he usually gave for women who were not his sister.

When he was finished he joined Muriel at the table. Between mouthfuls, they discussed her life in Walnut Creek. Bernie said she was crazy to live out there without a car. She should move back into the city. How did she expect to meet anybody? Was she planning to become a Jewish nun? And wasn't there something a little sick about living with a faggot?

Muriel interrupted him there, pointing out that everyone in the Bay area, including himself, knew many gay people; he could not possibly be serious about that.

He blinked. "You know, you're right," he said, surprised. But then he pointed his fork at her. "Dennis isn't on trial," he said. "You're on trial." He drained his bone china demi-tasse of espresso. "Don't you have a sex drive? Don't you want to go out?"

Muriel ate neatly, wiping her mouth often with the paper napkin. She had an urge to crawl under the table and hide, but Bernie would have seen her under there, because the top was made of glass.

"I go out," she said. "I seem to attract . . . profession-als. You know, architects, businessmen, lawyers. Men I don't have much in common with." For a moment she con-sidered adding, "Not lawyers like you, of course." But ac-tually the lawyers she had gone out with were very much like Bernie, without his enthusiasm for films and lovable ec-centricities, of course. They had kitchens and waterbeds like Bernie's. And they made breakfast like Bernie.

"Ah ha, I knew it!" Bernie said. "It's your damn clothes. Don't you ever take a good look at yourself?"

Muriel stared at him. Did he mean she was wearing the same dress she had worn yesterday? She hadn't wanted to bother carrying an overnight bag to work. Or did he know somehow that she had bought the same dress in different colors?

"I couldn't bring a change of clothes," she said defensive-ly. "It wouldn't fit in my bag. You know I'm using the bag to smuggle out photocopies."

"That's not what I meant," he said, looking at her incred-ulously. "I mean you look so straight. Goddam it, Muriel, it's Saturday. Every time I see you on a weekend you're wearing your office clothes. And look at those office clothes. What are you, some kind of young suburban matron? Do you want me to drop you off at your country club in Contra Costa?"

Muriel thought that somehow her clothes must look expensive, if he was talking about country clubs. But she had bought them out of a catalogue. "I don't see why I should have to defend myself for looking straight," she said.

This caught Bernie off balance. He thought for a moment, regrouping his arguments. "Why do you think you're attracting these architects and so forth? These godawful lawyers." So he had noticed the remark about lawyers. "You're sending out the wrong kinds of signals."

Muriel shrugged. "When I lived in the city I met Jesus freaks and burnt-out hippies. Now I'm meeting architects. I don't know. At least this way I get taken out for dinner."

"You're not doing it right, anyway. I've seen Sanford's wife, believe me, I know the score. You're not supposed to wear dresses on weekends."

"I'm not?"

"Christ, no. You're supposed to be dressed for tennis. You're supposed to wear goddam tennis togs."

He was serious but Muriel did not answer him and after a few moments they both burst out laughing.

\* \* \*

Bernie drove Muriel home to Walnut Creek. She was going to pack her bags and leave on the Trailways bus on Sunday. That night, her last evening at home, she and Dennis were going to watch a movie together on TV. Dennis was interested only in movies with trains in them: his favorite was a Doris Day film called *It Happened to Jane*, an obscure movie that Muriel had never seen. It had a locomotive in it. But the movie they were going to watch tonight was *The Scarlet Pimpernel*, the thirties version with Leslie Howard and Merle Oberon. Since it was set in the eighteenth century, it obviously had no trains in it, but Muriel had convinced Dennis that it was worth watching anyway.

* * *

After dropping Muriel off, Bernie headed back to San Francisco. The traffic was slow on the Oakland Bay Bridge: in front of him was a Capri with a bumper sticker that read, "I'd Rather Be Driving A Packard." This plunged Bernie into a fit of depressed self-consciousness. He had begun to suspect that the proper thing was to keep the antique car in the garage and use it only on special occasions; tooling around town should be done in a modest brown compact. He did not doubt for a minute that the owner of the bumper-stickered Capri also owned a Packard, probably one in better condition and with more luxurious appointments than Bernie's. It was so humiliating. An arcane system was operating here, of which the rules were known only to the rich. It was like wearing costume jewelry to a party and keeping your real gems in a safe somewhere.

Bernie drove doggedly, fixing his eyes on the road, fearful of the scornful glances of other motorists. He should never have sold his small American car when he got the Packard. Now the only thing to do, obviously, was to sell the Packard and buy a sports car. Or better yet, sell it and keep the money. Then he could take Chuck's Targa as payment for legal fees. That would work out better at tax time.

He parked the massive car in his garage, climbed out and yanked down the overhead door, brooding about why things that were obvious to others so often escaped him. That was the way it had been at summer camp, under the stars. The other boys had seen the constellations. "There's Cassiopeia!" they cried. "There's Ursus Major and the Plei-ades!" Bernie had squinted upward, wondering why God had chosen to paint the sky with a clogged spray can. "There's Orion!" the boys called. Bernie had moved in circles, staring at the sky until he became dizzy and fell backward on the grass. He couldn't see them.

*   *   *

The following day was Sunday. Lourdes Pagano walked her small dog past the apartment building where Bernie was just reaching to pick up the newspaper from the mat before his door. She had already gone to early Mass, where she had said a prayer for Arno, who went to Mass only with Lourdes' family in Buenos Aires.

The dog sniffed the grass growing near the curb. *Ya* he was used to the smell of the United States. But when did people walk their dogs here? These residential streets were always deserted. For blocks she had seen no one, except for a glimpse of that man taking in the newspaper, that neighbor with the elegant old car. She felt homesick for Buenos Aires whenever she saw that Packard; often she saw it in the mornings as she sat sipping sherry at her window. There had been many cars like that in Buenos Aires. Here everybody drove the practical little *compacto*. Here when things were old, goodbye! Out into the trash! She was still waiting for her possessions to arrive by ship. Arno had promised to call the freight agents soon.

While the dog relieved himself, Lourdes admired the look of her burnt sienna fingernails against the brown leather leash. The young woman at the Revlon counter in Macy's had helped her pick out the color. The salesladies at the cosmetic counters were pleasant. Lourdes frequented only the Revlon counter at Macy's and the Estee Lauder counter at Magnin's. The salesladies there knew her and greeted her effusively whenever she came in. On small cards they noted information about her complexion, skin type and eye color. They sent her birthday cards: this startled her until she remembered that they had also written down her birth date. The Macy's saleslady had added a brief handwritten note to the printed Hallmark greeting: since then Lourdes had found herself buying more from Revlon than from Estee Lauder.

The salesladies had both been about to note down the color of her hair when she stopped them and told them with a smile that that information would change frequently. At this they lowered their eyes, afraid apparently that their question had embarrassed her. These *estadounidenses,* these North Americans, were so frightened about changing their looks. In Buenos Aires everyone experimented: hennaed curls and kohl around the eyes one season, then straight raven hair and pale white faces. Here everybody pretended not to notice when you dyed your hair. Now this month, March, Lourdes' eyebrows were pencil-thin and her hair, like her fingernails, was burnt sienna.

There was a small bald spot on Arno's crown now. He did nothing to hide it; he could have thought of ways to comb his hair over it. Although he still wore his beautiful European clothes, he paid little attention to his appearance. But he was always telling Lourdes how to dress. He said she should not change her hair and her makeup all the time; people in San Francisco did not like it; it was considered lower class. But around Union Square Lourdes had seen stylish women wearing dramatic clothes. She told Arno that he did not know what he was talking about.

"They're probably secretaries or receptionists," Arno said. "Out shopping on their lunch hours."

Lourdes didn't understand that. Why should secretaries dress better than the wives of executives? Sarah Westfeldt wore big boxy shoes. Lourdes believed they were actually nurse's shoes which Sarah had had dyed brown.

"The secretaries at your place don't dress well," she said.

Once, while Arno ran in to get something, she had waited for him in the car in the Lovell parking lot and watched the women walking across the macadam. When Arno came back he pointed out a few of them: Francine, *la grasasa,* the greasy-faced one. The woman from Customer Service, *la ruca,* the wasted old woman with the hair of an ostrich.

"A different kind of female works out there, in the industrial zone," Arno said. "In the city, people dress well."

Arno talked down to her when he explained these things; he thought she should have it all figured out by now. But everything was different here. There were no seasons. There were no social seasons. At first there had been dinners with the other managers at Lovell, but now they avoided one another. Once there had been Cuban-American visitors, people Arno had known in his early immigrant days in Miami. They wore diamond rings on their little fingers and picked their teeth with matchbooks. Even Arno had been disgusted by their table manners and their mocking references to a past that they had somehow shared with him. What a waste of an evening, and a shrimp paella!

Arno didn't talk to anyone on the telephone now. He went to work only in the afternoons. In the mornings Lourdes rose from her seat near the window and went to bed, to sleep; she didn't know what Arno did in the mornings.

He had asked her to give up her volunteer work at the Historical Society—although it had been his idea at the beginning for her to work there. But she could not leave. She had been taught from childhood that a wife should obey her husband; she had no intention of being resistant but she could not give up this volunteer work because it would upset her sense of balance. Arno wanted her to leave the Society so that she would not see any more of Sarah Westfeldt. The executives at Lovell did not see each other socially any more, and so the wives should not see each other either. Arno had told all this to Lourdes as he stood before the window in the morning. She had closed the curtains and gone to bed, but now he opened them again; she had to throw her arm over her eyes to shield them from the morning light. When he told her to give up the Society she had murmured, *"Voy a ir. Voy a sobrevivir . . .* I am going to go, I am going to survive." But had he really been there? Was it possible it had been only a dream?

The little dog was growing tired: they had walked through many empty streets. Lourdes had noticed that few people walked out on Sunday. In Buenos Aires on Sunday everyone went outdoors, large families with children. Lourdes' family was growing smaller, not larger. Arno had troubles with the government. Would he become *un desaparecido,* a "disappeared person", like people who had troubles with the government in Argentina? And the stepson Jesus, Chucho as he was called—he was already *desaparecido.* Only Arno had given up looking for him because he had begun receiving postcards from his son which said, "I am all right. Do not worry about me." The postcards had no return address, but they were postmarked San Francisco, so Arno knew the boy was close by. The postcards were a very good thing: Chucho stayed away but Arno no longer hired private detectives to look for him, and Lourdes did not have to look sad and upset when the ladies at the Historical Society asked her about "the unfortunate situation". Chucho's mother, who did not seem to have worried much, must have received postcards too, because she no longer wrote to Arno on her orange stationery in her awkward handwriting.

Yes, the postcards made everything better. Sometimes

Lourdes wondered whether it had been she herself who sent them, mixing them in with her homesick letters to her family in Buenos Aires.

After all, there was an element of fantasy in the mail. When you posted a letter to Argentina who knew if it was ever delivered? Maybe there was no more Argentine mail service. Lourdes had heard nothing from her family for a long time. Perhaps the stevedores were on strike, although such things were forbidden now under *la presidente* Isabela's state of siege. Or the stevedores might be fighting the army. Things had been boiling for a long time. The Peronist Left had gone underground since the death of Juan Peron. Lourdes' father had rejoiced when Peron returned from Spain, older, wiser, more conservative, ready to purge the radicals from his ranks. But now Peron was dead and soon the widow would falter. Surely *el General* Videla must be tiring of sipping tea with Isabelita, explaining maps to her, giving her avuncular advice. Soon Videla would want to change seats with Isabelita. The generals would be back. And Lourdes' father, though a Peronist at heart, would resign himself. He had always been careful about what he said. He, among many other things, was the Lovell Munitions agent in Argentina, but he had never been stupid enough to sell guns to the Rightists. The guns were for hunting on the pampas. Lately Papa had been very busy with a yarn factory which he owned in the suburb of Avellaneda. It would be messy for some when the army returned, but not for Papa. But no mail. What a bother!

She had come very far from Jackson Street. She must turn back soon. The dog was panting; he would have to be carried part of the way home. It was late morning now and Lourdes was tired too. On Sundays she did not sleep in the morning, which meant that she did not sleep at all. Nevertheless she would have to cook the heavy Sunday dinner. She and Arno observed this Hispanic ritual, a ceremony which was meant to reunite the family after the work week. Sunday was a family day.

The pantry was stocked. During the week she shopped late, after Arno had come home, and she had finished her work at the Society. At that time of day—almost evening—it was difficult to find good meat and produce. Lourdes walked all over the Marina, visiting the greengrocers, the coffee and spice stores, and finally the butcher, who saved fine cuts for her. By the time she came home there were only a few hours left for talking before Arno became sleepy and went to bed. But the liquor stores stayed open late. When she walked the dog in the evenings, Lourdes often went out of her way to search for fine Chilean wines. Already she had quite a collection of them, stacked in a garish brass wine rack, a memento of the *maldita* first wife. It was pleasant to think of the bottles lying there with their little corked necks stretched out, each eager to be selected.

She picked up the dog, who gratefully licked her face. She laughed and automatically smoothed her cheek, so that her makeup would not look uneven. Her head was beginning to ache. It was possible that her leg muscles were becoming heavy, unattractive, from all this walking. She should have learned how to drive. But in Buenos Aires it had not seemed necessary. She had avoided the crowded buses and the *subte* which roared underground, satisfied to walk during the day and ride at night in cars driven by her brothers or her young men. She had been brought up to consider public transportation unsuitable for a person of her class. Thus in San Francisco too she refused to board buses. As she walked back to Jackson Street she thought suddenly of the money her father sent her four times a year. If there was bad trouble in Argentina, this money might be seriously delayed.

She thought about learning to drive, and wondered if it

was the same here as in Argentina, if cinema tickets could be sent in to the lottery office as chances to win an automobile. She had always considered film-going a plebian pastime; on Sundays fat parents jammed the galleries with their runny-nosed kids. But here in the *Estados Unidos* going to movies seemed more respectable. Her co-workers at the Society often spoke about movies. Her head throbbed. Maybe she should try going, especially if she could win a car. She wanted to win *un Packard*, like the neighbor's. It would look just right in Latin America, where it belonged, where people would appreciate its size and age. Maybe it would find its way home, like a pigeon. Maybe it would point itself on course, bumping down the dusty roads of Mexico, steaming through Central America and finally reaching Buenos Aires to sweep proudly down the Avenida Nueve de Julio, the widest boulevard in the world.

# Eight

Whatever Muriel had expected when she boarded the Trailways bus for Salinas, she had not expected to spend seven days holed up with Omar Herrera in his monkish apartment, watching him make selections from his library of books about weapons. He was coming toward her now carrying *Ballantine's History of the Violent Century*. A cheerful title. She wondered if he would sit closer to her on the cot this time. He didn't.

She had always thought that Dennis had an odd hobby, but this guy took the cake. Not that she blamed him really. A few more weeks in Salinas and she too might have started collecting something: maybe a pile of police magazines.

Of course she did not have to spend a few more weeks here. Just one more. One down, one to go. It would be a deep pleasure to beat it out of this burg and its tropical heat wave. Or would it? She watched Omar's long fingers move delicately through his unpleasant book, while he searched for a particular illustration. She had spent a week as audience to Omar's morbid show-and-tell. He was fascinated with guns, and she was fascinated with him. She wondered what it would be like to stroke those cheekbones, sharp as bayonets. To brush against those lips, dry as ... sand ... Sandblasting ... He was talking to her.

"Look at this Sten," he said.

Oh, yes. Stens were those makeshift rifles produced in England during World War II. They were lousy little guns, but very easy to manufacture. Every British bicycle and lawnmower factory had pumped them out.

"This one's got a sandblasted stock," Omar said. Like Muriel, he was slight, and the cot barely squeaked when he shifted his weight. He had to sit on the cot with her; there was no other furniture in his apartment.

"See," he said. "They probably sanded the stocks on these Lovell sporting guns. A shiny stock is all right when you're out in the woods hunting deer, but for military use you don't want your stock flashing reflections all over the place."

"I most certainly don't," Muriel said.

Omar closed the book. "This is serious, you know," he said reprovingly. He never used her name. Did he even know her name? "If you don't understand the conversion process you're never going to find the trans-shipment point."

Muriel thought she should probably be annoyed at his tone. But then on the other hand perhaps she should laugh. This entire "vacation" in Salinas was ridiculous.

Omar opened the book again after a pause and showed her another picture. "See," he said, "this is what the levers for an automatic are like. It's not all that difficult to convert a semiautomatic to an automatic."

Muriel laughed.

Omar closed the book again and lit a cigarette. "Are you going to pay attention or not?" he said. The cigarette hung enticingly from his lower lip.

"You've probably noticed," Muriel said, looking at his

hands holding the book, "that I'm not very mechanically inclined. Plus I don't see why I should even try to learn all this. I don't see what good it will do."

The cigarette smoke wafted up to the gas masks hanging from the bedroom ceiling.

"Guarino and I went through this with you already," Omar said patiently. "Eventually you will find this background knowledge very helpful."

Guarino had not been helpful at all. And he wasn't good-looking either. He was short and squat, like those colossal Olmec heads sticking out of the ground in Tabasco. The region, Muriel thought wildly, not the sauce.

"Call Guarino if you feel like it," Elba had said. Damn her. He was waiting for Muriel when she got off the bus.

Of course it was Guarino who introduced Muriel to Omar. Turned her over, so to speak, to his tutelage. She could not understand why these Chicano guys were so anxious to involve themselves in this Lovell thing.

"Migrant workers in the U.S., migrant workers in South Africa . . . Can't you make the connection?" Guarino had yelled at her. But the only connection she really wanted to make was with Omar.

He had gotten up and was back at his bookcase again, his narrow back to her.

"The trouble with you guys is you never worked in an office," she said. "All I have to do is locate a secretary who works in the office at Pardee. Someone in your group must know somebody who works there. Salinas is a small town, right? I mean, after all, Pardee must be a major employer here."

Omar nodded, riffling through a stack of magazines.

"So we find this secretary," Muriel said. "She tells me where the Pardee cattle prods are sent in Mexico. She gives me an exact address."

"And?"

"And that's it! That's the conversion point. See, I don't have to go nosing around machine shops all over Mexico. I've already told you—Lovell subcontracted Pardee to send the cattle prods to South Africa. Mean, horrible electric cattle prods, just like the ones in one of your books over there. Torture devices."

"Right. But how can you be sure that the Pardee prods went to Mexico before they went to South Africa?"

"Because you said so. You said that the gun conversions were probably done in Mexico rather than in Austria because labor is cheap in Mexico."

"*Life* is cheap in Mexico," Omar said. He was looking through a machine gun catalogue.

"And you told me that the shipments to Austria would have had to be by air which is expensive, so probably lots more guns were trans-shipped via Mexico."

"Right," Omar said. He came back to the cot carrying a magazine. Its headline, a yellow gash, read: "A Special Report on OJUS Barbed Wire."

The room seemed to be growing hotter and Omar was not paying any more attention to Muriel than he ever had. Don't do it, she said to herself, don't do it. But she did it. She began to whine.

"I really don't see why you and Guarino can't help me find a Pardee employee. I came all the way down here just for that, and nobody's giving me any help at all."

"Because the prods weren't trans-shipped through Mexico," Omar said, flipping through the magazine.

"But they were! I am sure, I am positive that my boss at Lovell made arrangements with Pardee. The dealer in South Africa was dying for some prods."

Omar looked directly at her.

"Sure," he said. "But there was no reason to send them

through Mexico or any other interim point. They went directly to Johannesburg."

"It's not legal to send weapons to South Africa."

"Cattle prods aren't weapons."

"I know that. But they're classified as non-military arms. I'm telling you I know all about this. I did research on it. Exports of non-military arms to countries that violate human rights have to be reviewed by a special board—"

"At the Commerce Department," Omar said. "I know."

Somehow looking into Omar's eyes was not as pleasant an experience as she had expected it to be. She shifted her gaze to the helmets hanging on the coat rack.

"Here's how it goes," Omar said. "Pardee, or any other U.S. company, has this nasty stuff it wants to ship to human rights offenders. So the company goes to the review board at the Commerce Department and says, 'We got some non-military arms we can get a good price for.' And the board says, 'What have you got there? Blackjacks for Thailand? No problem. A couple of thousand shock batons for Joburg? Go ahead.' See, licensing is not the same as restricting. They license everything. I've got a list of the things they approved last year. You won't believe it."

She believed it already. The helmets on the coat rack were German. How come this guy collected German military gear? Weird.

"So I came all this way for nothing," she said. "The Pardee prods don't have anything to do with my investigation."

Omar got up to find his list of licensed exports.

"Cheer up," he said remotely. "You didn't come here for nothing. Look at all this stuff I showed you. It's going to help, you'll find out where the conversions are taking place. You'll be able to catch them in the act."

He returned to the cot with some more gruesome books. He and Muriel chatted for quite a while about billy clubs and truncheons and curdler sirens and, best of all, the counterinsurgency chemicals that police threw against walls to light up the night. Muriel found that very cinematic.

All in all, it was a pleasant archival evening—much better than watching television in the modern motel room across the highway. The sun went down, and a wisp of air coming through Omar's window became a breeze that made the windowshade jiggle and dance in delight.

# Nine

Arno Pagano sat hunched in despair at his desk, his face cupped in his hands. His elbows slid slowly outward and knocked an ashtray onto the floor, reminding him that he needed a smoke. He sat upright and patted his jacket pockets, to locate his cigarettes and lighter. He did not need to stand up; he carried objects only above his waist, because his trousers were cut close, Argentinian style. He finally found some Pall Malls and a book of matches in his desk drawer. He puffed slowly, holding the cigarette in his palm in the continental manner.

He wondered what to do with the ash, since the ashtray lay shattered near the leg of his chair. He wondered also how the pack of Pall Malls had gotten into his desk drawer: he never used either American cigarettes or matchbooks. The cigarettes tasted vile, as he had expected they would, and stale, which he had not expected. He tried to remember if any of his acquaintances smoked this brand, exactly how long it had been since he had worked in his office, and who besides himself had a key to it. He could not think of the answers to any of these questions and he was also anxious about the lengthening ash; he was not enjoying his smoke.

There was a knock on the door. He started and one problem was resolved as the ash fell onto his trousers. Francine entered the room without waiting for a response. Arno stopped brushing off the ashes and smiled at her. After all she could only see him from the waist up and he knew that he looked as charming as ever.

"Well!" she said. "Long time no see!"

"Ah, yes," he said, puffing on the cigarette. He hoped that was the right answer. Francine always used slang. She was poorly bred.

She told him how glad she was to see him, complained about her new boss Randrup and made little jokes—the same little jokes she always made—about the word-processing machine. He smiled, nodded and looked concerned. When she began to talk about the computers he realized that he was smiling in the wrong places, because she stopped and explained, "You know—the *byoob* tubes."

"Ah, yes," he said, smiling with his teeth lightly clenched. He drew deeply on the cigarette and listened to her attentively. She began to talk again and then broke off suddenly. "Watch out for your ash!" she cried. "Where's your . . . oh, I'll get one."

She was in and out of the room in a flash, returning with a paperclip tray. She dumped its contents all over his desk and put it down in front of him. He flicked the Pall Mall into it and thanked her politely. Francine scraped up the paperclips apologetically and said that she had better go now, because she knew he had a lot to do. "Keep the tray," she said. "Muriel won't mind." Then she murmured something about Sharon doing a good job, and was gone.

Arno stared vacantly after her. She was a silly girl, but she admired him. If only he could receive such warm glances at home! He had no luck in marriage. His first wife had been a hellion. Now he had a shy one who peeked at him around corners. His only child lived somewhere within walking distance of his house, but corresponded with him only by postcard.

He sighed, and stubbed out the cigarette. Perhaps he should have married an American girl. Possibly with time one could become accustomed to the gum-chewing and the greasy face. He should have thought of the future. The authorities would not consider deportation if he had an American wife, no matter how many felonies he had committed. After all, a little powder would hide a greasy face. Who knew, maybe Lourdes' face was greasy under all that make-up. He had rarely seen her in bed, washed and undressed. A little powder would be better than deportation. What life could there be for him in Argentina now?

He had made a big mistake. He should never have sold arms to Enrique Cernades, the gun-supplier to an anti-communist league—he had done it just before Peron returned from Spain. Of course he could not have known that a month before Peron's death Cernades was going to be kidnapped by Leftists. Papers may have been seized. The Leftists, who had their own reasons for knowing Arno well, may have noted his name in the correspondence about the gun orders. A trap might be waiting for him if he returned to Buenos Aires. Right now the situation appeared tranquil. There was a state of emergency; the Leftists had gone underground. But eventually they might surface. And they would remember Arno. There were certain eventualities . . .

It was insane to be a commercial arms trader in Argentina and meddle in politics. It might be just as profitable, and safer, to work with the police, but he lacked the skills. He just sold weaponry; he didn't know how to use it. The police would find out now that Arno was in disfavor with the U.S.

Government, their source of loans, grants, technical training. Only a rich man like Lourdes' father could afford to sell guns safely in the Argentine. He kept his nose clean by selling only to hunters. It was a diversion for him, a hobby. Why should he have to care about money—he had his inheritances, his real estate, his yarn companies. Arno's father-in-law would enjoy seeing him crawl back home, disgraced, defeated, begging for a clerkship in one of the factories. And of course even that might not be possible.

Arno squeezed his hands together nervously. It was amazing that things could have come to such a pass. He was actually back where he started from when he had first come to the United States, a know-nothing, a greenhorn, walking the streets of Miami in his elegant pants with their empty pockets. Desperation must have exuded from him like the odor of an animal. But he had gotten some work from older men—Cuban-Americans. Before he had even learned English, he knew a thing or two about the Miami underworld.

Now he was far from that life—in miles and in years of respectability. He had no criminal record; there was no proof of anything. But Baziotis knew something. He had made veiled allusions. The question was, would he play that card?

Baziotis was pacing around outside the office. The sound of his steps receded; he had moved down the corridor. Arno began to relax. Then he stiffened again as the footsteps returned. Now Baziotis was standing outside the office door, near the secretary's desk. Arno decided that he would not behave like a caged animal. He ground his cigarette into the paperclip tray, making the plastic sizzle, stood up, straightened his clothes and walked boldly out of his office.

Baziotis was flipping through the "in" basket on the desk of their mutual secretary. He looked up, startled. "Ah, Arno," he said. "How goes it?"

"Fine," Arno said genially. "Fine." He forced a smile.

"Westfeldt's girl is holding the Latin American mail," Baziotis said. "Well, I'll see you, Arno."

He hurried away down the corridor again, his loose clothes flapping around him. Arno watched him, wondering what the bastard was doing at the secretary's desk. Playing the grand supervisor, no doubt, always checking up on the clerical staff.

Paperclips were scattered all over the desk. That was Francine's work, of course; the new girl was very neat. What was her name? Mariel. No. Muriel. He had paid little attention to her these last few months, only pausing briefly by her desk to pick up messages on his way to the conference room. She was thin and unsubstantial, something like his wife Lourdes. He remembered hiring this Muriel. Perhaps she had reminded him of Lourdes. Why was he always drawn to women who eluded him? Her desk looked uninhabited. Was it always like this or was she out sick? Baziotis had said that Westfeldt's girl had his mail. Arno went to look for Francine.

He found her sitting in front of a computer terminal, which emitted high beeping noises as she struck the keys. She cooed loudly at Arno. Muriel was on vacation, she said; she herself was delighted to help out. Muriel had one week paid, one week unpaid, which was really amazing on that salary. Francine herself could never afford that unpaid week. In the meantime Sharon would help him.

"There isn't really all that much to do," she confided in a lowered voice. She added that she wished that she could work with him instead of Sharon, but she was helping to typeset a brochure. Randrup was coming back soon from a marketing meeting.

Arno retrieved his mail from Sharon and took it into his office. The letters, all unopened, carried stamps with aquamarine and fuschia backgrounds—colors rarely used on

North American stamps: they were from Bolivia, Paraguay, Guatemala. Minor accounts. One was from Haiti. That would be an order for clay ducks for Baby Doc, president for life and afficionado of skeet shooting.

Sitting at his desk, Arno held the unopened letters in his hand. His job was slipping away. No one needed a twenty-five thousand dollar a year manager to sell guns to backwater accounts. His work would be absorbed by Jules Baziotis, African sales manager. Then, when Arno was gone, sacrificed, the foreign police would start ordering again. The Feds would vanish from Lovell, and the "all clear" signal would be given to police barracks in Chile, Nicaragua and El Salvador. Big orders would start coming through again, and Baziotis would line his pockets with the commissions.

Arno began to look through his drawers for a letter opener. Perhaps there were other strange objects in there as well. So far as he remembered, Baziotis did not smoke. Although he might have taken up the habit recently. Baziotis had been working his regular hours in the office while Arno and the others had been spending their mornings in a suite at the Jack Tar Hotel, discussing strategy with the corporate lawyers. They had all been assured that there would be no indictments. There had been plenty of time to shred the documents. No grand jury would indict on the flimsy evidence that was left, and very few people would be called to testify. Unfortunately Arno would be one of them, but his personal lawyer had told him what he should say. As more and more of the executives began to retain personal counsel, less and less of substance was discussed at the Jack Tar meetings. Lately the managers just sat quietly and listened to the corporate attorneys ramble reassuringly on. The only indictment possible, the lawyers said, was an indictment of the corporation itself. No individuals would be named. The corporation would enter a plea of *nolo conten-*

*dere*, and the whole dirty business would end. There would be the small matter of a fine.

So the corporate lawyers talked to the roomful of impassive ghosts, pale executives from Customer Services, Sales, Accounts Receivable, Advertising, all of whom had been told by their personal lawyers to say nothing. The meetings were like deadly poker games. Finally they ceased altogether. Arno was telephoned and told to resume his regular full-time duties.

Baziotis had been present at a few of these sessions. Westfeldt had not attended any. That was probably because Westfeldt was safe: the Austrian connection would never be discovered. But why had Baziotis been excused? After all he was the manager of sales to Africa. The finger had to point at him.

A familiar icy feeling of fear flooded over Arno; he reached for another of the stranger's cigarettes. Baziotis was going to turn state's evidence; he would testify against Arno, who was going to be the scapegoat for the company. No matter how lightly the Lovell lawyers talked about the possibility of an indictment, they did not want one; there was more at stake than a fine. Lovell could lose its gun manufacturing license.

Arno's own lawyer had told him that this idea was ridiculous. He had said that if Arno was indicted there would be a trial and then Arno's defense would expose the company. "They'll open up a can of worms." That was what the lawyer had said. And it was true. Lovell was full of worms. The worm Jules Baziotis would eagerly bore into Arno's territory after he was gone. And there were ways to silence Arno if he went to trial—the company would think that way. They might try to bribe him, they might approach him with money. But it was more likely that they would blackmail him somehow. He would be deported. Everyone knew he

was afraid of deportation. Stupidly he had talked about it
openly when this whole mess began; he had said that he
should have gotten his citizenship years ago.

Now the company would consider him a security risk.
They would be convinced that he would turn state's
evidence and testify against *them* in order to avoid deportation. Westfeldt had not looked at him when he went in to ask
Sharon for the mail.

The mail. He had forgotten about it; he was still holding it.
He got his letter opener and slit the envelopes. A letter of
credit from Haiti. To be routed to Accounts Receivable. An
order from Paraguay for .22 magnums. Hunting guns. The
secretary could easily handle this. How was he going to
justify his job with this kind of stuff? A letter from the
agent in Costa Rica inquiring about the cartridges they had
ordered.

Nothing from Brazil, Nicaragua, the big accounts. Baziotis had undoubtedly taken them over. There was an inter-
office memo from Engineering mentioning the technical
assistance arrangement with the Colombian government.
That seemed to be proceeding well without Arno.

The last letter was from Robles, one of the Guatemala
agents. He read it quickly and then re-read it slowly.

Dear friend Arno:

Everything has been destroyed in this tremendous
earthquake. Fifty per cent of the buildings in the capital
have been damaged; entire populations have virtually
disappeared in the interior of the Republic. More than
twenty thousand dead rest under the debris of their
humble houses; sixty thousand people have been
maimed or wounded. Highways were impassable, mountains collapsed, bridges broke into two—in short, it was
something terrible, and to think that it all happened in
36 seconds!

It was an awakening that I will always remember in nightmares. We were asleep. It was three in the morning. We felt everything falling in the house—the lamps tumbled down, pictures fell to the floor, no electricity. The entire city was plunged into darkness and we couldn't even stand up straight. Doors that were opened slammed shut and those already closed became jammed. It was horrible.

Good friend Arno, we are grateful for your consideration worrying yourself about us. I beg you to excuse us for not having answered your cablegrams these two months, and I hope you understand the powerful reason for this. Be assured that my family and I have been fortunate and lost only our home.

Your friend who esteems you,
Juan Carlos

Arno sat stunned. He had not known anything about the earthquake and so he assuredly had sent no cablegrams. Perhaps there would be no need after all for Baziotis to take over the Latin American accounts: that sales territory was a landscape filled with coups, sieges, assassinations and natural disasters. Possibly before long all the agents would be gone: murdered, imprisoned, fallen into cracks in the earth.

He took another cigarette from the package, a gift from a phantom.

# Ten

Willa leaned against the door and dug into her handbag, searching for the office keys. It was Monday and her weekend had been anything but relaxing. As she inserted the key in the lock she noted wearily that a new sign had been painted onto the glass. Squinting through pinkish eyes at the long flowing seraphs of the shiny black letters, she read "ckerman & xelrod." Something was definitely wrong. After a moment she noticed a large capital A that was evidently meant to serve both names. Ackerman and Axelrod. The hell with both of them.

She hung her coat on the clothes tree and unlocked the center drawer of her desk to take out the aspirin bottle. On her way to the watercooler, brooding deeply about having had to spend Sunday until the wee hours nursing her sick cousin Charlene in Dolores Park, she thought she noticed black marks on her raincoat. She pulled it off the hook and examined it. Then she walked quickly to the door and swung it open. The paint was still wet. Her coat was ruined. And the lettering was unmistakably smudged. Bernie would be there in half an hour. No—today was Monday. Sanford would be in first. Or wait a minute. Maybe it was Bernie after all.

With four aspirins burning a hole in the lining of her stomach, Willa was working feverishly on the door when she heard footsteps down the hall. She froze, a Q-Tip in one hand and a bottle of Liquid Paper thinner in the other. Then she slumped in relief. It was only a client, a slim young man wearing a suit.

"Is this the office of Attorney Bernard Axelrod?" the young man inquired.

"Attorney Axelrod will be in soon," she said, waving him in with her Q-Tip. "Won't you please take a seat?"

She went back to work and stood back after a few minutes to survey the repairs. Not bad. Some of the edges were a little wavy, but they could blame the sign painter for that. She went back into the office, carefully closing the door, and sat down at her desk.

"May I smoke?"

The young man's formality was amusing, especially on this day which had started out badly.

"Yes, of course." She pointed to the ashtray on the table next to the couch and he thanked her gravely.

"Attorney Axelrod will be here soon," she said again. She opened her big black appointment book. That was funny: there were no appointments for first thing Monday morning. Maybe this kid was not a client after all. Maybe he was a salesman.

"Did you have an appointment?" she said.

He didn't answer that, but he gave her his name. So this was the elusive Chuck. Bernie would be overjoyed. He had told her about the Porsche. Now he would overlook the paint smudges. She wished that Bernie would not take her into his confidence over superficial things like the Porsche. Maybe he thought he was flattering her, but she wasn't interested in cars. She wanted to learn how to prepare briefs so she could apply for a job at the courthouse. They had a terrific benefits package.

Bernie appeared behind the glass door, obviously admiring the new sign. She watched him nervously; he seemed happy. He came into the office with his shoulders thrown back, smiling broadly.

"You saw it, right?" he said, in greeting. "Classy, no? I got a calligrapher to do that. We had to have the old glass taken out; we couldn't erase the old sign. Pretty nice, huh?" He turned back to look at it again. "They came in over the weekend, the calligrapher and the whatchamacallit. The glazier. Bozo in yet?" This was a reference to the law clerk.

"No, he'll be coming in late for the next couple of weeks. He's cramming for the bar."

"Oh, right, right." He started down the corridor and paused again. "By the way, be careful," he said. "The paint might still be wet. The calligrapher wanted me to pay for lacquer, but I told him nah, use what you got. He's charging an arm and a leg as it is."

He had ignored Chuck who sat watching him coolly, with his legs crossed. Willa waited a few minutes and then buzzed the intercom a little harder and a little longer than necessary.

"Awright, awright," Bernie's voice crackled through the box.

"Chuck is out here, Mr Axelrod," Willa said.

"Are you kidding me? Where were you hiding him—in the closet? I just walked past your goddam desk."

"You overlooked him." Willa switched off the intercom immediately. She fitted a sheet of paper into her typewriter. Bernie's door flew open; he rushed out, extending his hand to Chuck.

Willa followed them down the hall and thrust Chuck's file into Bernie's hands just as he was about to close his door.

"*Very* efficient," Bernie said. He looked after her as she returned to her desk. Always wearing loose-weave clothes, he thought.

Bernie waved Chuck into the chrome-plated director's chair and settled himself behind his big clean Monday-morning desk. "You're lucky you found me in," he said. "Why didn't you phone first?"

"Unfortunately I have no telephone at the present time. Do you mind if I smoke?"

Bernie ran through his repertoire of frightening possibilities about the outcome of a trial for possession of narcotics. The dark face remained impassive. Cool as a cucumber, Bernie thought.

Chuck languidly ground out his cigarette. "You can bargain the plea, can't you?" He folded his hands, raised his eyebrows slightly and looked at Bernie expectantly.

To give himself time, Bernie flipped thoughtfully through Chuck's file. How old was this kid anyway? Twenty-three. Why wasn't he quaking and trembling like the rest of Bernie's clientele, especially since he was facing charges for the first time? Bernie lowered his chin into his collar and began to deliver his frank speech about how, just between you and me, the district attorney's office has been known to show bias. The kid had a dark tinge to his skin; it was like a woman wearing a dark slip under a light skirt. And that name. He was taking a chance; he couldn't tell whether the kid was white or not. He played it safe, not saying "black" or "white". Just "ethnic". He should have asked Muriel what she thought the kid's name showed about his family. And what about Muriel? Why hadn't she called?

"Well, you get my drift, no?" Bernie said. "I mean the D.A.'s name is Haywood Cooke. To a guy like that *I* seem foreign, you know?" He wasn't sure he was getting through. "What I'm saying is that these guys at court have more sympathy for guys who are exactly like them. The same background and so on."

"You're saying that they might discriminate against me because I'm Hispanic."

So. Chuck was Hispanic. He wouldn't have known it from his name, but then what did he know? Once when Muriel told him "Guzman" was an Hispanic name, he had gone into stitches. It sure sounded Jewish to him.

He nodded solemnly. Yes, it was sad but true. He didn't want to say it in so many words—he didn't even like to think about it. But there it was. It was his duty to warn his client.

Chuck remained impassive, still listening. God Almighty, what would it take to scare the shit out of this kid? No scare, no Targa. Bernie flipped through the file again, more slowly this time. Minor girls. Chuck had been picked up selling quaaludes to minor girls. Terrific! Now Bernie could talk from a firmer position. True, he said, quaaludes weren't heavy drugs, but selling to minor girls was heavy indeed. The D.A. would take a dim view of that. Between this and the Hispanic factor, the thing might have to come to trial. Not every plea could be bargained. Once in a while the D.A. had to put someone on trial. After all that was what the taxpayers were paying him for.

Chuck began to look uncomfortable for the first time. Bernie had the feeling that he had discussed all this with someone else already—was he considering changing attorneys?—and he knew that charges involving minors were serious.

"I will tell you one thing," Chuck said. He uncrossed his legs and leaned forward intently. "I do not want this to come to trial. Not so much for myself." He paused. "Someone else is involved. Not involved in the case. It's my family.

I don't want them to know anything about this. Please tell me now, are there are chances at all of having these charges dropped? Can I avoid trial in any way?"

After that it was a piece of cake. Bernie was subtle. He didn't mention the Porsche for a full fifteen minutes. When Chuck showed signs of agreement, Bernie kept his air of sober restraint. He was in control now. As he talked he absently opened and closed the center drawer of his desk. This action reminded him pleasurably of one of the exercises he did on a machine in the health club. It relaxed him.

As he escorted Chuck to the outside door he gave him a little good-natured talking-to. He told him he had better stay in touch, whether he had a phone or not. There were always pay phones. He reminded him that he had gotten him out on his own recognizance at the arraignment, simply by giving the high sign to the D.A., who now became magically transformed from a racist, anti-Semitic ogre into Bernie's best buddy.

He bade the boy *adios* with a clap on the shoulder and called down the hall after him: "Drive carefully, kid. We don't want that car getting wrapped up." He winked slyly at Willa. She met the wink with a curled lip, which he did not see because he was lost again in admiration of his name on the door.

"Sanford see this door yet?"

"Yes," Willa said. She sighed. "He came in about ten minutes ago."

"Wait till I tell him about my boy Chuck." Bernie trucked toward Sanford's office making "vroom-vroom" noises. He gave two quick raps on the door. What a pompous bastard, making his own partner knock. Before Sanford called out "Come in," Bernie's smile faded. It occurred to him suddenly that the story he had told Chuck in order to frighten him was actually true. The D.A. would not be willing to drop all charges. Minor girls. He would have to come up with a deal and it would have to be a pretty good one.

Two days later he was in the office, washing his hands and looking at himself in the mirror over the sink. God, he looked worn-out. Haywood Cooke had driven a hard bargain that morning. And that cabbie had charged a mint just to bring him back from court. He examined his hairline closely. Yes, there was no doubt that it was thinning out. God, his hair was falling out from all the strain. On Sunday he was supposed to pick Muriel up at the bus station and take her to the flicks. In what? He had better have Willa call Hertz. Anything would be better than using the Packard.

Cooke had agreed to dismiss all the charges against Chuck, but one of Bernie's other clients had to stand trial. That was the way it was: Bernie had to find a sacrificial lamb. There was only one choice. The only client Bernie had who was obviously innocent was Eddie from the St Francis Wood party, with his nervous tics and his lint-picking. Bernie was going to have to let this kid go to trial. It wouldn't take long, and the jury would acquit. The parents would bounce all over the walls when they heard this news. It would mean the loss of all referrals from St Francis Wood, especially if anyone out there knew anything about the law. And there was always the chance that the kid would take a leap off the Golden Gate Bridge before the thing was over. The whole thing was a colossal drag, but there was a Porsche Targa purring at the end of the rainbow.

# Eleven

Lourdes Pagano sneezed into her lace-trimmed handkerchief. She was cataloging the San Francisco shipwrecks for the Historical Society, and she was allergic to the dust on the old drawings. They were cheap pictures of grounded vessels, taken from old magazines by some previous volunteer, or "docent" as these unpaid workers were called by the Society ladies.

The corner of one of the illustrations was bent. Lourdes tried to smooth it out. "The tanker Lyman Stewart, rammed in the fog in October, 1927." She would have to take it over to the ironing board in the corner and press it down carefully. Death, destruction, disaster. Mrs Westfeldt had commented before she gave it to Lourdes. "Not a very cheerful subject," Mrs Westfeldt had said. But Lourdes had been eager to get the pictures ready for a maritime scholar who had applied to borrow them. She had even offered to mount the illustrations on mats. The Society would make money from lending them out for reproduction.

Another young docent had demonstrated the use of the

dry-mount press to Lourdes. But she was a student at San Francisco State University, and she had left for school after telling Lourdes vaguely that the wrinkles had to be pressed out before the pictures could be mounted. When Lourdes had asked Mrs Hardenburgh and Mrs Westfeldt if someone could show her how to iron, they had given her strange looks.

"Why, yes, dear," Mrs Westfeldt had said. "Of course servants did that sort of thing for you. But how do you manage in this country? I'd love to know your secret."

Ah yes, Sarah Westfeldt would undoubtedly love to know all of Lourdes' secrets. But Lourdes had no intention of telling her that all the Pagano laundry went to Chinatown for washing and ironing. That would invite a *commentario* from Mrs Westfeldt about how her husband had not seen Lourdes' husband at the office much lately, and wasn't the cost of living becoming outrageous? Mrs Westfeldt had already said that once, staring at Lourdes' new clothes from neck to hem. And shoes.

"Oh, this inflation is nothing, I think," Lourdes said. "In Buenos Aires inflation is frequently 200 per cent, 300 per cent."

Mrs Westfeldt averted her pale blue eyes from Lourdes' dark, thick-lashed ones. "Oh, I'm sure everything is bigger in Buenos Aires," she said in her dry, confident voice. "Bigger and better than what we have here." And she left the workroom quickly on her sensible heels, no more than an inch and a quarter high.

It was dangerous to work the dry-mounting press. The docent from San Francisco State had showed the healing burns on her hands to Lourdes, who recoiled in horror. Forewarned, she had brought little white cotton gloves from home; she unplugged the iron now and pulled these on. The drawing of the *Lyman Stewart* was wrinkle-free: Lourdes arranged it neatly on its mat and inserted it onto the platen. Carefully avoiding the hot spots on the press, she pulled the top down and secured the latch. A pleasant odor of melting wax wafted from the machine. It made Lourdes think fondly of her old-fashioned Spanish grandmother, who had always sealed her letters with wax. But she did not allow herself to be distracted from her task. At the correct moment she opened the press and pulled out the work. It was perfect: the ruined ship was bordered in dove gray, a mourning color.

She took off her gloves and returned to the worktable where she sorted out the pictures to find a smooth one. She disliked working at the ironing board; it made her feel like an American wife, someone who would never return to Argentina to resume her old life. She put on her gloves again and opened the press. The gloves reached only to her wrist and provided insufficient protection, but she could not risk ruining her long leather gloves. The allowance from Papa was late. It was now mid-March and nothing had come from Buenos Aires since early February.

Lourdes lowered the lid with all the weight of her light body. Soon she would be able to ruin as many pairs of leather gloves as she liked, regardless of Papa's allowance. Arno had been back working full-time for three days, and with a substantial raise. Now Sarah Westfeldt would not be able to make any more *commentarios* about his absences from the office. Everything was, as the North Americans put it, "okay".

Actually, now there was no longer any reason to go on working here. There was no further need for escape. Arno was busy at the office. He stayed late and came home with little beads of sweat on his upper lip; he sprawled in his chair looking self-satisfied. Apparently the trouble with the Government was over. She could not read the newspapers with ease: perhaps there was a new American regime. Arno had promised to find out news from Argentina for her. One could not reach Argentina through the telephone lines. The lines were in confusion: that was not unusual. Nevertheless she was anxious about it, although Arno said there was no reason to worry. He was worried again about his son. He was no longer satisfied with the weekly postcards.

Mrs Hardenburgh, director of the Historical Society, came up to the table. "Shipwrecks, is it?" she asked, and began to shuffle through Lourdes' neat piles of mounted pictures.

"Yes, it is very sad," Lourdes said. She plucked another illustration from the file. This was quite a large one, which she had somehow overlooked. It appealed to her sense of the picturesque, and it was completely smooth. Lourdes did not want to iron in front of Mrs Hardenburgh. Carefully, she took the engraving out of its folder and began to trim it.

"What's that one, dear?" Mrs Hardenburgh pulled on the corner, almost causing Lourdes to slash into the picture. "Oh my, that is a gory scene, isn't it?" She clicked her tongue in sympathy. Massive waves rolled in the foreground; behind them tiny sailors spilled from the devastated ship. Mrs Hardenburgh tipped the half-trimmed picture away from her and squinted at the caption.

"Do you know all these words, Lourdes? Reading these captions can help you practice your English."

Lourdes knew exactly what she meant. On many occasions the Society ladies had thrown out hints about schools in San Francisco where people went to learn English as a second language.

"For instance," Mrs Hardenburgh went on, smiling fiercely, "do you know what the word 'reef' means?"

"I do not read the captions."

There was a pause. Mrs Hardenburgh rallied and put on the glasses she wore on a cord around her neck. "You see, it says here: 'In the worst maritime disaster in San Francisco history, the *Rio de Janeiro* was wrecked on Fort Point reef in 1901. One hundred and thirty-one lives were lost. In the hope of preventing such tragedies, the construction on Mile Rock Light began in 1903.' " She looked brightly over the glasses. "Now, I suppose some of those words are rather hard for you. 'Maritime . . . reef'. Those are nautical terms, you know. Now just feel free to ask any of us any time if there is something you don't understand."

There was another pause. "Yes," Lourdes said.

Mrs Hardenburgh handed the picture back to her. "*The Rio de Janeiro*," she said kindly. "I suppose that reminded you of home. The caption doesn't tell us whether this ship belonged to the Argentinian navy; perhaps it did." She turned away and took off her glasses and then turned back again. "Oh, by the way, I hear that you're joining us on the field trip to San Jose. That's lovely; I know you're going to enjoy it. The bus tickets are sold out already." She sighed. "But there are so many things to attend to, I don't know where the time goes. Oh, that reminds me—I have to phone the San Jose Municipal Rose Garden again. We'd better give them fair warning that one hundred rose enthusiasts are about to descend on them, hadn't we?"

Lourdes, who had understood only about half of this speech, said nothing, but Mrs Hardenburgh bustled off without waiting for a reply.

Lourdes resumed her trimming with short, angry snips. Behind her back they laughed at her English, these brilliant women who thought that Rio de Janeiro was in Argentina! Even the *Doctora*, the university professor who served on the Society's board of directors, had made ignorant comments about Argentina. How curious, she had said, that your husband's name is Italian. And all of them were always explaining British customs to *her*, a life-long resident of

Buenos Aires. "We enjoy the English custom of taking tea at four," they said. The cream saucer left rings on her work-table.

English this, English that. They dressed themselves in tweed suits in foolish imitation of the British whom Lourdes knew well in her native country. Hadn't she dined countless times with her friends *los* Wingate at the London Grill in Buenos Aires? These historical ladies knew nothing of the world. And they condescended to *her,* Ma. Lourdes Refugio Vega de Pagano!

She finished mounting the picture of the wrecked *Rio de Janeiro* and straightened the stack of work which Mrs Hardenburgh had disturbed. Pulling off her gloves she examined the mounted illustrations. Ships. She had loved to look at them when she was a little girl, holding her father's hand. Often her entire family had promenaded down the pier after a fine fish dinner in one of the seaside restaurants. La Boca was nearby, the rough Italian section, colorful like the Montmartre in Paris, but not a suitable place for persons like the Vegas. Lourdes had never told anyone, not even her favorite older sister, that she had spent furtive evenings there in tango bars, with her bold friend Luz and two university students. She lowered her head over the pile of pictures to hide her smile. Those were interesting times. Before she met Arno.

Arno was of Italian descent, but he came from a good family. Lourdes' parents may have preferred someone of Spanish descent like themselves, but Arno's ancestry was not included in their catalogue of objections to him. He was, after all, not an Italian workingman like those who lived in La Boca. But he was divorced, he was old, he lived in the United States! She should have listened to her parents. Of course their objections had made him seem more desirable.

Mama had been right. She would never adjust to the

*Estados Unidos*. It was only for the vulgar, like Dick Haymes. His friends and family in the British community in Buenos Aires were still ashamed because of his scandalous adventures in the United States. Here was someone who had had all the advantages—expensive schools, membership in the English rowing club at El Tigre, fine horses—and what did he do with it? He went to the United States to sing songs in cheap night clubs, get married seven times, and drink himself into unconsciousness.

Lourdes had mentioned him once to the pseudo-tweed ladies. One day they had exasperated her out of her taut silence by attempting to explain Victorian architecture to her as though she had spent her life in an adobe hut.

"Oh, yes, I know the English customs," she had said.

"Costumes?"

She repeated her statement carefully, exaggerating her pronunciation.

"Oh. Oh, *customs*!"

She told them that many English people had settled in Argentina and had kept their customs. For instance, Dick Haymes, the famous singer, was an Argentinian of English descent.

"Imes?" they chirped. "Dick Imes? Who?"

Lourdes could not make them understand. But then the *Doctora*, forgetting that she was too intellectual to know anything about Hollywood, suddenly said, "Oh! Dick *Haymes*! An Argentinian—is that right? You remember him, Edna; he married Rita Hayworth. Oh, yes, it's coming back to me now. That's right. The government wanted to deport him."

\* \* \*

Dick Haymes and Betty Grable were dancing and singing on the large color television set in the motel. The fibers of the wall-to-wall shag carpet waved in the blast from the air conditioner like a field of royal blue wheat. Muriel sat on the bed, holding a glass and staring vacantly at the screen. The movie was *Diamond Head*, the first film in a Betty Grable festival. It was Muriel's last full day in Salinas. She had a bad sunburn and a feeling of discontent.

Omar Herrera had just left. His indentation remained on the bedspread. Perhaps there was some way to preserve it, like a religious relic. It was an indentation made by sitting only; she had never been able to get Omar to lie down, even though she often got the feeling that he liked her. Sometimes sexual admiration came through the talk about ammo shells and rim-fire rifles.

But he was put off because he thought she was apolitical. She sucked the ice cubes left in her glass. He didn't approve of that either—drinking before noon. And he certainly didn't care for her remarks about how bored she was at the Salinas Civic Committee to Support the Farmworkers, where he and Guarino had parked her every day. It had been just what she expected: political organizing meant making phone calls and stuffing envelopes. And there was always a priest in the background, talking in a nasal voice and slapping something with a rubber stamp.

The Salinas Civic Committee headquarters reminded her of homework, of repression. She noticed that Omar didn't spend much time there himself. Too busy reading about ways to blow people up. He had no visible means of support, but he had apparently been a farmworker. Hadn't liked it. Gave it up.

She had told him she did not plan to contact the Contra Costa office workers group when she got back home. And no, he had not asked for her address or phone number.

Tomorrow Bernie would pick her up at the bus station. And next stop would be the Lumiere and *Johnny Guitar*. Movies could help a person get over a wasted vacation. And bourbon helped too. In fact it would definitely be more helpful to get hold of room service and order a fresh drink than to watch *Diamond Head*. Dick Haymes had never done much for her anyway. When she finally focused her attention on the TV, only the credits were there, crawling up the screen.

# Twelve

Muriel leaned wearily against the sink in the ladies room, and coated her eyelashes with brown mascara. She had arrived at work a ghost with pallid lids. It had been three weeks since her vacation and she felt more exhausted than before she left. Here she was coming in late on a Monday morning. The standard joke. Perhaps this failing would make her appear more human, less conspicuously perfect. Elba had told her she had to be perfect to keep from being fired; she had retorted that she thought her perfection might attract undue attention. But Elba was always ready with a counter-argument. "It's worked for union organizers," she snapped.

Muriel propped her elbow on the stainless steel ledge running across the wall beneath the distorting twin mirrors. Expertly she moved the brown pencil across her eyelid. The commuters on the BART and the bus had seen Muriel's face today as she never allowed it to be seen in public. It probably didn't matter. They were strangers, people she would hardly be likely to meet again, since she never took that late train. She did not know whether she had slept through the alarm or whether she had forgotten to set it. She had not gotten to bed until one in the morning with her head filled with ideas arising from—believe it or not—a Betty Grable movie. The Grable film festival was still continuing on the network. Three weekends of Betty Grable. A bit much. But the one last night had been really remarkable. *The Shocking Miss Pilgrim.* Maybe Bernie knew about it.

She added a touch of pencil to define the invisible down that arched over her eye sockets. There. Her eyes sprang into being, no longer naked. She was ready for another day of spying.

She turned off the light and her hand was still on the light switch when the door burst open and on the threshold loomed a large woman, her lacquered hair, illuminated from behind, pointing out in spikes like the crown on the Statue of Liberty.

She lunged for the switchplate, nicking Muriel's fingers with her nails. "You don't save one bit of electricity turning off fluorescent lights when you leave the room," she said, flicking the lights back on. Confused, the tubes flickered and sputtered as Muriel escaped from the room.

She groped for a tissue in her handbag and blew her nose. Now all she needed was a cup of coffee, and her day would begin. But which way to turn—left, to her customary post outside Pagano's office, or right, to the computer terminal in Advertising? The two departments had been sharing her since her return from Salinas.

She decided to open Arno's mail first. Surprisingly, he was back full time and generating paperwork like mad. She preferred to start on her old job, even though there would be a pot of coffee perking in Advertising and Randrup was probably away on a business trip. She knew she was procrastinating, avoiding something she knew she had better look into, something that had turned up in one of the electronic files.

She found Arno hovering around her desk, flipping through the mail that had evidently just been dropped off. He greeted her with his usual affected shallow bow, and she responded with her usual nervous giggle.

"So," he said, "they have word processing for you in the mornings now?" He slipped into a casual pose, with his head cocked to one side, and his hands clasped behind his back. He looked a little sheepish, probably because he had been caught poking at the mail. "Are they very busy over there?"

Muriel confessed that she was late; she had just gotten in. She preferred to tell the truth and save lies for more important purposes.

Arno Pagano smiled his smile that never reached his eyes, and shook a playfully scolding finger at her. "Watching too many late shows," he said. He made clucking noises with his tongue.

Muriel's mouth went dry. How did he know what she had been doing? Was someone watching her? But, she thought, that was silly—everyone must know that she was an avid movie fan.

She settled into her chair and daintily ripped the first letter open with her opener. Pagano lit a cigarette and rocked back and forth on his heels. He seemed unusually eager to see his mail. There were over a dozen flimsy airmail letters for him, typed on cheap, unaligned Latin American typewriters. Probably orders. Baziotis hurtled by toward his office, and the stack on the desk blew over.

Pagano's lips tightened around his cigarette while he bent gallantly to help Muriel pick up the scattered papers. Only a letter of credit from a Swiss bank remained on the desk, weighed down by its expensive rag content.

"Our friend Jules is in a hurry," Pagano said pleasantly. "Lots of orders from Lebanon this week. They are killing each other there, the Arabs. All the better for Israel, isn't that true?" He looked at her pointedly.

She kept her head down, rapidly separating the orders from the chaff. She handed them to him with a blank look. "I wouldn't know anything about that," she said. Why didn't he scurry off to his office now that he had his mail? He had seemed so eager to get it. He mentioned Israel to her so that she would know that he knew she was Jewish. People always did that. So. He knew she was a Jew. Perhaps Francine had told him. Redheaded and a Jew. Average weight, average height, average looking, but still she could not blend into the woodwork. The minute she was spotted poking around where she shouldn't be, alarms were going to go off.

But Pagano kept on, holding the orders in his hand. The Arabs were not civilized, didn't she agree? However the United States was a faithful friend of the Jews (there it was: that word). The civil war in Lebanon was a fortunate thing for Israel. And for Lovell also.

"That's interesting," Muriel said. "I haven't been reading the newspapers for a while. I'll have to catch up." She unslung her handbag from the back of her chair and got up. "The computer beckons," she said. Her laughter tinkled like broken glass.

It was true. She still didn't read the newspaper. The trip to Salinas had accomplished nothing. That's what she kept telling Elba. It had been a foolish idea, trying to trace the Mexican contact point through the Pardee shipments. She and Omar had talked to a Pardee mechanic, and Guarino had plodded on with his library research. But nothing had turned up.

"The only thing I found out," she told Elba after her

return, "is that the prod shipments are illegal. That's one more nail in Lovell's coffin."

"I doubt it," Elba said.

Muriel explained the Commerce Department licensing procedures for paramilitary items.

"Who told you that, Guarino? Well, I gave him that information, but it's wrong. Things like leg irons and gas masks have to be registered. But not cattle prods bound for South Africa. They have cattle there, you know. The veldt and all that."

"Well, but Elba," Muriel said, amazed. "How did you come to give Guarino the wrong information?"

"I thought that the idea of more illegal shipments would hold your interest. We didn't want you to get bored down there. We were a little worried that you might come back before your time was up."

Muriel began to sputter with outrage.

"It's a funny thing about guys who work for the Commerce Department," Elba said, raising her voice slightly. "They've all got these plastic pen holders in their breast pockets. I was having lunch near the Capitol the other day . . ."

"Elba," Muriel said. "I'm delighted to hear that the Foundation has enough money to pay for long-distance calls about this kind of drivel."

"Are you implying that we didn't pay you enough to go to Salinas? Now listen, we can make a much more generous contribution toward your trip to Mexico. And I hope you remember to register to vote, the way we told you to."

"The Salinas trip was a complete waste of time. You people threw away your money and it was the most boring experience I ever had in my life. I also got a painful sunburn. I'll go to Mexico only if you can tell me exactly where I'm supposed to go."

"Oh, you'll find the address, sweetheart. We have faith in you. And now you know what you're looking for—a machine shop. You found that out in Salinas, and you found out all about gun modifications while you were down there. It was not a complete waste of time. You also found out why people work together in organizations."

"I found out I shouldn't go out in the sun without a hat," Muriel said. "And that's all I found out. Information on gun modifications you can look up in a book. I should know; I saw enough of them. And as far as organizations are concerned—no. I am not going to join an office workers group. All that would do is destroy any chance I have left of keeping all this confidential. As it is everyone in Salinas knows what color underpants I wear—and don't think I don't know who told them. I should have stayed here and picked Gerardina's brains. Now she's gone—off on a free yachting trip around the world. There's no use in my getting the voter's card because *I'm* not going *anywhere.*"

"Get it." Elba hung up.

This phone conversation ran through Muriel's head as she tried to read the computer manual. She had been left to study by herself amidst the "upbeat" decor of Advertising. Lovell sporting arms pointed their barrels at her from posters on the walls.

Francine's light table glowed in a corner, but Francine herself was nowhere to be seen. Probably off flirting with Pagano. Muriel put down the manual and picked up her coffee cup. She couldn't help feeling a twinge of guilt about the voter's card. Elba had asked her to register in San Francisco under a phony name. All she had to do was bring a postmarked envelope bearing a fake name and address to the Registrar of Voters and they'd make out a card for her. It was strange but true that the Border Police in Mexico would accept a voter's card as adequate identification for a visa. Thus Muriel could run all over Mexico with phony papers.

The question she had tried to ask Elba was, where would she run to? Where was this conversion shop? There were no more clues to pursue. Gerardina was gone, along with her nonsensical information about payments made through a blood bank. Now Pagano was back and another pair of eyes were watching Muriel as she worked in Sales—not that Pagano's eyes were as keen as Baziotis's. And now she had to waste half her day in Advertising—time she could have spent dipping into records.

Still, this Advertising thing might not be a complete waste of time. In her fledgling attempts at word processing and typesetting, she had noticed something interesting flit by on the cathode ray tube. If only she knew how to operate the machine! She picked up the operator's manual again, forcing herself to concentrate on the pattern of the control keys.

*   *   *

Unlike Muriel, Pagano read the newspapers. He had mentioned the civil war in Lebanon because it was on his mind. That damn Baziotis ringing up fat sales in the Middle East. Just a moment ago he had told Arno that he was looking for the secretary; he wanted her to book him on a flight to Beirut.

There were no business trips in sight for Arno. True, most of his accounts were now back in his hands and the heat from the Government was off, but the Vice President of International Sales still seemed to want to keep an eye on him.

They had actually sent Engineering off to the Columbian ball powder factory without Arno! Those technical idiots wouldn't even have been able to line up a translator if the redheaded secretary hadn't helped them by calling ahead to Bogotá. Francine would not have helped them; she would have given them the cold shoulder. Of course Francine did not speak Spanish. And it was too bad they had gotten the translator.

Arno looked over the morning paper. The orders could wait for a little while. They were just routine stuff from Brazil and Nicaragua. If this were the old days, before the Federal investigation, he would be scanning the papers avidly for news about insurgency in South America, ready to cook up a deal with a police force down there for some cut-rate supplies. He had always been able to walk into the VP's office with some promising newspaper clippings in his hand and arrange for a little travel. Now they had him on a short leash; he could no longer develop that kind of business. Still, he was lucky to be sitting in his executive swivel chair instead of on a hard seat across from the grand jury.

Arno smoked a leisurely cigarette, turning the newspaper pages. His eye caught a little item on page seventeen; he had seen many items like that in recent weeks. A right-wing vigilante group in Argentina had kidnapped another trade union leader. The item said this was about the seventieth such incident reported in recent months. The name of the kidnapping group was not mentioned, but Arno thought it was probably the Anti-Communist Alliance. The newspaper was right to omit it; the name was an unimportant detail. The Alliance was merely a front for Argentine military intelligence. Nor did the article say whether the kidnappers were armed. But of course they were. Arno blew half-circles of cigarette smoke toward the ceiling. They were using Lovell automatic carbines, which had not been carried in the Lovell catalogues since the Korean War. Arno had personally made the warehouse arrangements a few months ago.

* * *

"So how's it going?" Francine asked, coming in the door.

Frantically Muriel scanned the keyboard. She had to get this stuff off the screen and quickly. The tricky part was removing it without erasing it. Francine was coming toward her. Muriel hit the key that read "scroll down". The computer emitted little protesting beeps; but the lines on the screen did not change. She pushed the shift key, then "scroll down" again. Still beeps and no change. Muriel hit some more keys at random and tried to move the cursor. The keyboard was frozen. She had pressed a wrong key somewhere and now all the operations were stuck. What to do? Desperately she hit "reset". Mercifully the screen went blank just as Francine arrived to look over her shoulder.

"What a fool I am," Muriel said in a trembling voice. "Here I was going along fine and I hit the reset key. Now I lost everything."

"Actually, I think you were putting in the wrong code. I could tell from the beeps. You would have had to reset anyway. The keyboard was probably stuck."

"Does this mean I've erased the file?" Muriel held her breath, waiting for the answer.

"No, Muriel." Francine's patience was beginning to wear thin. "The only way you can erase the file is to read over it or press control X."

"But I've erased files before by mistake."

"I told you why that was, don't you remember? You read the file into the bugger and then made your changes, but you didn't scroll down to the end before you put it back in the same file. So you cut it short."

Muriel nodded. She still didn't understand.

"We can't do any word processing now. The daisy printer is down," Francine said. "God knows when we're going to get service. I swear, half the repairmen at Datacomp take a long weekend every weekend. Oh, I forgot—we're not supposed to call them servicemen. They get huffy about it. They're 'customer engineers'. Oh—talking about engineers, you'll never guess what Arno told me . . ."

Muriel looked sad and sympathetic while Francine told her indignantly about Arno's lost trip to Bogotá, and then finally returned to work at her light table.

Francine was not a good teacher, but she was a whiz on the word processor-typesetter in any language. She had discovered her skill almost by accident: Randrup, the head of Advertising, had gone berserk at a trade fair buying all this typesetting equipment so that Lovell could save money on setting its own annual catalogue, which had to be printed in Italian, French and Spanish as well as English, and also on setting the tables of sales statistics produced by the Marketing Department. A problem arose, however, when the equipment arrived: no one knew how to operate it. For five long months it sat under its canvas covers in Advertising. Finally Randrup persuaded Personnel to create an "advertising assistant" position, with a salary high enough to lure several top-notch executive secretaries to apply. Francine, fed up with Baziotis and wanting the money, had been the lucky winner. But at the moment she was disillusioned with the job. She hated pasting up the copy for the catalogue, and in fact she was not good at it: most of the work produced at her light table had to be peeled off and set straight by the printers. The only good thing about the job was that Randrup went on frequent promotional tours, leaving her free to socialize.

A week earlier Francine had taken a floppy disk from the vertical rack that held the little disk library, in order to show Muriel some tabular matter she had set for the Marketing Department. The floppy looked like a 45 rpm record encased in a square black cover. "You never take the cover off," Francine had said. She played the disk by opening the tiny door of the turntable slot, inserting the disk and closing the door again. "They look like square records," Francine said, "but actually the cover doesn't spin. The floppy moves around inside it and somehow the electronic thingies pick up the impulses right through the cover."

She had pressed the keys to access file M of the diskette. A jumble of words and codes appeared on the cathode ray tube.

"Here it is on the TV—a marketing table. See the heading? 'U.S. Exports to Country XXXXXX'. File M is a master file; all the information is entered as XXXXXX or as OOO. See, this way you can make a table of exports to any country without even thinking about your tabs. Pretty clever, huh?"

A mass of confusing information had appeared on the screen: little "t's" inside squares, four digit numbers, and, interspersed throughout, phrases: "Rimfire Rifles . . . Centerfire Rifles . . . Arm Parts."

"I know it looks like a mess," Francine had said sympathetically. "Look. I'll play it out for you."

The camera and the spinning silhouettes of letters clacked and whirred inside the computer cabinet as the chart was photographed at high speed. Then Francine removed the circular cassette of photographic paper and took it to the processor to develop it. She waited with folded arms for the paper to be mechanically conveyed through the fluids beneath a light-proof plastic cover. The foul odor of churned chemicals seeped into the air. Muriel coughed. "This thing stinks to heaven," Francine said. At last the "repro" emerged, a shiny, slightly damp image of the marketing table. Muriel studied it while Francine complained about its yellowish background and expressed the hope that she would not have to muck around cleaning that damn processor again.

"Gee," Muriel said carefully, "this looks awfully hard to understand. I don't know how you ever learned about it all."

The table was entitled "U.S. Exports to Country XXXXXX". Beneath the title were ten columns, each headed by a year: 1966 to 1975. Running down along the left-hand side were printed "Shotshells" . . . "M Units" . . . "M $" . . . "RF & CF Ammo" . . . "Bolt-Action Rifles" . . . and "Semi-Automatic Carbines". The table was divided into two parts: the upper table, subheaded "All U.S. Exports", and the lower one, subheaded "Lovell International—South San Francisco Exports".

Muriel realized that she was looking at the master table for the dollar value of Lovell exports: a concise compendium of all the information she had seen but had been unable to correlate, on dozens of interdepartmental memos. But since the chart was a dummy the dollar signs it contained were followed only by triple zeros. Thus there must be a chart detailing the inordinate amount of sales to Austria. There was that row for dollar amounts of sales of automatic carbines—the kind of gun that Omar had said was probably being converted in Mexico! Now if she could find the chart for Mexico . . .

This morning Muriel had found the export chart for Austria in file A. She had been reading it when Francine appeared. But she had not had time to jot down any of the information which appeared in a somewhat confusing form on the screen. The ideal thing would be to print it out on the photographic paper—but even if she knew how to get the chart photographed, which she did not, she could not put the paper through the processor without running the risk of discovery. Francine or Randrup might wander over just as the chart was emerging from its chemical bath, and pull out the repro to check it.

And she did not know how to find Mexico. Austria was the A file, but Francine had said that "M" stood for master file. So what stood for Mexico?

Now the reset key had done its duty and the screen was a blank.

Francine was back, holding a little looseleaf notebook filled with typesetting exercises. "I decided we have to have more of a system with our lessons," she said. "So I spent part of the weekend making lesson plans. Well, to tell the truth, it was Randrup's idea. He made me do it. But I think it will really be a help."

Muriel expressed gratitude. She hoped to God Francine wouldn't stand over her when she started the exercises. The floppy with the Marketing tables from file A was still on the turntable where a practice disk should have been.

Francine flipped through her notebook. "Most of these lessons are for the word processor," she said, "but we can't practice them with the daisy printer down." She stopped at a page. "Oh, good!" she said. "Here's one for the type-setter—a lesson in storing data strings. See, you're going to store all the lines in 'Three Blind Mice'." She leaned over the turntable. "Have you got your practice floppy on the turntable? Okay, good. Now we can start."

Muriel waited.

"Hit 'store, data, zero'and type in 'Three Blind Mice', then 'store, data, one' and 'See How They Run.'"

Francine paused and looked at her expectantly.

Muriel felt sick. She didn't know much, but she knew that if she opened a file on that Marketing floppy and wrote "Three Blind Mice" in it, all the previous information would be erased.

"What file shall I write in?" she asked, stalling.

Francine wrinkled her brow in thought. Muriel felt faint.

"How about A?" Francine said. "We may as well start at the beginning."

Wretchedly, Muriel put her hands on the keyboard, ready to destroy the Austrian file.

"Wait a minute!" Francine said. "Why open a file? This isn't a lesson in file-writing. Just store the data strings in immediate memory and then recall them right on the screen."

Dizzy with relief, Muriel stored all the data as Francine directed. Then she pressed "recall, data, zero" and the lines "Three Blind Mice" arrayed themselves on the bottle-green screen.

Muriel was careful to make enough mistakes to make the data string lesson last until lunchtime. She told Francine to run along without her to the cafeteria; she herself needed some fresh air. "I've got a terrible hangover," she said. As soon as she was alone, she ejected the Marketing floppy and inserted a blank one in its place—one that would seem to have been on the turntable all morning.

Then she threw on her jacket: March had been hot in the Salinas Valley, but it was chilly in the Bay Area. She was going outside the fortress gates of the Lovell Company to find a pay phone. She knew she needed help. This job was getting too big for her. She was going to call the office workers group. Someone there could undoubtedly help take the mystery out of the wizardly workings of the electronic keyboard.

Actually she had decided to make this call before she had these close calls at the video display terminal. She had decided to do it when she saw Betty Grable in *The Shocking Miss Pilgrim*. Miss Pilgrim was one of the first female "typewriters"—as typists were called at the turn of the century—who invaded the all-male domain of the office. She invoked the wrath of her male co-workers and her boss—played by Dick Haymes—with her good-natured efficiency. When her boss attempted to embarrass her by setting her up to address a suffragist rally, she won the crowd over with a stirring speech.

Muriel felt that her lack of respect for the office workers group had stemmed from ignorance. The film demonstrated clearly that office workers had once been considered skilled, serious workers—when they were all men. Now that they were women no one respected their skills. She was anxious to discuss the implications of the movie with someone—maybe someone of the Contra Costa office workers group had seen it. She certainly couldn't discuss it with Bernie. He bragged repeatedly about how little he got away with paying his own secretary. He also made lurid comments on her see-through clothes. But that was beside the point.

She opened her telephone memo book to find the number Elba had given her months before. It was amazing: a minor musical starring a second-rate actress had helped to raise her consciousness. Besides, she had to have some help in learning how to read the jumble of codes and words on the screen without freezing it there for the whole world to see. She had no desire to go down in history as The Shocking Miss Axelrod.

# Thirteen

"Coffee! She's the head of an office workers group, and her name is Coffee!" Dennis shook with his usual silent laughter.

"It's spelled with a y on the end. Barbara Coffey. She spelled it out for me." Muriel frowned over her toaster waffle. This was a serious matter. She was almost sorry she had told Dennis she was going to meet with the Contra Costa group that day after work.

Dennis composed himself with difficulty and sipped his coffee.

"And what did you say the full name of that group was again?"

"Contra Costa Office Activists," Muriel said stiffly.

"No, there's an acronym," Dennis said. "God, it's COCOA!"

He practically slid out of his chair in silent hysterics.

"These waffles are pretty good as frozen food goes, don't you think?" Muriel asked, changing the subject.

"Yeah, I like them. They taste a little like cardboard, but I kind of like that. You can't enjoy food in the morning anyhow." He began to talk about the trouble he was having painting bricks for a factory model he wanted to put next to his railroad tracks. One of the computer programmers had been helping him mix the paint. "This guy Hank has his own model railroad back home in Idaho, but there's no room for it upstairs. There are seven guys living in that flat, can you imagine that? They're all from out of town. Remember I told you they're working at Munson Electronics in Lafayette? They're scabs, is what they are. They get like one hundred dollars a day for crossing the picket line."

"Does this guy Hank know you're gay?" Muriel asked. She buttered another waffle.

"Are you kidding? He'd be out of here faster than a speeding bullet if he knew. He already told me everybody in Boise thinks San Francisco is Queer Paradise. He'd probably like to take one of those homophobe tours down Castro Street on Saturday night with his pals—they could throw potatoes at the perverts."

"Then I guess he hasn't seen Jeffrey coming to visit you."

"What do you think—he hangs out the window upstairs to log Jeffrey in in the evening and then log him out again the next morning? Anyway, I don't care. If Hank decides I'm poison ivy, I'll find someone else to play trains with. If worst comes to worst I'll join the Richmond Model Railroad Club again. Maybe that old fart has died by now—the one who only wanted burros and cactuses on the layout."

He hopped up to wash out his breakfast things. He was going on a field trip by himself to Suisun Bay to look at the old World War II freighters rotting in the water behind Benicia Arsenal. He had heard about this marvelous sight from one of his fellow shoppers at the hobby store and he was anxious to get going. He was still looking for his car keys when Muriel left for work.

She felt anxious: she dreaded going to a meeting with a

roomful of humorless radicals. Of course Omar—whom she was trying not to think about anymore—was a radical and he was certainly interesting. He had no sense of humor that she could detect. But he was mysterious. She did not see how office workers could possibly be mysterious; she was one herself. She was really dreading that meeting, and she was also dreading hearing Elba say, "I told you so."

Francine and she spent the morning doing exercises on the typesetter. Francine was teaching her how to access the file directory, a neat little listing of the first twenty-five key strokes of each file on the disk.

"See, the reason I told you to always key in a slug line without any coding when you start writing in the file is that way the file titles will read out in plain English." Francine demonstrated by pressing a sequence of keys to make the directory for the practice disk appear:

A   THREE BLIND MICE THREE BL
B   JACK BE NIMBLE JACK BE QU
C   LITTLE MISS MUFFET SAT O

There were blanks from D to X. Muriel wondered if Francine knew enough Mother Goose to fill all twenty-four files. They had indented lines of nursery rhymes, centered their titles, started them with small caps, and moved their phrases around until Muriel was ready to run up the clock.

After lunch when Randrup, who had just returned from a business trip, was closeted somewhere with salesmen, Francine went off to make her conversational rounds. Muriel, alone at last, seized the Marketing floppy again.

Her hands trembling a little with anticipation, she inserted the disk and turned to the section in the manual that read "accessing file directory". Now in a moment she would know where the export information on Mexico was stored. She might even be able to find data on South Africa. Frowning, she looked from the manual to the keyboard, punched three keys and waited for the computer to respond.

"What are you up to, Miss Axelrod?"

Muriel's heart leapt wildly into her throat. It was Randrup. He had come up behind her and was speaking in that fastidious, insinuating voice which always reminded her of Basil Rathbone playing Greta Garbo's horrible husband in *Anna Karenina*. She swiveled around to look up into his bony face. His eyes narrowed in interest as he looked past her straight at the screen.

"It's the file directory," she mumbled through dry lips. But it was the only screen display in ordinary English: "Exports to Austria . . . Exports to Brazil . . . Exports to Canal Zone . . .". He would know instantly why she was looking at this information with Francine out of the room. He was no fool. He had organized promotional shoots in South Africa and accompanied Westfeldt on those trips to Obergurgl. And the heat was on him.

She swiveled back again, with her eyes down and her body curled into itself as though she expected a physical blow.

"That's quite some directory."

He sounded almost amused. She looked at the screen. It was blank except for two flickering words: PRESS RETURN. Press return! She had not finished the entire keying sequence; the directory was one command short of being accessed.

She wanted to say, "I guess I goofed," or something equally airy, but she could not trust her voice. She leaned her narrow body over the keyboard and with her last reserve of strength touched her fingertip to the reset key. The words vanished from the screen; the computer's innards clacked and then made high soprano spinning noises like schoolgirls at a birthday party.

She coughed and cleared her throat. "Oh, drat! Now I've got to put the program in again." Her voice was shaking, but Randrup was used to shaking voices. He liked to humiliate people. She began busily looking for the program diskette. "Looks like you need a little more practice," he said, with contempt. She heard him stalk out of the room— off no doubt in brocaded coat and astrakhan hat to meet the train from Moscow.

To Muriel's relief she was needed back at her old job for the rest of the day: Baziotis was swamped with orders from the Middle East and even Arno had some telexes to send out. The backlog of sales work piled up at her elbow. She wondered if Baziotis finally realized that he had made a mistake when he decided to send her to Advertising to learn typesetting for half the day. It was going to cost him a lot in lost commissions if these orders did not get out on time. Francine had been helping out when Randrup was away, typing telexes for Arno and even taking dictation from him in his office—but now Randrup was obviously going to spend time in the office and Muriel could not handle all this work alone. Something would have to be done.

She would offer to work overtime. Perfect. Only eager beavers asked to work late, but that fit Muriel's image: following Elba's orders, she had been a model employee for a long time. Of course if she started now she would have to skip the COCOA meeting tonight. But it was the only way to avoid being pulled off the Advertising terminal. And the information on that Marketing disk was worth five hundred COCOA meetings.

She began to prepare a little speech in her head for Baziotis—she would point out that the company would not have to pay her extra for overtime work because she was a salaried employee—when Francine buzzed her on the inter-com line.

"You've got a personal call on eight six. A young man."

If it was Bernie, she had no time to talk to him. The orders from the Middle East were stacking up like Mount Sinai.

"Is this Ms Axelrod?" It was a stranger. Tentatively Muriel agreed she was indeed Mizz Axelrod.

There were brushing noises on the other end of the wire; the phone was being passed to another hand.

"Muriel?" A woman this time. "This is Barbara Coffey, from the office workers. I have some information for you. If anyone is listening don't answer—just say yes or no. All right?"

"Yes," Muriel said, idiotically obedient.

"When you called us from the phone booth yesterday, you said you had a problem pulling information off your video terminal. You know, you had trouble turning it off fast?"

"Mmm hmm."

"Well, we called the office workers group in San Francisco to ask them about it, and they linked us up with one of their members who's a word processing instructor. She says that the solution is to *turn down the intensity*." She gave a soft self-deprecating laugh. "I don't know what that means, but that's what's written down here on our note. I suppose it makes sense to you."

Muriel mulled it over until she was roused by the sound of the dial tone. "So long," she said dimly and hung up.

Turn down the intensity. Did that mean "calm down"? Was it some new northern California expression like "mellow out"? No, probably not. She flipped through the loose sheets of the typesetting manual, which she had fortu-nately xeroxed so that she could study it in Sales when she had a rare moment to spare. Yes, it was in the index: "Inten-sity. P. 6."

At half past four on the dot Muriel was racing down the staircase toward the security checkpoint, her shoulder bag pumping back and forth like a metronome set on allegro. Telexes lay unsent on her desk; correspondence still balanced atop the metal lip of her "in" basket. She was not working overtime.

Lurking inconspicuously on the underside of the cathode ray tube was a knurled knob that, when turned counter-clockwise, blacked out the entire screen. It was something like the brightness dial on a television set. If Muriel had known about it, it could have saved her skin during that brief encounter with Randrup. Instead she had been saved by a fluke. A miracle.

But she could certainly not go on trusting in miracles. She had to have the certainty of something solid—like the intensity dial. The phone call had come a little late that day, but it didn't matter. She was leaving the office and making a beeline for the COCOA meeting.

# Fourteen

The herringbone pattern of Mrs Hardenburgh's skirt writhed like the spine of a netted fish, as its wearer hastened toward the student docent who was audibly botching up a telephone conversation.

The student clutched the phone to her ear and shrank back.

Mrs Hardenburgh smiled a terrible smile and clenched her fist. "Insist on May the third," she said softly, pounding the desk in a playful parody of anger.

The telephone jumped in tiny increments toward the corner of the desk. The student docent, now speechless, looked at her, wild-eyed. Mrs Hardenburgh plucked the receiver from her nerveless fingers and put it to her ear.

"Hello! Yes, well, now you're speaking with Edna Hardenburgh, the director of this Society. I know that you're going to find us two charter buses for the third of May, aren't you? Oh, no, no, the date cannot be changed. Someone may have said it could, but that's simply not the way it is. We need our buses on the third. We must have them on the third. Do you understand? Yes, all right. Yes, well, I'm sure you can 'scare some up.'" She turned amused eyes around the room. "Now you *must* call us back about it today, before five. All right then. Before five today."

She hung up and made a general announcement.

"Well, everybody, it looks like it's all set for the third. There will be about one hundred thousand flowers in bloom in the San Jose Municipal Garden on that day. And I know none of us would want to miss the first bloom."

She left the office, leaving the staff feeling like petals withered in the first frost.

The maritime scholar was leaning over Lourdes' shoulder, examining the pictures she had mounted for him. "Feisty old bitch," he commented under his breath.

Lourdes did not know what "feisty" meant, but she understood what he meant. She looked at him in assent through eyes heavily ringed in mascara.

He left a little while later with a large portfolio under his arm. He was anxious to return to the salty atmosphere of the Maritime Museum: this place, he thought, was stuffed with large ladies in tweed and the Dragon Lady from *Terry and the Pirates* was working the dry-mount press.

Mrs Westfeldt came beaming to Lourdes.

"I'm so glad that depressing shipwreck project is finished," she said. "Now you can help us with these pesky mailing labels."

She radiated confidence that the trip to San Jose would go forward on the third. They had not yet heard from the bus company, but Sarah Westfeldt felt that Mrs Hardenburgh would always eventually get her way. The disgraced student docent was steeped in fluid fumes at the mimeograph machine, cranking out invitations.

Mrs Westfeldt showed Lourdes how to fold the flyers in thirds and affix a mailing label to them. "It's a shame we have to use these," she said. "I realize they look sort of shoddy. But it's cheap. And I don't think anyone will care. We're just inviting our members and some of our closest friends." She paused. "And of course some of our benefactors. As a matter of fact . . . maybe we should . . . just for the benefactors . . ." She took the photocopied mailing labels from Lourdes and shuffled through them hastily. In a moment she was heading toward the director's den with the label lists flapping in her hand.

Lourdes did not want to fold the invitations. She had just had a manicure at Magnin's and she did not want to chip her nails. It was a pleasant color; in fact it was called pleasant: Pleasantly Plum. A strand of hair had worked loose from her chignon; as she swept it back into place she noticed with mild surprise that she was a brunette again. She was not sure she liked it; it was too much like the real color of her hair. She had told them light brown this time, with auburn highlights. "Highlights." She had first encountered that word on a shampoo bottle. And "auburn"; another nice word. That was on the color charts near the cashier's table in the beauty salon.

Lovely words. The only English words that she liked. Most of the others were like scrub brushes on a linoleum floor; they reminded her of the sounds she made when she had to wash the bathroom between visits from the cleaning woman. She sighed. The manicure would be chipped anyway in a few days because she was going to have to cook another big meal soon. Arno was beginning to complain about leftovers. Now that he was working regular hours again he had gotten his appetite back. He was criticizing things around the house too. Hair in the drain, disgusting things like that. Too disgusting to mention, but Arno mentioned them. And the check from Papa had still not arrived.

She was going to go on this trip to see the rose gardens in

San Jose. It would be an entire day away from home. Arno
wanted soup and fancy steaks. Cooking made her hands
smell of onions. One of the women at the Society had advised her to try lemon juice. "Try lemon juice," she had said,
shrugging and turning away. She evidently thought it an inconsequential problem. And of course later at home when
she pulled her hand out of the little china bowl she saw that
her nail polish had curdled.

Would she end up like them with pared, unpainted nails?
With bare nails and square shoes, like coffins? She decided
to try again in the morning to get a call through to Buenos
Aires.

\* \* \*

It happened on a Wednesday, but it was Thursday before
Arno found out. The newspaper was routed to him only after
Westfeldt and Randrup had seen it, so it was a day late. The
little routing tag obscured part of the word "Peron" in the
headlines. At eleven o'clock Arno was given the newspaper
and by noon he was a fiery gray-and-red dot in the center of
his smoke-filled office. Muriel, returning from her stint in
Advertising, knocked hard at his door but he did not
answer.

He looked again at the blurry wire photo through the
Gauloises cloud. There was the dim outline of a helicopter
hovering over the Pink House in Buenos Aires. Mrs Isabel
Peron was being ushered away from the seat of government
with a military escort that she had not requested. Not in the
photo was what Mrs Peron would see from the aircraft: columns of tanks advancing from the base in Magdalena. Isa-

belita was not having a presidential journey. School was suspended. Civil servants picked up their paychecks and left their offices. The trade union banks were closed. The junta had taken over.

The newspaper said that most of Buenos Aires was watching a televised soccer match against a visiting team from Venezuela; they did not care that Mrs Peron had been plucked into the skies by a whirlybird.

Later Arno received the day's newspaper. Apparently Westfeldt and Randrup had not read it. It was lying still folded on the secretary's desk on top of a pile of unopened mail. The secretary was gone, evidently working in Advertising. She was small, almost weightless: even when she was there one had to look twice to see her. Arno took the newspaper and retreated to his desk, like an ant with a bread crumb.

He really did not want to open the newspaper. He dropped it still folded onto his desk, but staring at him was a column-wide indistinct photograph with the caption: "Submachine gun hanging from his neck, a soldier feeds the pigeons in Buenos Aires."

* * *

"I recognize the park. That's the kind of thing I know about. The gun? I have no idea. Perhaps an Auto-Ordnance, maybe Savage Arms. Guns don't interest me."

Baziotis coughed. "That's what we all say, Arno." He waved his hand before his face. "You're going to kill yourself with all this smoking." He peered at the photograph again. The news from Argentina was now on page two. One day after the coup and on the front page was only this ironic picture of the innocent soldier with the sub-machine gun around his neck.

Baziotis turned the page. The headlines over the Argentina stories were rather small. "This should be good for sales, huh? The police will be tooling up now, am I right?"

"That may be," Arno said. He picked up some papers from his desk, wishing Baziotis in hell.

"No more of that penny-ante stuff with the vigilante groups." Baziotis lowered his walrus-sized body into the extra chair. Settling in for the duration? "Now you can go for the big sales at the barracks. The money all comes from the same wallet anyway. Isn't that true?" Then without waiting for an answer he said, "How did you launder those payments anyhow?"

"What do you mean, launder?"

The old language-barrier game. Maybe Baziotis would believe he didn't understand him and lose patience. What the hell was he doing in here anyway? The Israelis were ringing his phone off the hook, not to mention the brisk business with Lebanon. But Arno was afraid he had already shown his hand by locking himself in his office all day with a carton of cigarettes. Baziotis was hot on the malodorous scent.

"What do I mean, launder? What do you mean, what do I mean? Don't tell me you don't know what I'm talking about after all we've been through with the South Africa orders. No one will ever be able to figure out how we got paid for those. And God, were the Feds grateful that we handled it like that! Not a trace. Hey, but listen. I've been reading *The New York Times:* it says that the vigilante groups are working for the police and the Army. That is the way it works south of the border, isn't it? Didn't our pals in the State Department give you a little ring-a-ling about that?"

"They opened up a separate account. '*Liberadores de la*

*America,* I think it was. Or *Alianza Anticomunista'.* I don't remember which one they decided to use."

"You don't remember! Well, I remember that it was your bread and butter a few months back. But now you can get the jelly. Are the phones working down there?"

Arno jogged a stack of orders into a neat pile.

"They should be straightened out in a week or so," he said.

"Well, I rejoice for you. Too bad you're still grounded. Which reminds me, Travel should have my tickets to Saudi by now. Christ Almighty, I'll probably have to pick them up myself. That redhead of yours better come back from Advertising for good now. Things are picking up."

And whose idea was it to send her over there?

Baziotis got up. He was finally leaving. "Well, next week will find me in Mecca. Good old Saudi. It's a great place if you like lousy booze. It's really too bad you can't get away yourself."

"Oh, I was away long enough," Arno said.

"I hope the phones start working soon. It really is a shame you can't wing down to B.A. You must have relatives you want to see—if the left wingers haven't gotten them yet. Those terrorists ought to be shoved up against a wall and shot." He gave a dry laugh. "You see what I'm saying?"

"They are," Arno said quietly.

"They are what?"

"Shoved up against walls and shot. Quite often."

This caught Baziotis off guard. But he quickly regained his balance. "Anyhow, personal contact is best. I've always said that. In fact I was just saying that to G.F.—he was squawking about the Sales travel budget. Nothing, I said, *but nothing* replaces a face that the customer can recognize."

He stood over Arno, searching his eyes for a sign. But Arno was ready for him. He exhaled a plume of smoke which rose like a screen between them.

"Well, so long." His hand was at long last on the doorknob. "And you ought to watch that nicotine. Haven't you heard that it's not good for you?"

# Fifteen

Someone in the fifth or sixth row kept crushing a styrofoam cup and rubbing the remains together, producing a horrible sound, like human screams. Muriel sipped her cocoa, the mascot beverage of the Contra Costa Office Activists. She wondered idly what would happen if she proposed a resolution prohibiting the use of styrofoam cups at meetings. The speaker did not even seem to hear the noise. She was discussing occupational hazards in offices.

"And how many of you have to operate a photocopy machine in an unventilated room?"

Some hands shot up.

"That's really hazardous. There's nasty stuff coming out of the toner that can ruin the linings of your lungs. Have you noticed that you can't breathe after you've been in that little room for a while, copying out Mr Blitzo's two hundred page report?"

She wrapped her hands around her own neck, coughing and making strangling noises.

There was laughter. Muriel sipped the cocoa. The cup

crusher had apparently been distracted; the noise had stopped.

There was more hilarity to come. The speaker ran through the carcinogenic dangers of liquid white-out, eye fatigue possibilities from video display tubes (here she crossed her eyes) and back problems from secretarial chairs which, she said, were adjusted to the height of non-commissioned officers in the U.S. Air Force.

"Really, that's how they test them."

Eventually there was a spatter of applause with some reminiscent chuckles, and it was over.

Barbara Coffey resumed her role as chairperson to introduce the real surprise of the evening: an enormous checkbook with four human legs gingerly entered the side door of the church auditorium. The room was abuzz with exclamations of admiration and delight. Muriel could not believe her eyes. It was a resurrection of the 1950s Old Gold ads, except that the legs wore corduroy bell-bottomed pants instead of black-seamed stockings.

"This is our kick-off for the banking campaign," Barbara announced triumphantly. Under her breath she murmured to the checkbook, "Can you see all right?" Two pairs of eyes darted back and forth inside square cutouts near the upper edge of the book.

Barbara pointed to a name emblazoned on the giant checks below the ledger. "See," she said, "this is the ledger page for Ms Bank Teller." The COCOA members seated toward the rear of the auditorium began to pop their glasses on as she read the ledger entries.

"Look at the deposit column. 3/20/76. One hundred thirty dollars. See the explanation on the next line? Weekly pay!"

The audience made sounds of agreement.

"Now look at the lines for checks made out. Check number 33, 3/21/76. One hundred seventy dollars to Larry Landlord, rent! Check number 34. Twenty dollars to the Safeway, groceries! Check number 35, 3/28/76. Fifteen dollars to Donald Druggist. Prescription medicine!"

The audience was mumbling and moving about. Muriel was afraid they would kick their chairs over and start the revolution on the spot. "Don't forget babysitting costs," someone yelled. "You forgot the utilities," from someone else.

Barbara Coffey pacified them all with a shake of her long, oily hair. "It could just go on and on," she said, smiling. "But you've got the idea. And the press will get the idea. Now watch this."

She stood aside and lifted Ms Bank Teller's check, turning it up to reveal its underside. After a few false tries, she succeeded in attaching it to a clamp located at the top of the structure. The eyes peering through the cutouts were now blinded and for a moment one pair of legs wobbled in confusion beneath the checkbook.

The flip side of the bank teller's check was another ledger page; the check below it bore a name imprinted with letters about three times larger than Ms Bank Teller's. This was the checkbook of MR WELLS FARGO BANK PRESIDENT.

"Now look at *these* entries," Barbara said to the hushed audience. There were some millions of dollars in yearly assets, some thousands of dollars expended to buy stagecoach replicas for first-time depositors and tidy sums for expense accounts and office renovations.

"My brother-in-law got one of those cheap little stagecoaches," a woman said. "What a piece of shit!"

"The point is," Barbara Coffey raised her voice over the din of comments on the shitty stagecoaches, "the point is, these promotional gimmicks cost plenty. We actually got the prices from our sources at the factory. And the thing is, *when was the last time the Wells Fargo employees got a raise?"* She answered her own question quickly: "We happen to know that the last time was over two years ago, and it was only five percent! COCOA knows this because our members on the Banking Committee have told us. And at this time I'd like to ask the Banking Committee members—and among their ranks are some real, live Wells Fargo employees!—to stand up and take a bow."

They did, to wild applause and laughter when the legs under the checkbook curtseyed in acknowledgement of their committee affiliation.

A folding chair creaked near Muriel.

"What will we see next?" a bored voice drawled into her ear. "A bellhop yelling, 'Call for Philip Morris!'?"

It was Harriet Warren, reading Muriel's thoughts again. There she was, out of place in her chevron-striped sweater and pale blue stockings: everything designer-labeled and made of natural materials in this sea of polyester suits and vinyl handbags with peeling yellow clasps that clicked open and closed as their owners retrieved Kleenex and cough-drops.

Just Harriet's hair left something to be desired. In the awful illumination of the room—dozens of images of square overhead light fixtures reflected in masonite panelling—it had the texture and some of the color of straw. Too much exposure to chlorine, no doubt.

The general meeting ended and most of the audience drifted out. Now it was time for the steering committee meeting. Barbara Coffey sighed as she picked up the pathetic sweaters left behind. "We really ought to get a lost-and-found box," she said.

"Either that or tell the church to keep the goddam heat down so people can keep their shirts on," Harriet said. As usual, Barbara ignored her. She sat down at the head of the aluminum cockle-finish table and ticked off items on the agenda.

"Old business, report on progress of grant writing, evaluation of general meeting, plans for next general meeting, Muriel."

So she was at the end of the agenda and she could not escape until the meeting was over. Muriel smiled gratefully. She knew that it was an honor for the steering committee to take the time to discuss her problem. That's what Barbara Coffey had called it: a problem. "The telephone line is tied up with women who call us for referrals or advocacy. We really don't have the necessary staff to help you by phone with your problem."

The treasurer was discussing the grant writing problem. Her frequent nasal asides about "asshole foundations" and "sexist bigshots who want asskissing", interspersed among her flat reading of requests for a larger postage allocation, and data culled from the *Foundation Directory,* produced the effect of a dialogue between a ventriloquist and his dummy. Barbara and five or six of the others nodded while she talked, and made notes. Harriet removed the tortoise-shell barrette that anchored her washerwoman hairdo and redid the whole thing, right in the middle of the steering committee meeting. Trying to hide the split ends, Muriel thought.

They began to evaluate the general meeting.

"I think it was just super," said a short plump woman with rheumy eyes who was seated at Barbara's left. She was the head of COCOA's Board of Directors, and a clerk at a Contra Costa office of California Blue Shield.

Everyone agreed. "Fantastic. . . Our best yet. . . Really well planned. . ."

"The only negative criticism I would have," the treasurer said in her ventriloquist voice, "is that we overdid it. *Both* occupational safety *and* the banking campaign kickoff. It was too much of a good thing. What are we going to have left to show them next month?

There were murmurs of agreement. A breach had appeared in the wall.

"You're right," Barbara Coffey said evenly. The murmurs stopped. "But there's a very good reason why we had to do it this way. In fact there are several very good reasons."

"All the Coffey's reasons are *very good* reasons," Harriet whispered.

The speaker on occupational safety could fit COCOA into her busy schedule only that month. And the giant checkbook could not be postponed because the press conference to kick off the banking campaign was already scheduled for a date *before* the next general meeting. "And what is even more important than the press conference," Barbara said, "is the morale of the banking committee members. I mean, they worked very hard and they just finished constructing the thing two days ago. . . ."

"Egad," Harriet said loudly, "the glue must have been dripping on those poor girls' feet."

"Women's," someone corrected severely.

". . .And they were absolutely chafing at the bit to show it to the membership. We just can't afford to put off that kind of positive reinforcement."

"Positive reinforcement!" said Harriet more loudly than before. "Excuse me. I must have taken a wrong turn coming from the pool. I thought I was at a COCOA steering committee meeting in the Methodist church, but I find myself in the middle of a B.F. Skinner lecture."

"Harriet," the head of the Board of Directors said meaningfully. She bobbed her head significantly toward Barbara Coffey.

Harriet paid no attention. "Positive reinforcement! Chafing at the bit! Tell me, Barbara, have you been dipping into behaviorist theory lately? Or is this more of the gospel according to National Headquarters?"

Barbara Coffey threw a pencil across the table. "All right, I've had it!"

Everyone looked uncomfortable. Muriel had been present at only one other steering committee meeting. She had witnessed a similar scene then.

"Maybe I don't know what I'm doing," Barbara said. The others rushed verbal consolation to her. "Maybe someone else from the staff should sit in on the banking committee meetings."

A flicker of feeling passed over Harriet's well-chiseled features. But she refused to back down. "Tell me this," she said slowly, "we all applauded the committee's ingenuity in constructing that checkbook, but what was their accomplishment? The idea or just the execution? Didn't I see that same goddam checkbook—a little more neatly constructed, I might add—in the newspaper from the Seattle group? Are we running these people through arts and crafts sessions or are we operating on an adult level here?"

"There's nothing wrong with coordinating events nationally," the head of the Board of Directors said heatedly. This remark was echoed in a ragged chorus. Harriet pushed her chair back from the table. The chorus died out; all eyes were on Harriet. But she merely crossed her sheer-hosed legs and composed her hands on her lap.

Barbara Coffey broke into the silence to remind everyone that there was a long agenda to be gone through before ten o'clock. Someone tactfully handed Barbara a pencil to replace the one she had jettisoned, and the meeting resumed.

COCOA's newest member was anxiously awaiting the last agenda item: herself. Muriel felt an irrational sympathy toward Harriet Warren, whom she had met only once before. She had of course read about her in the newspapers: Harriet was a diving champion who apparently had to support herself by office work. At the same time Muriel was annoyed with Harriet for delaying the meeting. Because of her interruptions they might postpone the "Muriel" item to the next steering committee session. By that time she would be dead, she would be in a coffin. Randrup would find her sitting before a video screen with corporate secrets flashing on it like neon signs. They would search her apartment and find photocopies of Lovell memos next to her camisoles in her bureau drawer. They would stomp on Dennis's H-O railroad, splintering the little warehouses and freight cars, just as the Gestapo destroyed the French boy's model ship in the new Truffaut movie. "Don't tell me anything more about it," Dennis had said, "I don't want to see it."

But the end finally came. Barbara Coffey's voice was tired. The table was littered with crumpled papers, mutilated styrofoam cups, hairpins (a strand of Harriet Warren's brittle hair curved toward one hollow cheekbone). Barbara said hoarsely, "The staff has had a meeting about this with the full Board of Directors."

The rheumy woman from Blue Shield nodded. It was true.

"They've given us the green light on this whole thing. So now we're going to go ahead." She paused dramatically.

What's with the suspense? Muriel wondered. Everyone seemed a little livelier now, especially Harriet Warren, of all people.

Barbara folded her hands on her notebook. "We're going to enlist the support of the San Francisco group on this."

Muriel wondered how many people were on the Board of Directors of COCOA, and whether the San Francisco group could fill a stadium. Had all these people been told what she was doing? It was just incredible.

The other women at the table seemed to find it incredible too. They shifted in their seats and muttered to one another.

"They've got the know-how," Barbara Coffey was explaining. "Not one of us has ever operated a typesetter or a word processor. They've got members who know these computer manuals inside out and upside down."

"But they're not affiliated with National Headquarters," a woman objected.

"That's true." Barbara smiled slyly. "And they never will be. They're not a real office workers group. They've spread themselves too thin. But that will be helpful to Muriel in this case."

"How?" Muriel asked. Everyone looked at her. It was the first word she had spoken aloud all evening.

"We've already set up an appointment for you with their computer expert. She's going to give you detailed directions on how to. . . Let me see now." Barbara glanced quickly down at her notes. "On how to access and print out the information you need. How to get the stuff off the screen if you're subjected to surveillance."

"When?" Muriel asked. She felt a twinge of excitement, or fear.

"Next Tuesday, March 30th." Barbara slapped the notebook closed. "In our office at seven o'clock. One of the staffers will stay late to lock up afterward. Also, there might be someone from the airlines there."

The airlines?

"To help you plan your escape route. *You* know. To get you out of the country.

Muriel cleared her throat. "Does everyone in this room know what we're talking about?" she asked, in a strangled voice.

She thought she saw them nodding. There was a lot of motion in the blur before her eyes; it looked like nodding. Harriet Weaver came into focus, looking at her and saying, "Yes, we all know about it. And we all know about apartheid in South Africa."

"Harriet wouldn't go there to dive," someone said. Harriet waved her to silence.

"We're *all* going to help you," she said, "At our interim steering committee meeting we voted unanimously to help you." She spoke to Muriel, but she faced Barbara. "There will be a woman who works at the TWA reservations desk; she will help you too. She's a member of the San Francisco office workers group. Which is why we had to cut through all this *political bullshit rivalry with San Francisco in order to help you.*"

They were all back in focus. The Board of Directors woman was nodding reassuringly at Muriel; each nod was like a pat of her little plump hand.

"But I wasn't planning to fly to Mexico," Muriel said weakly. "It would be much safer if I went by land."

"Yes, of course," Barbara Coffey was impatient. "But you want it to *seem* as if you went by plane. To Europe. This TWA woman is going to fix all that up for you. She'll put you on a passenger list. You'll be checked in."

"It was your own idea, Muriel," Harriet Warren said kindly.

"And we need a dead person," Barbara Coffey said. "For your voter registration card. Yes, I checked it out already with the Mexican embassy. That's all you need for a visa. Can you believe it? All we have to do is pick up a piece of mail addressed to someone who died and we'll take it down to the registrar of voters."

Muriel, rooting around in her large handbag, found a compact and opened it. There was one big eye in the mirror. She closed the lid and dropped the compact back into the bag. It was the kind of large handbag that small women are advised not to carry: accessories should not overwhelm. She had to think for a while to remember why she had been told to buy it. For smuggling documents out of the Lovell plant.

Barbara's voice was very hoarse now. "Liz, you live in an apartment building. Hasn't anyone in there died lately?"

\* \* \*

"Spike heels on this torn-up linoleum. She's going to fall and break her ankle before she gets out of here. And you should have heard the jewelry jangling! And the perfume, my God! Sales is going to stink for days."

Muriel kept her eyes on the video display screen. "I'll take your word for it, Francine. I'm in the middle of a return address now. Do you think I indented it enough?"

"Oh, Muriel. You've just got to come and take a peek. It won't look obvious at all. Say you're working on the Lebanon orders. We shouldn't be stuck in here anyway. The switchboard is lit up with calls for Baziotis. Look—it's not like knitting. You can drop it in the middle."

Muriel, very tense, found herself being hustled down the hall with Francine babbling behind her. "A real hot tamale. And mad! They must have had some fight. She came in here like gangbusters, clipping along in those heels at sixty miles an hour. I wonder how she got by the security checks. Maybe she mowed them down. Do you suppose she ran into 'the other woman'?" Francine was running out of breath, trying to say it all before they reached Sales. "Arno probably has a girlfriend, huh?" she asked with plaintive urgency.

Muriel sat down at her desk and raked some mail out of the basket. Rhythmically she slit envelopes with her letter opener, hoping that Baziotis would not turn up at that moment and make her sit there for the rest of the day. Although, really, it didn't matter if she couldn't return to Advertising today. There were still several days to go before she was meeting the computer whiz—and the airline woman.

Francine fussed with the stapler, oozing jealousy about Arno's wife. If only she would stop and go away so that Muriel could clear away these Lebanon orders and get back to the video terminal.

She started to get up. Francine pushed her shoulders down.

"Stay, stay," she said desperately. "She'll be out in a minute, I bet you anything."

Muriel started to protest with talk of letters of credit, Accounts Receivable. Then she thought better of it, and sank back in her swivel chair.

Throughout Sales suspense-filled whispers reverberated off the file cabinets. Knots of secretaries formed around the Mr Coffee station, cradling mugs and glancing back toward Arno's door. A junior European manager, one of Westfeldt's flunkies, hesitated on the threshold of his office. This was no time for Muriel to play the wet blanket. She pushed her letters of credit aside and tried to smile.

Francine winked at her.

Arno's doorknob moved. Across the room someone pulled the glass coffee pitcher away before the machine had finished. Drops of liquid fell onto the plastic burner, sputtering excitedly.

Infected in spite of herself by collective curiosity, Muriel swivelled her chair around: the door had opened slightly. A man's hand at the end of a familiar worsted-wool sleeve could be seen holding the inside doorknob. Then the sleeve disappeared, the door opened, and a small dark-haired woman emerged, swathed in furs. She was ridiculously overdressed. But as the woman calmly closed the door behind her, Muriel felt impressed. The expensive perfume; it always produced the awesome effect that the ads promised. But no, there was something else. The way she met the dozens of eyes staring at her was impressive. Ashamed, Muriel swiveled back to the orders on the desk, but that was even worse. As if on cue, they were all running back to their work stations, and beginning to shuffle frantically through their papers. And Arno's wife had looked straight at them. *Brava*, Muriel cheered silently, and slit another envelope.

"There is a ladies' room here?" The voice spoke near her ear, thickly accented and surprisingly deep. Muriel looked up into dark eyes under mercilessly plucked eyebrows; there was something vulnerable about the face that could be glimpsed under the layers of cold-white powder.

"Around the corner," Muriel said, pointing. Mrs Pagano left, walking in a kind of sea roll on her insanely high heels.

Francine made cryptic gestures until Arno's wife had negotiated the turn into the corridor. "Thank God you took care of that," she said, as if someone had suddenly turned her volume back on. "I was so busy looking at her that I didn't even hear her. Cheap looking, huh? I hope Arno hasn't jumped out of the window. I bet she really gave him the business."

"Why don't you go in and check?"

"No, no. I want to talk to her when she comes back. Come on, help me think of something to say to her. What do we know about Argentina?"

"Absolutely nothing."

"Oh, I know. Say something to her in Spanish."

"Francine, I have nothing to say to the woman. Why don't we leave her alone and get out of here?"

"No, I really want to say something to her. I've been dying to see her all this time, and now she's going to split after we've only seen her for two minutes."

"Ask her if she'd like an escort to the parking lot," Muriel suggested. It would be a way to get rid of Francine for a while. "Tell her it's a lousy neighborhood and we had to put up barbed wire to defend ourselves."

Francine brightened. "That's a super idea. Only, wait. She doesn't drive. Arno told me. I wonder if she took the bus here." She frowned. "Gee, you'd think Arno would drive her home. They must have really had some fight."

"He's probably four feet deep in the sidewalk—just like you said."

Arno's wife appeared at the entrance to Sales. This appearance was an anti-climax. A few people turned to look, but everyone was back at work now, immersed in shipping arms to Europe, ammo to Australia. No one was interested in watching Mrs Pagano make her slow way back to Muriel's desk. Except Francine, of course.

"I'm going to ask her for an idea about what to name the new rifle." Advertising and Marketing were developing a name for a new model, always a major undertaking.

"That's stupid," Muriel whispered, skimming a letter from a distributor in Syria.

"All right then. I'll ask her about makeup. God knows we spend enough time ordering it for her. Personal errands. We're not supposed to do that. . . Those office worker groups. . ."

"Hello," Mrs Pagano said to them both, inappropriately. Then, to Muriel: "Please be kind and order a taxi to me. I return for San Francisco now."

"Certainly." Muriel dropped her letter and reached for the phone. She wondered whether she should address the woman in Spanish, since her English was so poor. But that would be insulting. "The taxi will have to wait outside the gates," she said, in English. "On the street. They won't let it come to the door here. I'll get someone from the Maintenance Department to take you outside."

Mrs Pagano nodded. Perhaps she understood better than she spoke. Francine glared at Muriel; she had wanted the escort job herself. Muriel dialed the cab company, hearing Francine ask the inevitable question. What a boor she was.

". . . so I've often wondered what made the Mexican makeup so special. They must have extra good stuff down there. I always thought you could get just about anything you needed in San Francisco. But Arno always said no, my wife wants this really special makeup from Mexico."

Mrs Pagano's face looked stiff with rage.

"You confuse with his first wife. A Mexican. *I* am *not* Mexican. I am from Argentina. I never go to Mexico in the life."

"Oh, I know you're not Mexican. I'm not saying you're Mexican. I'm talking about the makeup. The makeup you ordered from Mexico. I used to type the letters. See, *I* was Mr Pagano's secretary. Now *she* is Mr Pagano's secretary." Francine was talking slowly and distinctly and pointing. This was turning into You-Tarzan-Me-Jane. Muriel could feel her face beginning to burn in vicarious embarrassment.

Mrs Pagano narrowed her eyes and clenched her fists. She was actually falling into the 1930s spiteful woman role for which she was costumed. Muriel hung up the phone, wondering how Francine had the nerve to persist. Those three-inch-long fingernails could easily scratch an eye out. Could they extend and retract like a cat's?

"*Ella esta hablando del maquillaje que Ud. pide a un salon de belleza en Mexico,*" Muriel said. Anything to end this stupid misunderstanding. "And someone from Maintenance is coming. I called a taxi for you."

"I understand the first time," Mrs Pagano said, through

clenched teeth. She kept her narrowed eyes on Francine, who looked gratified at having caused this scene. "I know this words. *Makeup.* I know makeup," she spat, curling a lip outlined in one shade and painted in another. "I buy my makeup in I.Magnin. In Macy. No in Mexico. You confuse with his first woman, his Mexican woman."

An overalled *deus ex machina* from Maintenance appeared at this point and Arno's wife arranged her furs and followed him, without a backward glance.

"She's crazy," Francine said gleefully. "He's married to a crazy woman. You know as well as I do that we ordered pounds of that makeup from Mexico for her in the past year. And those magazines. Unless. . ." Francine's face clouded over. "Unless it was for a girlfriend."

Or unless it wasn't makeup we were ordering at all, Muriel thought, holding a letter opener which was suddenly vibrating like a Jew's harp. As soon as Francine left, she was going to note down a certain address in the Personal Correspondence file—a file which had been standing untouched throughout the Federal investigation.

# Sixteen

Omar Herrera splashed cold water on his face and reached for a towel. Its nap was gone; it clung to his sharp features like a wet Kleenex. Impatiently he peeled it off and folded it, sopping as it was, from an old habit of orderliness. Wearily he made his way to his narrow bed and pulled off the laceless, gaping old black oxfords which he wore as bedroom slippers.

The mechanical clock had stopped. He lifted it and it started ticking; then it stopped again. No, it could not be three o'clock. It was eight, or maybe seven. Long ago his neighbors had taken the bus to their work in the fields. He himself had driven all night from Los Angeles, and just arrived back in Salinas. He reached out and pulled a newspaper at random from the pile on the floor near his bed.

He lay on his back and began to read, holding the front page directly over his face until his arms grew tired. With a groan he turned on his side and continued his perusal. This was last Wednesday's paper. Soon Guarino would take all these papers. *New York Timeses* from the past week, the

Sunday *Los Angeles Times,* plus various leftist quarterlies which were published sporadically. It hadn't been easy to find a copy of the *NACLA Latin American & Empire Report,* and none of the vendors carried that East Coast Puerto Rican paper any more. *Pinche Guarino.* Why couldn't he be content with the Chicano papers? He should get off his ass and travel to L.A. himself once in a while.

He was beginning to get very sleepy. Lazily his eye caught a small headline in a lower left-hand corner of the front page. "Field Marshall Montgomery Dead at 88." He stopped reading and fell back on the bed, feeling strangely saddened by this news. Montgomery, the Viscount El Alamein. It was like hearing of the death of a distant relative, one you had always disliked. Lucky bastard, Montgomery. He made his reputation on Rommels' misfortune. Imagine choosing the name of a place in North Africa for a British title. Arrogant imperialists.

He fell asleep. The newspaper, carrying a wide headline proclaiming Mrs Peron's overthrow, slid against a buff-colored pile of army field manuals.

* * *

There was a late March chill in the apartment. Dennis had opened all the windows in his room. Breezes wafted around Muriel's ankles in the kitchen, where she stood near the wall phone looking through her telephone memo book.

"God, I'm thirsty," Dennis said. He filled a glass with water from the faucet and stood drinking it by the sink.

"God, I'm cold," Muriel said irritably. "Would you kindly remember to keep your door closed while you're in there?"

Dennis opened his eyes wide, and put down his glass. "Excuse *me!*" He walked back into his room and shut the door firmly behind him.

Calm down, Muriel told herself. She flipped through the pages of the memo book for the third time. Was it under "S" for Salinas or "C" for Citizens Committee? Ah. She found it. It was under "S" for "Support Committee Headquarters". Dennis' air compressor was running in his room again. She would have to apologize. She dialed the number with nervous fingers and held a photocopy from Lovell—a new one— in her hand as she listened to the rings.

Someone answered. "*Bueno.*"

They never used to answer in Spanish. "Is this the Support Committee Headquarters?" Her voice sounded thin and childish.

"*Comité de Apoyo,*" the male voice responded. Oh God. A monolingual.

"*Esta Omar Herrera?*" Now she sounded furtive, like an obscene caller.

"*No. No está.*" Muriel asked for Guarino. He was there.

"Guarino? This is Muriel."

"Muriel! How are you? We were going to write to you." We? "We couldn't turn up anything on the Pardee connection. It's been pretty busy here."

"Forget about Pardee," she said, through dry lips.

"Yeah?"

"But listen. I have to talk to Omar. About munitions."

"He's not here. I think he's in L.A."

Muriel's heart sank into the brown espadrilles which had just arrived in the mail from Spiegel's.

"I've got something important to talk to him about," she said, as if this would induce Guarino to bring him out of hiding.

"I think he'll be gone for another day. I don't . . . Maybe he came back last night." Ah. So Omar might be produced after all.

"Could you leave him a message? It's really crucial."

"Sure. Who knows? He might stop by here later. He's supposed to have some stuff for me."

"Okay, I'll give you my number. Have you got a pencil?"

"Just tell me. I'll remember."

Oh God. She gave him the number. "He has to dial the area code first. It's the same one as for San Francisco." She was not going to trust Guarino with nine digits.

"Yeah. 415. I know."

"He should call collect, of course."

"Okay. Collect. So how have you been, anyway?"

Surely the numbers were becoming garbled in Guarino's head with every new word that was spoken. Muriel told him she was fine and ended the conversation as soon as she decently could.

This time it was she who was drinking a glass of water next to the sink when the noise of Dennis's air compressor stopped. In the silence she could hear two voices behind the closed door. Dennis came out, one of the programmers from upstairs walking behind him like a dim shadow.

"Oh, Muriel. This is Hank Blundon from upstairs. Hank, Muriel."

They exchanged nods. When had he come in?

Hank left by the back door. Dennis stood in the doorway and called after him. "Try to come over tomorrow night and we'll see about weathering those gondolas." There was a response, a faint cry like a sheep's bleat. Muriel shivered by the sink. The flimsy house shook under Hank's footsteps as he mounted the outdoor stairs. "Nothing like letting in a little more cold air, Dennis," she said.

Obediently he closed the door. "I'll shut the windows in my room as soon as it airs out a little more. We've been getting a lot of painting done."

"Do you really like that guy?"

"Not to talk to." Dennis disappeared into the pantry and emerged with a box of crackers. "He's a real straight arrow. Typical sys-anal."

"What?"

"A systems analyst. Bor-ing. The kind of technical freak that made me want to drop out of school. Plus, he'd probably dash out of here in ten seconds and take a bath in Lysol if he found out he was playing trains with a faggot."

"He sounds enchanting."

"He knows quite a bit about model railroading though. He's pretty interesting to run trains with. He told me about the new transistor throttles; he's into electronics. If he was planning to stay in Walnut Creek longer he said he'd even rig one up for my layout."

"Oh, is he thinking of leaving soon? Eat over the table, Dennis. I just swept the floor."

"Yeah. He's just here for the duration of the strike at that electronics plant in Lafayette. I told you, he's scabbing."

"That's not very nice."

"Ha. I'm the one who told you about that too. You didn't even know what it was."

Muriel wanted to say that she had learned a lot about it in Salinas, but she was trying not to worry about Salinas. She didn't want to think about Guarino forgetting her telephone number or Omar not returning her call.

"When is that strike going to be settled anyway?" And when was that man Hank leaving? With his neatly pressed flannel shirt and jeans on a Saturday morning. Studiedly casual.

"How should I know?" Dennis folded down the flap of the cracker box. Muriel noticed that he forgot to crimp together the inside cellophane bag first. "You're the one who's supposed to be reading the newspapers. Didn't those people in Washington tell you to read the newspapers?"

"I don't think they meant the Walnut Creek papers," Muriel said. She didn't read any newspapers.

"Well. Back to the National Railways of Mexico. I've got a turnout repair problem."

"Dennis!" Muriel called after him.

"What's the matter?"

"Did that guy Hank come out into the hall when I was on the telephone?"

"Were you on the telephone?"

"Yes, I was. I hung up just before you and he came out."

Dennis thought for a while, rubbing his eyes. A contact lens popped out. Expertly he retrieved it from the floor. "Well, he did go to the bathroom but I don't remember exactly when. I think I better pay a visit there myself and wash off this lens."

He disappeared.

Muriel thought. It seemed to her that on another occasion she had seen Hank standing in the hallway when she was talking to Elba on the phone. Always going to the bathroom. Did this guy have a kidney infection or what? And could he hear anything over the noise of the air compressor? Although that wasn't so loud when Dennis's door was closed. She walked into her bedroom to get a sweater and put her new photocopy back in the bureau drawer under some clothes. Maybe she should buy a padlock.

*   *   *

She was just entering the house, back from her walk to the hardware store, when she heard the phone ringing. She tossed the paper bag onto the table and ran for it.

Her heart leaped. It was the operator with a collect call.

"Yes, I accept the charges." She wound the phone cord around her body as she swiveled to face Dennis's door. Closed.

Omar's voice was soft. She had almost forgotten what he sounded like.

"I called you about something very important."

"Yes?" She wondered if he knew who she was.

"The Lovell thing," she said significantly, watching Dennis's door. There was a pause. If she didn't say something soon, he might hang up. She plunged in. "Look, I found a really important document." She cupped her hand over the phone and whispered into it. "Can you hear me?"

"Yes."

"I think it's about directions for the gun modifications that were done in Mexico. I have them in a letter, but it's in code."

"Oh?" Omar sounded interested. "Can you read it to me?"

"Yes. No! Listen, I think someone is spying on me. Right in my own house. Maybe I should call you back from a pay phone. Are you at headquarters? Are you going to be there for a while?"

"Tell me in Spanish."

Muriel had already thought of that. "I can't. I don't know the words for those things."

"Oh." Another pause, to underline Muriel's feelings of inadequacy. "I may be in San Francisco later this week. Maybe I can see you and look at the letter."

"I can't see you here, it's not safe."

"I'll give you my friend's address. It's 3550 . . ."

"Wait! I have to find a pen." She stretched the phone cord

to its limit, reaching her purse on the chair. There was a pen. No paper. She wrote the address on her arm. Thursday at eight o'clock. He said goodbye.

"*Oye,* Omar!"

"*Que quieres?*"

"Omar . . . *cuando se convierten los rifles* . . ." It was no use. She did not know the Spanish terminology. Incautiously she switched back to English; she couldn't let him go before he answered her question. "Didn't you say that the barrels are changed? That the shine is taken off them?"

"Right. When they're converted from sporting arms to paramilitary weapons, the barrels are sandblasted. That's so they can be camouflaged more easily."

"Would you say that the barrels then have a *matte finish?*"

"Dull finish, matte finish. The gloss is removed."

"And," Muriel's voice was trembling with excitement, "didn't you say that their capacity for ammunition is increased?"

"Yes. What did you find? Did you get the specifications on that? Did you find out where it's being done in Mexico?"

"No, no. Please, just answer my question. Is their capacity for ammunition increased?"

"Yes, the magazines are enlarged. The carbine is changed from semiautomatic to automatic. I explained it to you. Remember? The automatic gun fires as long as the trigger is squeezed—not one bullet at a time like the hunting rifles. And naturally it carries more ammo. It needs a big magazine."

After the *hasta luegos* Muriel hung up, walked to Dennis's door, took a deep breath, and flung it open. Dennis leaped six inches into the air and then grabbed for the switches to stop the trains.

"You want to give me a fucking heart attack? Why don't you try knocking?" He glared at her from under the visor of his Union Pacific engineer's cap.

The tracks of the model railroad were laid out on a chest-high wooden platform. Muriel bent to peer under the structure. No Hank.

"You've been acting peculiar lately," Dennis said. "You know that, don't you?"

"What's this?" Muriel asked. She pointed to a boxcar stamped with a decal that said, "Southern Serves the South". "I thought you were making a model of the *Ferrocarriles Nacionales*. Why is this printed in English?"

Dennis moved a switch and set the trains back in motion. "They use American boxcars." The annoyance faded from his face and voice; he was in his element again. "Say a freight shipment was sent down there in the 1950s or '60s. The Mexicans never bothered to send the boxcars back. No one ever kept good records on the boxcars. They're all over the place."

The trains shuttled around the track, making soft noises like the patter of raindrops. Muriel stared at them, wondering if she, like the boxcars, would end up abandoned in Mexico. It wouldn't be long now.

She went into her bedroom and dug out of a drawer her own personal ticket to Mexico: a copy of a letter from Arno—similar to many of his letters which she and Francine before her had typed during the previous year. This one had been sent to an American businessman in a small Mexican city. Muriel remembered Arno handing her a draft of one of these pieces of correspondence, in his slanting handwriting on a yellow legal pad. "Women. They're impossible," he had said, with what now seemed to her to have been a nervous giggle.

This was addressed to Salon El Porvenir, Calle de Cornejo No. 52, Zacatas, Zac., Mexico.

Dear Edward,

I hope this letter finds you and your family well. My wife thanks you for your recent shipment of Maquillaje Exquisita, which arrived exactly on time. We've been very pleased with your recent promptness in filling orders. This is a definite improvement over the delays in the past. I am pleased to place another order for five more jars of Alpine Formula Foundation, matte look of course. We would also like some more of those excellent leather belts, which are now satisfactorily priced, per our conversation. Just one little complaint, my dear Edward: the magazines you sent. You know that my wife must have her magazines, the same ones she has always read. In the last shipment you sent, the magazines seemed somewhat smaller, and this will not do at all. Are you certain that these are the same magazines that we specified? I hope that this question will be answered in the very near future.

I remain, your friend who esteems you. . .

It was an awkward letter, by anybody's standards. That silly business about the size of the magazines hadn't even been noticeable, sandwiched in between the Latin courtesies—wishes for the recipient's good health clogging the beginning, obsequiousness obscuring the end. Muriel had a dim memory of trying to straighten out the English in one of these letters. And hadn't Arno, his hand poised to sign it, warned her never to change a word?

Now she held the address in her hand. A beauty parlor on a street in a provincial Mexican capital. If she went there she would not find any women drying their hair under heated domes. She would find men sweating in a cloud of sand, blasting the shine off gun barrels. There would be the sound of grinding wheels biting at levers, modifying them so that bullets would spit out in a continuous stream. And somewhere there would be a pile of finished automatic carbines—"similar to assault rifles," Omar had said—with matte finish barrels and inexpensive leather straps to be slung . . . over whose shoulders?

"This guy sends the stuff to my home. He already knows the address," Arno had said, reaching into his pocket for a cigarette.

So these were the guns for Joburg. Muriel sank into bed, satisfied. The puzzle was solved. Sleepily she turned over onto her side. There was something written in ink on her wrist. She raised her head to peer at it. Omar. She would talk to Omar on Thursday. And before that was the meeting with the computer expert and Barbara Coffey and the airlines woman. And Elba. Elba would call. Muriel pulled the bedspread around herself and closed her eyes, listening to the sound Dennis's model trains made, racing too fast.

# Seventeen

Lourdes stabbed at the lock of her Jackson Street house with the ill-fitting square key. Finally, it made contact with the tumblers, and the door opened. *Idiota,* she cursed herself. Why didn't I take the original and let *him* struggle with the spare? The hall was dark. Lourdes groped for the light switch. So, he was out. She wondered where he had gone, leaving his fancy sports car parked on the street. Then she saw him, seated in the corner of the living room, making himself at home.

"You want to take a big chance?" she asked. She shrugged out of her fur and walked to the hall closet to hang it up. "Arno is going to be home at five-thirty."

Without turning, she could see in her mind's eye that self-satisfied smile. "I'll be out of here before then. Come and have a cocktail."

"Oh, very good! Now you drink all the liquor. It's going to look like I am *alcoholica.*"

"Relax," he said in his lazy voice. He held out a full glass to her.

But she could not relax. Animosity still washed over her whenever she saw him—although, strangely enough, in the last few days she had actually been glad to see him. Anything was better than being alone. Or being with Arno.

She flung herself onto the sofa. The movement disarranged the gold pendants hanging on her chest.

"What did you find out today?" he asked. He crossed his legs in the European style. Like Arno, she thought with disgust.

"Nothing." She sipped the drink. Hard liquor. She set it down on the marble-topped coffee table. "I no have time to think about these things all day. I am busy with the Historical Society, I explained you that."

"Tired out from a hard day volunteering again?" His voice was filled with contempt.

"Look. We not going to be enemies, remember? I need you, you need me, and everybody going to be happy, right?" She got up, picked up her glass and his and started for the kitchen.

"Where are you going, Lourdes?" he called, always composed. "I haven't finished that drink."

"The drinks go in the sink and you go out of here. Your father will be home soon. Now you hurry yourself and go away."

She came back into the living room and pulled the stopper off the sherry decanter. "Why you park your car near the house? I told you park around the corner." Why didn't that *bruja* of a Mexican mother teach this Chucho—Chuck, he called himself now—to speak Spanish? She poured sherry into her glass.

"I like to be near my car," Chuck Pagano said. He got up slowly. "I'm going to lose it soon enough."

"Yes, good," Lourdes spat at him. "You be a hero and pay this lawyer five times what you should pay. Save your father the disgrace. *Niño mimado,* I could get to Buenos Aires and back ten times for the price of that car!"

"Sure you could," Chuck said. He picked up his coat from the back of a chair and pulled it on. "But what would you go back to? They've got your name, Lourdes. You'd better think of a plan."

She sat silently in her chair. When she heard the door close behind him, she lifted the lid of her wrist watch. Five o'clock. She had found a Mexican station on the radio; should she turn it on? Last week the Spanish news broadcasts had been filled with broadcasts from Argentina. Then, after Friday, nothing. Mrs Peron was at La Angostura, a lake resort in the Andes, awaiting possible trial. The government was being run by Videla, Massera and Agosti. It was said that the transition had taken place without the firing of a single shot.

It was an old story in Argentina; anyone could have predicted it would happen after the old man died. Only not this soon. It was too soon.

Lourdes sipped her sherry. There was one consolation. As soon as the workers faced the bayonets, the strikes would be over. Her furniture might arrive any week now. She glanced around the room. (Did Chuck think of his mother whenever he looked at these low, uncomfortable chairs, cheap garish furniture with orange flowers?) And she would get mail. The checks from Papa would arrive.

But what use would the checks be, now that she could not go back? She stared into the sherry. It was dark yellow, like the sun in late afternoon on the Calle Florida, where she and Arno had met secretly three years before. He had been still married then, and in Buenos Aires on business.

\* \* \*

"What's the matter? Arno reached over the table to take her hand.

He was not yet balding, not so thin.

Lourdes turned back in her chair to face him. She touched the orchid at the side of her coiled hair. "Nothing. I thought it was my cousin Luis."

"Don't worry so much. No one will see us."

Through the open doors of the old-fashioned sidewalk cafe came the sounds of a small band playing the seven movements of the tango: *el paseo, la marcha, el corte, el paseo con golpe, las tijeras, la rueda, el ocho.*

Arno cut his beefsteak, and transferred his fork from his left to his right hand before he began to eat, in the American style. Lourdes touched her mouth with her napkin and wondered about the United States.

The band played *La Nostalgia.* Arno finished eating and pushed back his chair, relaxed and ready for a smoke. The sun was setting; the match lit up lines on his cheeks. Lourdes' skin was like the petals of her orchid. Hastily she looked down at her plate, but not before she had seen the wedding band glinting on the hand that held the cigarette.

They spoke little until they finished dessert. After the waiter had cleared away the cannoli, they returned to a familiar, and forbidden topic.

"You must remember one thing, my dear; they did not kill this man. He was kidnapped. Not executed. It was a warning, nothing more." He smiled at her indulgently over the candles that glowed now on the table.

"Yes, I know, a warning. That is exactly why I am worried. I hope the warning has been heeded."

Arno shrugged. "This man, the Ford dealer, what's his name? John Swint. He's dead. The FAP executed him without hesitation. Why don't you worry about the Ford dealers, the Exxon executives, the people at Phillips Argentina? Things are much more serious for them, I assure you."

"I don't know any Ford dealers! The only dealers I know are arms dealers. Two, to be exact—you and my father."

"Lourdes, you know nothing about these things. The man was an imbecile. Look at him now, mouthing off to the international press. Telling everyone that his sales were nothing compared to the deals made by Interarms-Interarmco. He's right, of course, but who asked him? He wanted to be a public figure, so he became one. And he got his reward. The FAP caught onto his game and kidnapped him."

"Not the FAP. The FAL."

Arno picked up the bill. He was ready to leave. "Who can keep track of these Communist groups? We can only hope they continue their infighting and kill each other off. They call themselves Peronists! Why aren't they content? Wasn't Peron inaugurated last month?"

"You don't understand things here, Arno. You have been away too long."

Arno reached across the table and took Lourdes' chin in his fingers. "*You* don't understand, little cat. Do you think that your father and I are so hungry for sales that we would sell guns to these groups that the leftists hate so much? I have told you a thousand times: my company makes sporting arms. Rifles for hunters."

It was a warm summer night, a sultry November in Buenos Aires. Inside the restaurant candles burned on the tables, behind a window swathed in white Austrian curtains, like bridal veils.

*   *   *

"That's what he said then," Chuck said, smiling. They sat on a bench in Union Square, that first day that she ran into him. She wondered what he was doing in Magnin's: his rain-coat was mildewed like an old shower curtain.

"Come to think of it, it was probably true at the time."

"What was true?" She untangled the leash from her little dog's paws.

"He probably wasn't selling guns to the far right then. Those were the days when he travelled down to Argentina pretty often. To see you, I guess. Mother had an idea that something like that was going on."

Lourdes studied the shopping bags beside her on the bench with narrowed eyes. Everything was there: shoes, scarves, blouses, perfume.

"What I mean is that it seemed safe for him to do it when he wasn't going down there any more. And he didn't intend to go down there again. Your father's been handling the distributorship just fine all by himself. The sporting sales, that is."

Lourdes thought about shopping for dinner. Perhaps she could pick up some after-dinner mints from Blum's while she was in this neighborhood. Sitting here where all the world could see her in this noisy park full of derelicts. But at least Chuck was not coming home to dinner. He was in some kind of trouble. He was saying something about his lawyer, some difficulties.

The little dog barked. He wanted attention. Lourdes bent over him. "Yes, I know. You need your walk. Don't worry, we go soon." She glanced at this tall, smug stepson to see if the hint had registered. Still that arrogant look on his common, dark-skinned face.

"Well," she said, "maybe Arno needs not go to Argentina on business. But he needs to go visit my family with me." She stooped over the dog again. "This little dog wants to see his brothers and I, too, want to see all my family."

"Have you heard from your family lately?"

"No," Lourdes said reluctantly. What business was it of his? "There is some problem with the mail. The political situation. As always." She gathered up the leash and wound it around her hand.

"The political situation!" His voice was oily, like the lard Mexicans use for frying. "I should say so. Poor Isabelita. Her government will fall any day now."

She hooked the end of the leash over her wrist and began to pick up the packages. "Oh, you think so? That's very good, you know the future. I wish you can tell me about my future too."

"Well, there's one thing I can predict, Lourdes." He rose from the bench. "You won't be going back there very soon. At least not as Arno's wife. That wouldn't be very safe."

They were both standing. "What do you mean?" Lourdes asked. "Explain me what you are saying."

"I'm telling you exactly what my father told me. He's been shipping guns to some of the same groups as that guy who got kidnapped back in 1973. You know those groups: right-wing, and they sound left. Peronist Syndicalist Youth. And that union, the Metallurgical Union. You might say that he picked up where the other guy left off. Dad's not very original."

Her nails tore into the paper bag in her hands. "I don't believe you," she said.

Chuck went blandly on, as though she had not spoken. "And what's even less original is that he also sold to the far left groups. To the guerrillas. The group that robs banks—the Montoneros. That's where the big money was. But it was a big mistake, you know, Lourdes. Because the military's going to take over, and they're sure to find out."

The dog tugged at the leash. Lourdes looked to the right and to the left. She felt suffocated, pressed in by the couples in their sloppy clothes who crowded the paths of the park.

Across the way some people were gathered to watch a mime whose face was painted white, like a corpse. She wished she could rise straight up in the air like a helicopter and escape.

And that was just what Chuck wanted her to do: to run away. He wanted his father to himself. He was using terrorist tactics.

He turned to go and then turned back. "Oh, and remember, don't tell Dad that you met me. After I iron out this little legal problem, I'll have a talk with him. But in the meantime you wait and see, Lourdes. What I said is true."

It was. Arno told her so himself when she surprised him, bursting in on his warehouse of an office. And now she had to think of a plan.

# Eighteen

Muriel had the figures on the sales to Mexico. They were on printer's "repros," the wet, slimy photographic paper which slid out of the photographic processor in Advertising. And a few inches below the Mexican sales was the table of sales to Austria—partially obscured by a light leak, but still legible. Muriel had passed through agonizing moments while the paper passed through the processor. At last this wet length of repro had emerged from the slot.

"That's where your real problem is going to be," Patsy, the computer whiz, had said at the meeting. "When you have the stuff thrown up on the screen you can turn down the density but—" she had held a warning finger in the air,"—if anyone comes up behind you while the power is rolling out of the processor, you're sunk."

Barbara Coffee was ostensibly knitting in her corner of the COCOA office. She gave Muriel a meaningful glance that said, Get the picture?

Muriel heard herself whining. "Can't I turn the machine off if someone comes in at that moment? The processor has a switch."

"They all do," Patsy said indistinctly. She was eating a banana. She had run over right after work and she had to eat what was left in her lunch bag or she would starve to death, she said. "The trouble is, what goes in the processor will eventually come out. It'll look suspicious enough if you turn that thing off suddenly—processors are mechanical, not electronic and the average person can understand them. But it'll look *real* suspicious if the person sticks around and sees two repros instead of one coming out with the next run."

Patsy finished her banana and dropped the peel into the brown paper bag. "You'd better be absolutely sure that the coast is clear when you put that photographic paper into the processor."

Muriel bent over the manual, nodding and chanting instructions to herself like her grandfather *davenning* in the Fairfax Avenue Synogogue.

When Patsy left, the woman from the airlines took her place. A surrealistic conversation ensued about passenger lists, about where Muriel would like people to think she had gone while she was actually in Mexico, and about border difficulties. "Oh, dear, you really should have a passport. Well, it's too late to apply now. Maybe you can get by."

It was eleven o'clock before they emerged into the windy street. Barbara Coffey groped for her car keys in the tangle of yarn in her tote bag. "You San Francisco people certainly seem to have oodles of resources," she said to the airlines representative. "I suppose it's one of the benefits of diversifying."

"Bon voyage," the airlines woman said. She was going to fly Muriel's spirit to the Austrian Alps. Muriel noticed that she was wearing a Peter Pan collar.

And now she had the sales figures. No one had sneaked up behind her. It had all gone almost too smoothly. At least until she got home and took them out of her bag. Patsy hadn't mentioned that they would stick together when they were folded. However, a little frantic sponging with water had fixed that. They smelled even worse than the photocopies.

But now they were in a registered envelope, on their way to the Foundation for Investigative Reporting, and Elba. All that remained of them in Muriel's room was a xerox made at the public library. And if Hank Blundon decided to investigate her bureau on his way to the bathroom, he wouldn't find even the xerox, because the xerox went with her to the rendezvous with Omar.

"If you really think he's spying on you, why don't you ask your roommate to stop seeing this man?" Omar looked shabby, but he blended easily into the peeling-paint look of this flat on Mission and 30th Street. Muriel, on the other hand, was aware of the pristine neatness of her work clothes (light blue pants set of woven polyester, rayon and flax; jacket has notched collar; front tucking; sleeves have roll-back cuffs; Penney Cat. # A 219-2938 B) contrasting with these depressing digs, the tenant of which, one Julio Calo, had tactfully left as Muriel entered. Perhaps he had gone to one of the Outer Mission cantinas, whre trombones laughed loudly from juke boxes.

Omar interrupted as she was beginning to answer his question. "Actually, it's better this way," he said thoughtfully from his perch on the edge of a leaking beanbag hassock. "You drag a herring across the trail."

A confused image of a fish in a straw handbag flashed across Muriel's mind.

"Your roommate will be told that you're in Austria, correct? So that's what he tells the spy, and the company wastes time looking for you in the Alps. Perfect."

But it wasn't perfect. Spies using her new soap dish, the bathroom towels . . . it wasn't a pleasant thought. Muriel began to babble, looking for reassurance. The guy probably wasn't really a spy, that was probably silly, wasn't it? Didn't Omar think that was probably silly? After all, that woman at Customer Service wasn't even paying any more attention, even though she had seemed so suspicious for a while there. The whole thing was probably a figment of the imagination. Wasn't it?

Omar shrugged. Muriel wondered what he had thought when she said that Dennis was her roommate. And she was carrying an overnight bag at this inconvenient evening meeting. Did he believe her when she said that she was going to stay at her brother's?

What did she care, anyway?

But she did care. She found it exciting to see him again, or at any rate it was one sort of excitement blending into the events of the last few days to make her heart beat like a triphammer in her chest. At the moment she had a cathartic feeling, a pleasant exhilaration. Possibly this was because the worst was yet to come: the solitary journey to Mexico.

"Yes," Omar said. "This is exactly what you need." In his almost transparent hand he held the yellow legal papers, facsimiles of the make-up order and the Mexican sales data—ghosts of the materials sent to Elba.

"Three hundred thirty caliber carbines going to Zacatecas per month." The papers pinged as he struck them with his index finger. "It's true that hunting is popular in Mexico, but this is absurd. And the State Department issued export licenses for every one of these shipments."

"See. I got the figures for the three years before," Muriel said, pointing them out. "It's a five hundred percent increase."

"That's good, that's very good. There's even a reference to the subcontracts with Pardee for cattle prods."

"Right," Muriel said, almost chuckling with excitement. "Was I ever surprised when that came up on the screen!

That's the first time I've seen a footnote at the end of one of these sales tables."

Omar looked puzzled. "The screen?"

"The video display screen. The tables were stored inside an electronic disk. Photography is involved. . . I really had a job getting this data printed out."

"I don't understand computers," Omar said. "But mechanical stuff. . . That's what this is." He pointed to the letter about the make-up. "Matte-look, magazines, leather belts. There's a machine shop in Zacatecas all right. And they must be very busy if they're converting three hundred arms a month from sporting goods to police weapons."

He read the letter again, while Muriel watched him. Then he looked up at her. "Does this make any sense," he asked, "the way it's written?"

Did he think she knew a lot about cosmetics? "Sort of," she said, blushing. "My boss doesn't write too well in English." Would he think that rouge and eyeliner were effete? She wished she could remain pale and blanched, like him.

Julio returned, to busy himself in the kitchen, opening and closing cabinets and washing dishes. Omar inclined his head toward the sound of running water. "He can be trusted," he said. He stared off into space. "Things are really getting hot in South Africa." he said. There had been a new language policy in the public schools. "The students were supposed to change over from English to Afrikaans in a day or so. Just like that! It's exactly the way they treat the Chicano children, forcing them to change from one language to another—whipping them for speaking Spanish in school."

Muriel picked up her jacket and suitcase. She had to take the bus to Bernie's apartment. Omar said that there had been language demonstrations, followed by a bus boycott and an enormous rally in Soweto where the black workers lived, outside Johannesburg. "A lot of white South African policemen are looking forward to receiving their rapid-fire carbines."

Muriel nodded, trying to think of a way to say goodbye. "Well," she said.

Omar got up and dreamily walked along with her to the bus stop. The San Francisco breezes whipped dark strands of his longish hair across his pensive, skeletal face. When they reached the stop he touched her hand, wished her good luck and vanished around a corner.

Muriel searched for her monthly bus pass in her wallet, shivering from Omar's touch mixed with the chill of the evening. How elegant he was, how mysterious, like the young John Gielgud in *Foreign Agent.*

As she mounted the bus steps, she thought suddenly that it was not Omar who was actually playing the Gielgud role; it was she, Muriel Axelrod, in her light blue pants set of woven polyester, rayon and flax.

* * *

Hank Blundon relaxed in his chair. It was comfortable, covered with real cowhide that matched the lush brown carpeting. It would be real easy to get used to this kind of luxurious living. Not that he had a chance of doing that, on the money he got from Munson Electronics. A lot of thanks he was getting for helping them out of a jam. He couldn't even afford to live alone down here, not while he had to keep his mortgage payments going in Yuba City. Between that and the car payments. . . The Company had made it seem like his salary was some kind of fortune, but it sure wasn't. Not by a long shot. And on top of that he had to pass by those screaming picketers every morning. What a lousy way to start the day. One of those damn freeloaders had scratched the finish on the Datsun. Lucky thing he had left the new wagon back home with Ellen.

"Care for a cigarette?" Jules Baziotis extended a rumpled pack; he was sitting under an oil painting that looked like the real thing. Class all the way.

Hank declined. Baziotis lit one for himself and held it in front of his eyes for a moment. "I never smoke on the job," he said thoughtfully. "Some people find smoke really annoying. I certainly wouldn't want to take the chance of annoying someone really important." He drew on the cigarette and let the smoke out in ostentatious rings.

Hank cleared his throat.

"I've got some more goods on her," he said.

Baziotis smoked silently.

Hank waited with an expectant smile until Baziotis nodded almost imperceptibly. Then he took a small notebook from the inside pocket of his double-knit sports jacket.

"Saturday, March 26," he read, in a sing-song voice. "She was on the phone to Salinas, to that Farmworker Committee."

Baziotis studied the high ceiling moldings. "And what did she say?"

Hank put the notebook away and ran his hand over his brush haircut. "Well, I'm afraid I can't tell you that, Mr B. She didn't get through to the party she wanted. And there was just no way I could stay down there any longer."

"Oh? You had another engagement?"

"Hey, are you kidding? No sir! This assignment gets top priority. No, but see, the way it works is, Dennis and I . . . Dennis is her boyfriend . . . Dennis and I start on a project. See, last Saturday we were painting a railroad depot with an airbrush. Now when we finished with that---"

"I know, I know. It's all right, Blundon. Now do you have anything else to tell me?"

Hank took a deep breath, swallowed and leaned forward with his hands on his thighs.

"No, I don't," he said, in a level voice. "I do not have any more information at this time."

"All right, Blundon." Baziotis began to get up.

"This is the way it is," Hank said quickly. His prepared speech, in which he had intended to accentuate the positive, flew out of his head. "This girl Muriel is onto me now, Mr B. I'm just about ninety-eight percent sure of it."

Ash dropped on the velvety carpet. "She's onto you," Baziotis repeated.

Hank regained his composure somewhat. "There wasn't a way in hell of getting around it. She saw me in the hallway. She was on the phone, and I was supposed to be on my way to the bathroom. See, the thing was, we had the air compressor on in the room there, and the damn things makes so much noise I couldn't hear a thing over it. So I had to go out into the hall."

"You're sure she saw you?"

"Yes, sir. She gave me a pretty funny look. And besides, since then she hasn't made any more phone calls. Not from the house anyway."

Baziotis got up and walked over to the window where he stood with his back to Hank, who inserted his finger inside his shirt collar to give himself a little air. Nice room, but it was kind of hot. Parts of his speech began to come back to him. "Now the way I see it—"

"I don't particularly care to hear about the way you see it at the moment. I'm trying to think."

There was silence for a few moments. A vacuum cleaner whined outside the door in the corridor. Baziotis walked back and forth, the soles of his leather shoes rubbing electrically against the carpet. The crackling noises sounded like distant gunfire.

"We've probably got enough on her now," Baziotis said. He sank back into his chair, lost in thought. "In fact we've definitely got enough on her now."

"That's just what I was going to say," Hank said eagerly. He ticked off items on his fingers. "We've got the name of her contact in Washington, we've got her connection with this bunch of Contra Costa secretaries, we know all about her farmworkers, and it is clear—it is absolutely clear, sir—that she intends to spill her guts to the press."

"Yes, I should think that is clear, Blundon. After all, the foundation that is supporting her investigation is headed by Jack Anderson. I hardly think he intends to write this information on a piece of paper and leave it under his pillow for the tooth fairy."

Hank laughed heartily and then sobered immediately, frowning. "That's pretty funny, Mr B.," he said, "but just the same it's a pretty rotten thing that woman did, carrying away confidential documents from the company that employs her. I mean, she was in a position of trust." He was improvising, but it didn't sound half bad, he thought. "Really, it makes my blood boil. The U.S.A. has come to a sorry state of affairs when things like this can happen to a company like this."

Baziotis gave him a look. Maybe improvising wasn't such a hot idea.

"You say she's leaving soon," Baziotis said.

"Yes, sir. I'm positive of that, sir. Of course I can't say where she's going."

'Umm hmm. But she's staying on a week or two more."

"That's right. And you know you can always put a tail on her. And phone booth or no phone booth, there are ways she can be listened in on."

"No." Baziotis was firm. "We're not going to do that." He had made a decision on that long ago. It was one thing to accept the help of this slimy neighbor of hers. This slug apparently wanted to play junior detective so badly that he had actually phoned Lovell and asked for Miss Axelrod's supervisor. Well, nobody in his right mind would turn down information, especially at a time like this. But to go so far as to hire a private detective to trail her—if this thing actually were to reach Jack Anderson's desk, an action like that could be an open admission of guilt. And it would cost money, and that would generate more records to hide. And it was obvious by now that some things were going to come to light no matter how much trouble was taken to hide them.

How in the world could a mousey little secretary uncover a plan that had taken years to develop? The best minds in the company had worked on it. Of course the girl had not worked alone. According to Blundon, she had the Farmworkers and some office workers union and some kind of subversive agency in Washington working with her. God knew who else was involved. But she had a lot of guts. Maybe she was getting a big bankroll for doing it. Or maybe she was pissed off at all those sales to the Arabs. She was a Jew, after all.

But whatever the reason, Baziotis was mildly surprised to notice that he did not feel personally hostile toward her. That could be left to Blundon. . . God, he was a nasty specimen. All that eager jovial crap didn't cover it up. There was something awful generating behind those little eyes. He enjoyed this. That's probably why he had asked for so little money. Baziotis had been able to take it out of his own pocket. And he had asked for a recommendation for membership in the Club. Evidently he intended to settle down here permanently. Not a bad break for Yuba City.

"You remember my suggestion, don't you, Mr B?"

He had that glint in his eyes. Baziotis did not answer.

"It isn't the worst thing in the world that could happen to

a person," Blundon said. "I'm not saying it's the best thing either, don't misunderstand me. But she was asking for it, Mr Baziotis. No one asked her to come here looking for trouble. Let's say we'll just slow her down a little."

Baziotis had had enough of this interview. He had reached a decision. "All right. Someone will be in touch with you."

Blundon rose with his wide grin. "I'll be talking to you soon, then. I've got just about all the details worked out. Believe me, it's sure-fire."

Baziotis walked over and put his hand on the doorknob, "Mr Blundon," he said. "I said someone will be in touch with you. This is goodbye. You won't be talking to me again."

A little confused, but still smiling, Hank held his hand out. A tiny charge of static electricity pricked him as they shook their farewell.

Alone at last, Baziotis went over the phone and dialed. "Arno," he said, "Jules. I've got something urgent I must discuss with you."

# Nineteen

Chuck sipped from the heavy Mexican cup. It was another afternoon visit with stepmother for coffee and conspiracy.

"I tell you what," he said. "That trial will be over any day now. Then all charges against me will be dropped. I'll sign the Porsche over to my lawyer and come home to stay with Daddy."

"Oh yes? And how you explain him why you were away?"

"I told you, Lourdes. He'll believe me. I'll tell him about the girl I got pregnant and how I had to sell my car to pay for the abortion. He'll *want* to believe it. Anyway, what I was saying was, after I come home I'll get a job and save money. It won't take long before I have enough so I can lend you what you'll need to go to Mexico and file for divorce from there. He won't contest it if you do that; he'll know you're serious."

Lourdes folded her arms across her narrow chest and looked away. "I am not interested in Mexico," she said.

"Okay, then go to Colombia. Just so it's far enough away. I know how Dad's mind works. If you do it from this country anywhere, he'll challenge it. He'll think you'll come back."

"You are understanding his mind, but my mind you are not understanding. I want to go to Argentina." If Chuck was moving back into the house she could ask Mrs Hardenburgh if she could work more hours at the Historical Society. The big field trip to San Jose was only two weeks away; the Director could use the help. And then Lourdes would not have to see much of Chuck. He was irritating, with his cocksure advice. Yet, strangely, she found herself looking forward to his visits. And oddly she wanted him to move back into the house. He would push the revolving door, so to speak: he would move in and she would finally rouse herself to move out.

"It's Mexico or Colombia. You'd better plan your escape route soon. You know as well as I do that Argentina is out of the question. Either the Government will arrest you because Dad sold to the Montoneros, or the Montoneros will kidnap you because he sold to the right-wing groups. You'd better face it, Lourdes. In Argentina, you can't win."

She began to scrape coffee cake crumbs from the table into the palm of her hand. "It is very late," she said.

Chuck took the hint and left. He would settle his legal problems soon, make up with Arno and move back here. It was getting very late for Lourdes.

* * *

The paint had long since dried on the glass door of Ackerman & Axelrod when Chuck Pagano once again sat in the reception room opposite Bernie's secretary Willa, who had buzzed Bernie. But Bernie was sitting in his office, making Chuck wait.

Sometimes he worried about his heart, the way it acted when something good was about to happen—like being handed the registration to a Targa. There were good palpitations and there were sick palpitations. These were sick ones, reflecting the old morbid dread that something would go wrong at the last minute. Or maybe these were just left over from the trial.

Getting that nervous wreck Eddie acquitted had been a piece of cake. He was innocent, and the jury knew it. Still, Bernie had had a few nightmares about the kid getting put away, just for the sake of a sports car. But it was all over now, thank God. The kid's father had stopped chatting with his lawyer friends at cocktail parties about how come something like this was going all the way to trial, and the mother had stopped having migraines. And the kid—well, the kid had always been a mess.

All's well that ends well. Bernie grabbed his coat off the brass rack in the corner. He had found a buyer for the goddam Packard and now he was off for a test spin in the little gray beauty. He could only hope that it would rev up as well as his heart was revving.

"So this means that all charges against me are dropped."

"That's what it means." Bernie slid the document into Chuck's file. They were back in the office after their little jaunt around the block. God, did that baby perform. And maybe Muriel was right about all that fatty French food. The old ticker might even be skipping beats. Yes, there were definite beats being skipped.

He winked at Chuck. "The D.A. never goes back on his end of a deal. And speaking of deals. . . I hope you remembered to bring the registration."

"Certainly."

Bernie scanned it. Everything was in order. Chuck signed

a bill of sale for a ridiculously low dollar amount. "We don't want to give the State of California too much sales tax," Bernie quipped. Then there was a paper which released Chuck from all legal fees. "Pretty shrewd of you to ask for this," Bernie said. "It's just a standard form. Sign at the bottom."

Chuck read it. "You haven't signed it," he said.

"With pleasure." Bernie uncapped his Montblanc fountain pen, and paused, holding it over the paper. *Jesus Pagano*. Jesus. Of course. That was Chuck's real name. He had noticed it ages ago, when the kid first came to his office. Even before that, at the arraignment. Why in hell was the kid named Jesus? A Jewish shimmer went over Bernie. The name might be a bad omen.

"Hey," he said with false jocularity, "I always thought Chuck was short for Charles. How come you call yourself Chuck instead of Jesus, or is the answer obvious?"

The kid just kept looking at the pen poised over the paper. Hurriedly, Bernie scrawled his signature.

"It's Spanish." Chuck folded the paper and put it in the inside pocket of his jacket. "Hay-zoos. Common Latin American name. The nickname is Chucho, like Pancho for Francisco, you know? My parents called me Chucho. In school the kids changed it to Chuck."

"You're Spanish? No kidding. I thought Pagano was Italian. I knew a kid in L.A. named Nicky Pagano—Italian kid."

"You're right. It is Italian. My father is an Argentinian of Italian descent. There are a lot of people of Italian descent in Argentina. About a third of the population." He turned to go.

"Oh yeah, Right." Bernie rushed out from behind his desk. "My sister told me the same thing. She works for an

Argentinian guy out at that big munitions plant in South San Francisco. Lovell."

"Oh?" Chuck turned to face Bernie. He looked surprised.

"Yeah." Bernie said. Suddenly he felt self-conscious. It was a pretty vacuous conversation.

In another moment client and attorney had exchanged farewells. Bernie went back to contemplate the car keys on his blotter, and Jesus Pagano, the prodigal son, made his way on foot to Jackson Street to await the return of his Argentinian father from the big munitions factory in South San Francisco.

\* \* \*

Muriel nursed a ginger ale at the corner table in Marshall Pétain's. She felt rotten. It had taken her an entire weekend to recover from loss of sleep at Bernie's and then what had she done? Tuned in to Channel 30 at two a.m. on a Tuesday night to catch the first half of *Odette*. The first half was the only half worth watching.

"It's like the world's first non-alcoholic hangover," she said to Harriet Warren.

"It's probably just from stress," Harriet said. She beckoned to the barmaid.

"Stress! If it's from stress, it's certainly come late. This is the easiest week I've had in ages. All I have to do is show up at work and actually work. No snooping, no spying. It's like a vacation."

Muriel decided to switch from ginger ale to bourbon. After all, it wasn't booze that made her feel like this. A few nights of early to bed and she would be as good as new.

Still, everything had a strange underwater look. Maybe it had something to do with Harriet's being a diver. Subliminal suggestion.

"How are things at your job?" she asked Harriet.

"Sucky, as usual." Harriet dug into her alligator clutch. "I've got invoices up to here. They're giving me the old speed-up routine so I can make up for being off a whole week next month. I have to dive in the A.A.U. semi-finals in New Jersey. Speaking of travelling. . ." She lowered her voice and handed Muriel a small envelope. "Here it is."

"Cheers." They raised their glasses, looking at each other significantly.

After some desultory talk about the traffic and the weather, they drank up and went for a walk in the twilit Clement Street.

"A terrific job, don't you think?" Harriet said. Muriel had just put the cards back into the little envelope.

"Who did it?"

"A woman lithographer, someone close to the San Francisco office workers group. I think it's a little better than trying to find a corpse to register. Looks like the real thing, doesn't it?"

"It really does," Muriel said. Actually the light was too dim for her to get a good look at it. "You know, I think most people couldn't describe their voting cards if their lives depended on it."

"I can't believe they'll accept that for a visa at the border."

"Oh, they do. I'm positive of it. I used mine every time I crossed the border. Oh, wait a minute. I want to stop in at this Russian bakery."

"We have to keep walking. It's not safe to stop."

"This cloak and dagger stuff is really ridiculous, Harriet. Walking won't stop anyone from bugging us. They use microphones with crosshair sites. Didn't you see *The Conversation?*"

"I don't go to the movies, I told you that. I'm too busy diving."

It must be nice to be tall, Muriel thought, stealing a glance at their blurred reflection in one of the plate glass windows. And then she thought, we really have nothing in common.

"What name are you going to use? You know, on the voter's card. You can type in anything you want. Just use an electric typewriter with pica type, like they have at the Registrar of Voters."

"I really don't think the Mexican customs officials know what kind of type they use at the Registrar of Voters. We don't want to get obsessive about this."

"But what name?"

"I don't know. I'll try to pick a good one. Maybe Barbara Coffey."

"Ha!"

"After all, she wants to get involved."

"Oh, right. Does she ever!"

"Why is she hostile to you?"

"Because I'm an athlete. She doesn't take me seriously as an office worker. She thinks any complaints I have about my job are trivial because someday I'll take a nice coaching job and leave all this behind me."

"Will you?"

"I suppose I might. But in the meantime I've racked up five years experience as a bookkeeper. Some of the other women in the group haven't worked as long as I have."

They walked all the way to 34th Avenue. The fog rolled up from Land's End, obscuring the outlines of the rocks, the unfriendly coastline of the Bay, fangs perpetually bared. They reversed direction and walked on in silence for a while.

"That's interesting what you said about Barbara," Harriet said thoughtfully. "About her wanting to get involved."

"Oh?"

"Yes, because . . . well, I'm not supposed to tell you, but I don't see what difference it can make."

A bus roared down Clement Street with large, diffuse halos around its headlights.

"Well?" Harriet said. "Aren't you interested?"

"Oh, yes!" Muriel said. She was wondering if there was a drugstore nearby where she could get some eyedrops.

*     *     *

By 9:30 she was under the covers, trying to push Harriet's voice into a dim corner of her brain so that she could set about following Ben Franklin's advice.

It was no use.

Anyway, she could close her eyes and rest them. That would help, along with the eyedrops. She would probably be fine in the morning. Healthy and wise, if not wealthy.

This stuff Harriet had told her about the blood bank was unbelievable. Rollins Memorial Blood Bank! She hadn't thought about that place since . . . when was it? . . . months ago. She had talked about it at Marshall Pétain's with someone. Gerardina.

So Barbara Coffey had been thinking about it all this time. "She remembers every single thing you told her in that first interview she had with you," Harriet had said. "She's like an elephant."

Some elephant. She took it down in shorthand. And then she decided to pursue the line of investigation all by herself.

"Why didn't she tell me?" Muriel had demanded. She had stopped dead in the middle of Clement Street.

"She didn't want egg on her face if it didn't pan out."

So. Muriel turned over again, trying to find a comfortable position. Barbara Coffey thought that weird Gerardina had her finger on something very important. In this age of computers evidently breaking into a secret part of the database is a challenge equal to climbing Mount Everest. And Barbara Coffey knew someone who worked on accounts in the Rollins Memorial Blood Bank.

So Barbara Coffey, girl detective, had contacted said accounts person. "A blood bank," Harriet had said, "is no different in principle from your regular money bank. The blood you get free in the hospital after you donate is not really your blood at all. It's like money. They lend your money out another window as soon as you deposit it. Blood doesn't keep, you know."

Harriet said she had been well briefed on this at a steering committee meeting presided over by a Coffey who had swallowed a canary. She even brought a blackboard. A blackboard!

Harriet said that patients who need blood in California hospitals have to pay a steep price for it. "It's really strange. Rollins doesn't pay the donors, but they charge the recipients. But you can get out of paying sometimes, either by donating pints to Rollins in advance and getting a credit in your blood savings account, or by having your friends donate while your hospital bill's still pending."

"Forty bucks a pint! Remind me not to get run over by a truck."

"And get this. Rollins is part of a big international blood bank network. It's like the Bank of America, with branches all over the universe. That means that when you donate blood to Rollins, you can credit someone else's account instead of putting the credit in your own blood bankbook. You just waltz in and say, 'Deposit this to General Hospital,

Tuskegee, Alabama. My Aunt Mary's in there with a hemorrhage."

Harriet and Muriel took the same BART train back to the suburbs. There, in a half-empty coach, Harriet finally revealed what all this had to do with gun-running to South Africa.

"Those conversions in Mexico," she said, softly, "were paid for in blood."

The rubber-wheeled train left the Civic Center station and slipped into the four-mile tube under the waters of the Bay. As it accelerated to its top speed of eighty miles an hour, the lifegiving fluids drained from Muriel's face.

There was an interlocking dictatorship. Someone named Gordon Nash was on the board of directors of both the blood bank and Lovell.

"That was easy to establish. Coffey found it in *Who Owns Whom*.

*Who Owns Whom*. Why did that sound familiar? From whom had she heard it before? Oh yes, from Guarino, those first days in Salinas. She had had an uncomfortable feeling with Guarino that her work was being expropriated, and that feeling was fast returning now.

Over the past two years, credits had been coming in to Rollins from a hospital in Mexico City. "Supposedly whole bunches of Mexicans were pouring out their arteries in order to transfer credits to San Francisco."

"Most unlikely," Muriel murmured.

"Most unlikely, you bet. So anyway patients up here in San Francisco are getting free blood left and right because of the credits. And meanwhile, down in Mexico, the Mexican blood bank is getting all the actual blood for nothing and charging for it. They're making out like bandits."

"*Bandidos.*"

"Right. So after a while—according to this accounts person of Coffey's—the accounts became so unbalanced that the Mexican blood bank had to agree to a system of repayments. In money, not blood. Which means, checks from Mexico were coming up here—and guess where they were going."

"Into Gordon Nash's pockets."

"Right. We don't have hard data on that yet, but we're working on it."

"We," Muriel repeated dully.

"That's right, *we.*" Harriet stared at Muriel. "The steering committee. COCOA. It's our project, too, and we've done you a favor."

"I see."

"Now look, Muriel." Harriet's voice was cold. "You know I don't like Barbara Coffey any more than you do. But she did a good job. She found out how the conversions are paid for. Do you realize what this means? It proves that *Lovell's board of directors were directly involved.* Now that's pretty important, don't you think?"

Muriel was near tears. "Why wasn't I invited to this steering committee meeting?"

They were at the Rockridge station. Harriet buttoned her coat, getting ready to get off at Lafayette. "There was no reason for you to be there. Barbara is going to call you soon. She's getting photocopies of the checks drawn on Mexican banks. Muriel, that money was undoubtedly deposited in Mexico by the South African dealer. That's the link you need."

Muriel did not reply.

"I'll talk to you soon." Harriet whisked down the aisle to the door.

Brooding, Muriel turned onto her stomach and finally fell asleep. She woke early and pulled back the curtains to reveal a sun circled with haze, low in the east. Wearily she opened the drawer to her night table and took out the small bottle. Sitting on her single bed in the cold morning light, she held her head back while the drops took effect and thought about Harriet Warren, a young woman already famous as an athlete.

* * *

A week later she was sitting once again with her head back; this time it was pressed against the headrest of the passenger seat of a battered Toyota. Her eyes were tightly closed—not that there was anything to see. In the wee hours of the morning she was being transported through the Southern California desert by two women she had never seen before.

". . . And I'm sure they'll wait for us for an hour at least," the driver was saying to her friend once again. She was a secretary from Compton, taking the day off to help a sister officer worker disappear across a national border.

Muriel opened her eyes. Had someone called her? No, the driver was still looking straight ahead, babbling on to the woman in the back seat about how she refused to speed, it wasn't *her* fault it was getting late, the car from up north had screwed up, she wasn't about to risk people's lives.

It was a great getaway vehicle. A squint at the lighted dashboard revealed that the Toyota was pounding along Interstate 10 at forty-five miles an hour.

This was the fourth car and driver. Or was it the fifth? Muriel had moved through all these confusing changes as though she were anesthetized. There had been a number of different people in different back seats who couldn't read maps. Walnut Creek to Milpitas, Milpitas over to Fresno and Interstate 5, Fresno to a place called Buttonwillow. Then Compton and this timid driver and her friend. It was the Great Trans-California Escape, engineered by Barbara Coffey and sundry UFW members to throw interested people off Muriel's trail.

"Where are we?"

"Oh, Muriel. You're awake." The driver's voice held the same tone of reverence that Muriel had been hearing all night. She was the precious cargo.

"We're about twenty minutes from the last change point," the woman in the back seat said.

"Which is?"

"Coachella. Someone from the UFW will take over there. Then—Calexico, here you come!"

A warm breeze floated through the open windows of the car and stirred Muriel's hair, which was now dyed brown. In the dark she tried to make out the profile of the woman beside her, whose hands gripped the steering wheel in the driving school "ten minutes to two" position. Poor soul.

"Maybe you could see the freeway better if you turned down your dash lights," Muriel said.

"Oh," the driver squeaked, "so you noticed that I'm not the world's most confident person behind the wheel." She laughed without amusement. "I'll get you there. I just like to be careful. I can see the road fine. It's getting light now anyway. And then will it ever be hot!"

"You're doing great, Trudy," said the mendacious friend in the back seat. She tapped Muriel on the shoulder. "Can you imagine, Muriel—I can't drive at all! They probably should have gotten two other members to do this. We really got LASSOED into it. Right, Trudy?"

"Yeah. LASSOED again."

They laughed loudly as Muriel winced. LASSO was the Los Angeles Society for Secretarial Organizing.

"Not that we would have missed this excitement for anything," gurgled the voice from the back.

I would, Muriel thought. Was it really getting light? Her hand moved automatically to her bag. She pulled out one of the three bottles of eyedrops nestled next to each other in the zipper compartment.

"Oh, gee. Eyes bothering you again?"

"This'll fix 'em." Muriel applied the drops expertly. And it did fix them. God help her if she was separated from her luggage. There was an entire carton of eyedrop bottles in her white Samsonite beauty case. Only one brand was really effective. And that was probably not available in a Mexican *farmacia*.

They were drawing near the Coachella Valley and the last stop in the U.S. on Muriel's exit itinerary. Agrarian smells blew into the Japanese car. The harvest was beginning here; far from the highway workers were plucking the grapes. One of them, sacrificing a day's pay for Muriel, would wait for her at a trysting point on a dusty barrio road.

After various wrong turns and much asking of directions, the Toyota bumped slowly down an unmarked street.

"Blue house with yellow doors. This has got to be it." The driver turned off the ignition and went limp.

"House?" the friend stared at the yard, strewn with sagging tires. "It's a shack!"

The three women unpeeled their wet backs from the car seats and got out. Roosters in a nearby yard crowed mournfully. Two small dogs ran by, scraping against Muriel, and almost causing her to lose her balance. The scene was devoid of human life.

"Don't panic. We won't leave you until we're sure you've

made your connection," the driver assured Muriel, who was longing to be rid of them both. The heat was drying her eyes and things looked hazy again. There were auras around her mundane companions. Feeling irritated, she pulled out her wallet and made sure the counterfeit voter's card was still there. It was, along with the fat wad of travellers checks, received at the very last moment from the Foundation for Investigative Reporting. She zipped her purse closed and tried to smooth some of the wrinkles from her shirtwaist dress. On impulse she bent to look at herself in the car's side mirror. Eyedrops streaked her white peaked face under the dead brown hair.

"I'll get a sunburn," she said. The women looked embarrassed. She noticed that the car trunk was ajar. They were holding her suitcases, waiting for her. Cicadas buzzed in the dry shrubs, sounding like someone walking on broken glass.

It was the wrong house. When they finally found the right blue house, around the corner, they were greeted by dozens of people. Children snatched the luggage from them and led them inside to a hero's welcome. Lemonade was served in chipped cups, under a huge red banner on the wall bearing a black Aztec eagle circled in white. There was plenty of time for a fiesta with accompanying noise and general confusion, before a couple named Figueroa drove Muriel to the border.

A young Chicano in Mexican-made bi-colored jeans told a story in English about how office workers and the UFW had worked in cooperation before. Something about the first farmworkers' contract with Schenley Vineyards. The secretary to someone named Blackie Leavitt had circulated fictitious memos saying the Bartenders Union would boycott Schenley unless the farmworkers got union recognition.

Muriel sat on a broken stool and watched the merriment. Her companions from the Los Angeles office workers group were enjoying themselves. Their bracelets jangled; they sang along with "De Colores", although they did not know Spanish. Guitars strummed and people came over and shook Muriel's hand and the hands of her two companions.

\* \* \*

"Ten bucks for this boxcar, and the plastic's chockful of flashing. Hand me that knife, will you?"

Hank Blundon searched through Dennis's miniature tools.

"The worn-out modeling knife," Dennis prompted. "When they get worn down so they look like fins, then they're just right for picking at flashing."

Hank found the knife and then, with his hands in his pockets, wandered over to the bookshelves. His mind on other things, he flipped through an old issue of *Model Railroader*. Overhead the ceiling creaked. Good. It gave him an opening.

"You sure can hear people walking upstairs, can't you?"

"Mmmmh," Dennis said, scraping away.

"Doesn't it bother you, all that noise from our place?"

"Nope. I don't even hear it. Bothered Muriel though. She's an insomniac."

A perfect opener. He had been going to say something about two people living together being quieter than four— but this was much better.

"Where's Muriel been lately anyway? I haven't seen her car around."

"Doesn't have a car."

Hank could have socked himself right on the jaw. Now what?

"There." Dennis coupled the boxcar back in place. "I

think it looks better with the scratches, actually. More real."

Hank put the magazine back and walked over the railroad layout. Time to look interested again. Not that it wasn't interesting; it was. He loved model railroading. But it wasn't going to help him find out where the little bird had flown.

"She's in Austria," Dennis said, reaching for the throttle.

"What?" Hank shrieked, unschooled in deception.

"Muriel's in Austria." Dennis flicked a turnout so the Baldwin Centipede could rumble onto an outer track. "Vienna. Did you see that new switching problem in the May *Railroad Model Craftsman*?"

"Vienna," Hank said, stunned.

Dennis straightened up and looked at Hank. A lot of interest in Muriel. Could this hayseed have a crush on her? Lord, it must be those prissy little outfits she always wore.

Hank cleared his throat. "Does she go to Europe often?" His eyes slid sideways as Dennis looked him in the face.

"Nope." Dennis decided to fall back on being inarticulate. God only knew that Muriel had strange tastes in men, but this was going a little too far. The guy was fine to run trains with, but he was a reactionary. He had said once that San Francisco would be a swell town if they would clean the faggots off the streets.

"She's going to Prague too," he said, on an impulse. "She wants to see this plaque they have in the middle of town. It has the names of all the Czech Jews who were murdered by the Nazis. Her relatives might be on it." He watched Hank's face for a reaction.

"Is that so?" So the bird had flown that far. Imagine. In her condition. Hank's jaw muscles twitched. Baziotis was not going to be happy about this.

# Twenty

Inside the Victorian house on Jackson Street the little Hispanic family with the Italian surname was reunited. Two of its members at least disliked each other, and no one was happy. But they were reunited. Now Lourdes had to cook for three people instead of two. She looked at the pores of the skin on her hands and pondered routes of escape. She put in long hours at the Historical Society up the street, licking and stamping the anguish out of her heart. Soon there would be the field trip to San Jose. To the south. The same direction as Argentina.

Arno had welcomed his son back to his bosom with few questions asked, as if he were a stolen bicycle. "It's all the better for me, this trouble he's having at Lovell," Chuck said to his stepmother. She was scraping food off dirty dishes. He was lounging against the kitchen counter, wearing a lambswool sports sweater and new front-pleated flannel slacks.

"Oh, yes. He always has trouble. But not much trouble. He works every day. Not like before."

Chuck watched Lourdes cover a plate with Saran Wrap. "It's worse," he said.

"What it worth?" She took off her dirty apron and put on a clean one. She hated wearing soiled aprons. The laundry bag in the pantry was filling up again already. Time to go to the Chinese laundry again.

"Worse," Chuck repeated. "Worse, not worth. Bad, very very bad. More bad than before."

Lourdes came out of the pantry tying her apron strings. "You tell me," she said.

Chuck strolled over the kitchen table and took an apple from the bowl of fruit. He bit into it with his strong white teeth. Lourdes shuddered with repressed anger, and reached for a Chore Girl scrubbing pad. Six pots tonight.

"It's just that now you *really* can't go visit your family."

"Oh, thank you very much. I think I know that now. The rightists and the leftists will shoot me, no?" She scrubbed with a vengeance. "The Government, it will look for me and the Anti-communist Alliance, and the Guardians of Liberty maybe, too."

"Don't forget the other side—the Montoneros."

"Oh, no. In Argentina we never forget the Montoneros." She laughed over her scrapings, thinking about the guerrillas.

Chuck went to the sink to throw his apple core into the disposal. "But now," he said, standing over Lourdes, "there's still another reason. Dad could never go to Mass with your family."

His reward for this dramatic announcement was a tinkle of laughter.

"He couldn't go," Chuck said, "because they will see he can't take communion."

"Your father is not a religious. This I know for a long time."

"No, but I mean he really couldn't. Not even once a year."

"Oh, no?" She sighed wearily. When would Chuck tire of these games?

"No." Chuck took a cigarette from the pack in his sweater pocket and turned on a stove burner to light it. "Because he can't confess what he's done. He's a very guilty guy these days."

Lourdes stopped scraping and looked at Chuck with interest. Maybe Arno was having an affair. She felt mild curiosity, as though she were reading a story in one of the first wife's comic books.

"He's been trying to kill one of his secretaries," Chuck said. He drew deeply on the cigarette. His face fell as Lourdes collapsed into giggles.

"*Fotonovela*," she gasped.

"No, you're wrong. I'm serious," he said. She wiped her eyes on her forearm, since her hands were dripping suds. "You see," he went on, puffing on the cigarette, "he's in big trouble with the Government up here as well."

Lourdes' rare moment of mirth was fading into familiar feelings of irritation. She resumed her work. "That is all over now. The Government does not want to investigate. They are guilty also. You explained me this yourself."

"The Federal Government, yes. But now he's in trouble with the state of California. A little case of attempted homicide."

Lourdes looked at him: he was studying the filter of the cigarette. Could he be serious?

"Dad told me so himself. That's one reason why he was so anxious to take me back into his arms. He's consumed with guilt. He needs someone to confide in."

She began to run the water in the sink and concentrate on the dishes with frowning efficiency. She did not want to hear.

"He had this little redheaded secretary, see? And it seems she was stealing corporate secrets. In fact she had enough on Dad and his boss and his boss's boss to send them all to jail for a nice stay." He reached past Lourdes, took a saucer from the drainboard and stubbed out his cigarette in it. "The only thing is, she made some kind of mistake or something. Anyway Baziotis found out about it—Dad's boss. So he told Dad that if this woman wasn't eliminated Dad would be blamed for the whole thing. Pretty nasty stuff." Lourdes kept grimly rinsing the dishes. "Deportation threats, and all that. Dad had to agree."

Lourdes opened the faucets wider. The water ran fast and loud. "Is she dead?" she asked.

"No, you didn't understand what I said. I said *attempted* homicide. He didn't succeed. At least, I don't think he succeeded. But if he did, she died in another country—trying to escape.

Lourdes snorted. "Oh! He missed them. I am not surprise. Your father does not know how to shoot."

"He didn't use a gun. It's very interesting, actually. It was a case of murder by electronics. She sits in front of this computer terminal at work, it's like a television screen. It emits microwaves—well, you wouldn't know what that is."

"Microwave. Microwave oven. Yes. I know."

"Well, they changed the inside of the terminal, understand? So the waves were too strong. But apparently it didn't work."

Lourdes twisted the faucets closed and said quietly, "They tried to cook her."

Chuck threw back his head and laughed. "Cook her! That's it!"

She reached for the disposal switch on the wall above the sink.

"Say, Lourdes, you're supposed to run the cold water

when you use the disposal, remember? I told you, you're going to ruin the whole mechanism."

She ignored him. The disposal made horrible noises, like a fierce grinding and gnashing of monstrous teeth.

\* \* \*

It was nine o'clock at night and the patrons sitting under the sign of the swan in El Cisne, a cafe at the edge of downtown Zacatecas, looked curiously at the table where Diane Adkins, Steven Sullivan and Gloria Russell sat drinking manzanilla tea. These Americans were attracting considerably more attention than the dandy of a ranchero, two tables to their left, who, decked out in black pants and shirt, and with a white bandana tied carefully about his slender throat, was languidly garnishing the lid of his beer can with lemon juice and salt. This kind of studied provincial rakishness was an everyday spectacle in Zacatecas. But English-speaking foreigners were not an everyday spectacle:

Zacatecas, inaccessible by air, lies on the main road between El Paso and Mexico City, and contains nothing to detain the tourist. It has the usual allotment of churches, one decent hotel and some nearly exhausted silver mines. It has no ruins, no beaches, no lake and no woods. Its setting, in a ravine at the foot of twin mountains, is picturesque, but its ranches and saloon brawls give it a spiritual resemblance to Texas in the eyes of vacationing Californians, and Texans prefer larger, rougher cities like Monterey and Chihuahua.

The three Americans sipping tea in El Cisne had business in Zacatecas. Diane Adkins taught English at the USIS school in a basement on Hidalgo Street. Steven Sullivan was a young Jesuit whose mission was tending to the needs of the workers in the nearly exhausted Zacatecan silver mines. Gloria Russell was there because she was Muriel Axelrod.

She had chosen Russell because of her admiration for Rosalind Russell, and Gloria because it was easy for Latins to pronounce. This pseudonym and the brown hair, which she was beginning to find flattering, were her only forms of disguise. Glasses might be next, she thought, looking past Steve, who was a definite contender for the title of World's Most Boring Conversationalist, and trying to make out the prices written on the cafe blackboard. "*Refrescos* $55." Sodas for fifty-five pesos? That couldn't be right. She reached for her ever-handy plastic bottle of eyedrops. If it were nearsightedness, eyedrops would not fix it at all. At least that was what her two myopic companions kept telling her. They said the nearest competent optometrist was in San Luis Obispo, too far away. She would have to suffer through the week and then find an eye doctor as soon as her jet landed in Washington.

In very bad Spanish Diane ordered another plate of beans. "That engineering student who signed up for my one o'clock class? Remember him?" she asked Muriel . "Today he came in wearing a Che Guevara suit!" The beans arrived; Diane wrinkled her little nose in disgust.

"Wait a minute!" she called after the waitress. "Tortillas! *Quiere* tortillas."

"*Quiero*," Muriel said.

"Oh, she understood me."

Steven Sullivan raised his wire-rimmed glasses to his forehead and rubbed at the red mark on the bridge of his nose. He was thirty-three years old, but he looked forty. He had not ordered any food, although his stomach rumbled audibly.

Diane Adkins had broken her diet, as she did every evening, and was lunging for the tortilla basket and scooping the beans into them avidly. Her glasses fogged from the steam. Muriel checked the blackboard again. The chalk lines were sharply defined. She had the familiar feeling that she had awakened from a nightmare.

Steve sat silent, as always. Either his religious mission filled him with quiet beatitude or, as Muriel had recently begun to suspect, he was looped on the various barbiturates available over the counter in Mexico. She sipped her tea and thought of guns, machine tools, photographs and fame. Even with these Ugly American companions, she could savor her satisfaction—or she could when the blur was gone from her eyes and Diane wasn't bending her ear with contemptuous stories about her students.

When all was said and done, it was a lucky thing she had run into the Uglies. They had spotted her instantly when she had arrived at the Zacatecas bus station after a hair-rising ride over the mountains from Mazatlán. They were waiting for the *Transportes del Norte* to pull in from Mexico City with their copies of the English-language *Herald*. They were delighted to receive a bonus in the person of a native speaker of English. Diane had taken "Gloria" under her corpulent wing, steering her to her own boarding house.

"The food's good, but they stop serving at eight. How come you're staying here anyway? If it's silver you want, you'd be better off in Taxco. Oh—art history. The cathedral? Sure, I've seen it. Well, to each his own."

Muriel had found to her relief that she could buy a sketching pad of sorts at the hardware store near the Jardin Hidalgo, the town square. As she shelled out twenty-five pesos for the pad and some charcoal, she prayed that no one who knew anything about drawing would ever look over her shoulder while she was trying to sketch. But maybe it would work out all right. If anyone stopped to laugh at her drawing, she could ask the way to the Calle de Cornejo and the bogus beauty parlor. Surely someone would know where it was, even though no one at the boarding house had heard of it and there were apparently no street maps of Zacatecas. There was always the police station, but Gloria/Muriel preferred to stay clear of the police.

She preferred to, but she had had no choice one afternoon when she was perched, trying to look scholarly, on a low wall across from the baroque seventeenth century cathedral. An officer toting an M-1 smiled at her from under the brim of his fatigue hat (U.S. surplus from the Korean War). *"Estudiante?"*

*"Si."* Muriel moved her arm casually across the sketchpad. She could not begin to fit the building onto the paper (it was the wrong shape), so she had started sketching the fourteen statues of saints in the niches on the northern facade of the cathedral. On her paper they looked like paper dolls in shrouds.

*"Norteamericana?"* asked the policeman.

Muriel nodded. He grinned lasciviously and strolled off. She sat wondering how to remove the charcoal from her sleeves.

A genuine student had stopped by and seized the charcoal from her hand, to show her how to draw properly He attended the Autonomous University of Zacatecas and was supervising the hanging of a banner announcing the Red and White Ball, the annual engineering school dance. By the time the banner billowed proudly over the Jardin Hidalgo in the strong winds that threatened a rainstorm, the student was escorting Muriel to the Calle de Cornejo, an unpaved back street carved into a steep hillside. The number 52, black and ornate against a white oblong tile, hung on an iron door set into a courtyard wall.

It was almost six o'clock. Too late for a machine shop to be open. But the next morning, when the banner announcing the engineering ball lay spattered with mud in the center of the square, Muriel had hurriedly climbed the stoney steps of Cornejo Street. The day began early for work in Zacateca. The door to number 52 was already open. As she approached she could hear a powerful hissing noise issuing from it. Cobras? Nervously, she stood to the left of the entrance and peered in.

Two wooden shacks stood in the center of the deep yard, which was strewn with the debris of light industry. Less than fifty yards from the iron door two men flailed about in a sandstorm. Then the hissing ceased, along with a chugging percussive sound that had accompanied it. Like snow-flakes in a paperweight, the sand settled at the feet of the two workers, who coughed, despite the bandanas tied over their mouths and noses. Gasping for air, they put down the nozzles of the sandblasting machine and fled. More sand sifted down. When it cleared Muriel took the Minolta out of her handbag and took a photograph of dozens of rifle barrels lying dull and nonreflective in the mountain sunlight. Matte-finish rifle barrels, suitable for paramilitary use.

Muriel had returned to the Calle de Cornejo several times that day. She looked up and down the muddy street to see if she were being observed before snapping the shutter of her brother's camera. Grinding noises came from the shacks. Somebody was enlarging the ammo magazines, while another somebody affixed leather straps to wooden stocks.

But those operations could not be photographed by Bernie Axelrod's Minolta. Muriel could not get inside the shacks, or even inside the courtyard. She had to settle for a roll of shots of dull barrels. Some of those were quite dramatic. One picture she had seen in the viewfinder showed the sandblasters working in clouds of rolling dust.

"Gloria!"

Startled, Muriel could feel her face burning. Did brunettes color so easily? Apparently she had forgotten to answer to her name again. She had really forgotten where she was, sitting in the cafe.

"I said, how are the sketches coming along?" Steve was giving her his beatific smile. There was a small aluminum foil packet lying beside his teacup. Mexican pills.

"Magnificent structure," she said.

He nodded. His face appeared to be sagging during the course of the evening—probably the relaxing effects of the drug. Good. Now he wouldn't ask a million questions about the lateral altars of the Santo Domingo church. She congratulated herself for having chosen the cathedral instead of the Jesuit church a block west of the square. He would have been going over her pathetic chicken scratches with a fine-toothed comb.

Diane plunged a spoon into custard. "Movies tonight?" Muriel asked Steve. He nodded. So she could count on this soldier of God as an escort once again. What could be more proper? It was a great movie bill, too. *Ten Rillington Place,* a British mystery, and *Las Puertas del Paraíso,* Muriel's favorite Mexican motorcyle flick, full of black leather and hard breathing.

A few more five-peso double features and she would be taking leave of Zacatecas. She wondered what the price of movies was in Washington, D.C., and whether the theatres there looked like the Lincoln Memorial. She would know in a week—it would take that long for the photofinishing place to process her shots. The hardware store manager had promised to have them ready in a week. Of course no one could promise that any of the pictures would come out well, although if Bernie and the ads were to be believed, the Minolta with its automatic exposure was absolutely foolproof. "Christ," Bernie had cried, "you can't hand in a Polaroid snapshot to the *Washington Post!*" In the week before she left, he had given her a crash course in 35-millimeter photography.

Now she sat in the Cafe El Cisne, damning her brother and his only-the-best consumerist philosophy. She couldn't find a Polaroid camera or a developing lab in this ranch town, so she was stuck here for at least a week. More, if the first batch of pictures came out lousy.

Relax, she told herself. No one is following you.

But when she lifted her teacup, it clattered against the saucer.

* * *

On the bus rolling south on the Bayshore Freeway, no one sang "Do You Know the Way to San Jose". It wasn't that kind of crowd. They preferred to sit quietly, this excursion group with its sprinkling of elderly gentlemen, but mostly with its ladies—forty or more of them seated in neat little rows, like Madeleine's schoolmates gone gray.

Lourdes sat near the back of the bus, next to a timid, silent intern she had met once or twice at the Historical Society. But she did not recognize all the faces on this bus, nor on the second one following it. Sarah Westfeldt had seemed to know everybody: she had spent a good half hour beaming at them, welcoming them aboard and assuring them discreetly that there was a restroom in the rear. Lourdes tried to keep away from her and from the taint of Lovell, which she now knew to be a factory of death and deceit.

"Oh, I see you found a seat," Sarah had cooed to her. "Oh, dear, where shall I sit, do you think?" The intern began to rise, but was frozen in motion by a look from the tail of Lourdes' eye.

"Palo Alto," someone called out above the twittering of polite conversation, as the bus roared through the smog. "It won't be long now."

Lourdes didn't care how long it was. It was a whole day away from Arno and Chuck. She fingered the Argentinian passport which she carried in the pocket of her pink silk jacket. She had brought it along on impulse, as if to rehearse for a much longer journey. The bus smelt of old women and lilac toilet water. It made her feel ill. She breathed from time to time into her handkerchief.

Mrs Hardenburgh stood up and faced the uplifted faces on either side of the aisle. "First, the old town." To the driver she said. "Now are you sure you know where St Augustine Street is?" He downshifted in reply. The bus left the highway and within minutes two busloads of ladies in very wrinkled skirts gingerly debarked.

Lourdes was one of the last to rise. When she stepped down from the bus she found a knot of women standing shocked before a little tin-roofed house covered with plywood siding. Their leader was gesticulating angrily at the bus driver, who merely shrugged and stamped out his cigarette.

"I think it's supposed to be the Peralta adobe," the intern whispered.

Valiantly, Mrs Hardenburgh knocked on the door. The crowd held its collective minted breath as its leader was granted access. She emerged with an ashen face, cupped her hands around her mouth like a megaphone, and called, "It's an utter disgrace."

Murmurs.

"It's the right address. Make no mistake! This is the adobe!"

A ripple of polite outrage passed through the throng.

"It's being used as a storeroom!"

A wild clicking of tongues.

Mrs Hardenburgh, growing hoarse, carried on. "A structure built in 1802, degraded in this manner! This all goes to show, dear friends, that these are difficult times for historical preservationists."

It was also a difficult time for the ladies who, distracted by the gravity of the situation, drifted off the sidewalk and into the road. A hot rod gleaming with black lacquer veered dangerously close to them and swerved away at the last moment. They scampered onto the curb as fast as their support-hosed legs would carry them. *OOO-GAAH*, the hot rod blared as it sped away.

Mrs Hardenburgh steadfastly boarded the bus, barking "Downtown!" at the driver. The troops followed, their faith unshaken. They were rewarded by the discovery that, through historical accident or the power of Mrs Hardenburgh's will, the rest of the landmarks were preserved inviolate. In front of the public library at South Market and San Fernando, they nodded approvingly and muttered "Richardsonian Romanesque" in chorus. St Joseph's Church was still neo-Baroque, and flashbulbs popped in front of the monument commemorating the site of the first state Capitol building.

Lunch was at a modern fern-hung restaurant on the Alameda. Lourdes' feet pinched as they swelled inside their linen pumps. Sarah Westfeldt swooped at her from behind.

"There's a war going on," Sarah said in a conspiratorial tone. She leaned over so far that her gold locket dangled in Lourdes' chef salad bowl.

"Yes?" Looking straight ahead, Lourdes took a dainty sip of water.

"Between the mineral springs enthusiasts and the horticulturists." Sarah, amused, raised her hand to her chapsticked lips. "The mineral spring people want to stop at a park and drink the medicinal waters. But the horticulturists are insisting that we run right over to the Municipal Gardens and spend the afternoon among the roses." Chuckling, Mrs Westfeldt retreated to her seat at Mrs Hardenburgh's left flank, throwing appreciative glances back at Lourdes.

All very well for Sarah Westfeldt to make jokes about war. Lourdes speared a mushroom. Didn't the woman know that her husband was a merchant of destruction, like Lourdes' own husband, whose name she now considered unmentionable? Where was the secretary that Arno had tried to murder with the *electronica?* While the wives of Lovell executives wasted the day on this silly trip, did she lie dying somewhere in Europe?

Lourdes pushed her decorative comb deeper into the wave behind her ear. The teeth stabbed her, and she winced.

It was announced after lunch that the rose delegation had proved victorious: the trip would proceed as scheduled with no sidetracking to Alum Rock Park. A smattering of the most arthritic excursionists could be spotted climbing into taxis at the side door of the restaurant. No one commented on this and the bus continued on down the Alameda.

"Rosicrucian Society first," Sarah Westfeldt announced. The horticulture contingent groaned, protesting that they wanted to get to the roses before the day got too hot. Sarah assured them that it was right on the way.

The paintings on exhibit in the Rosicrucian Society Gallery were done by a well-known artist from a good San Francisco family. But the Society building itself was nearly as much of an embarrassment as the Paralta adobe. Mrs Hardenburgh's assistants called, "This way, this way," trying to divert the crowd which stood agape at the sacred statue in the courtyard. What kind of paintings would be on exhibit in the gallery of a cult that worshipped a hippopotamus?

The most fervent rose-devotees plunged into the gallery as if their Naturalizers were track shoes. They reasoned, obviously, that the sooner this ended, the sooner they could get to the rose garden. Others followed, ignoring with difficulty the eerie moans emanating from a darkened room, through the entrance of which could be glimpsed a full-scale model of a temple. Lourdes wandered inside it.

A voice spoke in her ear.

"Hey, it's a gas, right?"

In the dim light of the temple she could make out his long dirty hair and the patches on his jeans. A hippie. She turned away and made her way to the altar. The tape recording gurgled and murmured in garbled, incomprehensible English.

"You here with the Historical Society? I mean, it's a real trip, isn't it?"

"I want to be alone."

"Oh, sure. It's this place, right? Hey, no problem. I'll give you your space. See you later."

"Goodbye," she said firmly, keeping her eyes on the altar.

"My name's Don. I'm on the second bus."

She felt her shoulders relax as he left the room. Hoping that she was not committing a blasphemy, Lourdes began to pray. She knew that she should pray for absolution for her husband, but she did not. She prayed for the well-being of his secretary.

The crowd stampeded through the corridor, drowning out

the crooning oracle. Lourdes crossed herself and left the holy place to join the excursion.

"Far out."

He was following her again, the hippie. He had found her away from the others, hidden away in a lane of blood-red roses.

"Too much clipping and cutting, though. I like wild roses, you know. They should grow the natural way, you know."

Lourdes walked quickly down the aisle, but he kept up with her, addressing her narrow back.

"Those pink clothes look good here, you know? You ought to stand next to the pink ones. That would really be a trip, you know."

Lourdes wheeled around, her eyes flashing. "I like red. And I like be alone too!"

The young man spread his hands, palm up, at chest level. "Hey, hey. Don't get so excited. I'm not going to molest you or anything. I just like you, you know? I think you're spiritual. Different. I mean, I saw you in the temple. Are you into that stuff? I think it's far out."

"I am Catholic!"

"Yeah, hey, you Mexican?"

Lourdes walked on, perspiring slightly in the three o'clock sun. The end of the row was a cul-de-sac, a gravelled half-circle in which a white wrought-iron bench sat under an arbor of roses. It was no use trying to run away from him. At least not in the new linen pumps. She sank onto the bench and crossed her legs, easing her heels out of the shoes. He took her dangling shoe as an invitation and sat next to her.

"You have really spooky eyes, you know that?"

"I do not understand."

"Spooky. You know. Scary. Mysterious. Like we're going

to the Mystery House next. You know. Mystery? Creepy. Like creepy."

Lourdes patted at her brow with her small handkerchief. There would be a ladies room in this Mystery House. She could fix her face.

"When were you born?"

"What?"

"What day were you born on? Like I'm an astrologer, you know? I'll do your chart."

She shrugged. "January sixteen. Nineteen hundreds forty seven." Maybe he would be shocked. She was so old, twenty-nine. Maybe he would go away. He looked as old as Chuck.

"How about the place?. . . Right. Bwayne-is Ear-ease. Argentina. Far out."

At least he didn't think it was in Brazil.

"Hey, you were born under the Southern Cross."

"Yes, the cross," she whispered. "I am Catholic."

"No, no, not that kind of cross. I mean the stars, the constellation. The sky is different down there in the Southern Hemisphere."

That sounded familiar. Yes, something she had learned as a little girl. Yes, it was true. The constellations were different in this alien northern world. In all those nights she had spent sipping sherry next to the dark window, she had never thought to part the drapes and look up at the sky. No wonder she felt so dislocated in these *malditos* United States. The *yanqui* stars were in the wrong place.

He was writing on the back of an envelope with a pencil stub. "January 16, 1947. Buenos Aires. You know the time of day?"

Lourdes shook her head. And no, she could not ask her mother. "These are bad times in Argentina in these days. Political murders, tortures. There are no letters."

He was still writing. He did not listen. "Wow, a Southern

sky chart. I mean this will be a real challenge, you know? I'll do the whole twenty-four hours for you. I mean it'll be a learning experience for me. Then when you hear from your mother you can tell me the time and I can finish it off. Okay. Give me your name and address."

"No."

He looked up at her. For the first time a real expression flickered on his amiably vacant face. It was the beginning of a look of annoyance. She did not appreciate the gift he was trying to give her.

On the other hand it may just have been a shadow flickering through the rose arbor, as the sun began to sink. "Okay, no problem." He beamed again. "Tell you what. I'll leave all the chart information with Mrs What's-Her-Name at the Historical Society. You can ask her for it. I'll just tell her it's for the little Argentine lady with the spooky eyes."

Lourdes narrowed these at him.

A stocky figure appeared at the far end of the row of roses, calling. It was time to go to the Mystery House.

* * *

"No way, Jose." Hank Blundon intertwined his fingers and cracked all ten of them at once. "You won't catch me in that faggot's apartment again. Anyway, it doesn't matter; there's nothing more we can get out of him."

Westfeldt gave his boozy chuckle. "Is that right? What have you been getting out of him?"

Hank's face turned purple. "Are you calling me swish?" He half-rose from his chair. "Listen, I don't have to take this crap—"

"Take it easy." Baziotis spoke from his corner.

His master's voice. Hank sat back. "I told you. I didn't know the guy was a fag. He sure didn't act like it. I guess he swings both ways. Now his girl's gone, he's got that fruit with a moustache coming in. Staying all night." He shuddered.

"That's enough of that." Baziotis got up and began to prowl the room, picking lint off the backs of chairs. "The point is, where has his girl gone to?"

"I told you. Austria. The Alps."

Randrup chortled, a graveyard laugh. Hank looked around, confused.

"I'm afraid not, my boy," Baziotis said, straightening a pleat in the drapes. "Not unless she's got the Green Lantern's ring and she can make herself invisible."

"Maybe she went skiing," Westfeldt suggested. "Maybe she's using our precious Lovell documents to wax her skis."

"Or," Baziotis said, looking at him, "maybe she died somewhere on the way."

"Oh, sure." Westfeldt stifled a yawn. "Maybe she died and slid under a seat on that plane she took. They should have smelled her by now."

Hank was sitting up straight again, a vein throbbing on his forehead. "Now, hold on a minute. Just a minute here. That's what I said: she took a plane. She was booked on that TWA flight to Austria. She checked in to fly to Vienna, it was verified. So what are you—?"

"There's just one little problem," Baziotis said. "No passport has been issued to Miss Muriel Axelrod. And how do we know that? We know that because an outfit in Washington known as the State Department is in charge of issuing passports. And we have what you might call a special relationship with said State Department. And said State Department would also like to know where our clever little secretary has gone."

"So what? She probably has a fake passport in another name."

"That's a bright idea, Blundon. In fact, that same bright idea occurred to some of the rest of us." Baziotis's eyes darted around the room. Westfeldt wasn't listening, the fool. He sat with his flaccid face, booze bags under his dull eyes, obviously half-asleep. He was the European sales manager; six months ago he had been over in Obergurgl arranging illegal arms trans-shipments and now it was all anyone could do to get him out to a meeting, and he dozed through it when he did come.

Then there was Pagano, looking even smaller and more bent over than usual, always dressed in undertaker black with his damned narrow ties, getting more grey-faced and bald by the minute as he sat on the rumpled bedspread. He was definitely one man who realized what a dangerous situation they were all in. Sensing Baziotis's eyes on him, he looked up and dropped some ash on the rug.

"The trouble is, Blundon," Baziotis resumed, "I don't believe it. I don't believe she has a counterfeit passport."

Hank cleared his throat. "Why not?"

"I'll tell you why. I think she planted that story about Austria to throw us off the scent. And don't worry about her homo friend there. You don't have to talk to him again. I think you're right, there's nothing to be gotten there. He probably does really believe that she's headed for the Alps."

Arno spoke for the first time, quietly, almost to himself. "How does she know about Austria? This is what I can't understand."

Baziotis ignored him. "We've got people ready now, in key positions. Austria, Mexico, even Joburg. They've got pictures, and they've got their instructions." He swerved suddenly toward Hank, and pointed a finger at him. "But what beats me is how she was feeling well enough to leave in the first place." Blundon's ears were engorged with blood. "I thought your—manoeuvre—with the display tubes was supposed to be foolproof. She was going to retire very young, suffering from a mysterious illness."

"Damn it!" Hank cried. The sound startled Westfeldt, who jumped awake. "I don't know what the hell happened. Those waves were turned up good. She should have been fried right out."

"You didn't suffer from concern about—the legality of the thing, did you? Weren't you the one who suggested something nasty. . . something about homicide?"

Hank leapt up and faced the older man.

"Now just hold the phone, Mr Baziotis. I hope you're not insinuating that I don't know my business. There was no question of homicide, just—incapacitation. I told you people that, and I meant it. I know what I'm talking about. And nobody knows those tubes can be dangerous anyway. They're turned down now, aren't they? So where's the legal trouble going to come from, you tell me that. Where's the weapon?"

"That's precisely what I'm suggesting. In your eagerness to circumvent possible legal problems, maybe you neglected to turn the waves up high enough."

Blundon clumped heavily to the door on his square-toed shoes. He slammed out, in a rage.

"He'll simmer down," Baziotis said calmly.

He looked, almost fondly, at Arno Pagano, sitting drawn and shriveled on the bed. Arno was going to be the man of the hour, because Arno was a desperate man. He was the man to set this botched-up job on the right track. He was terrified that he could be facing the end of his career. And possible deportation. And he had the right connections to do what was necessary, from his shady old days in sunny Miami.

# Twenty-one

It was dark when Lourdes came back from San Jose to her house in Jackson Street. In the morning she would talk alone to Chuck. There were signs; she was going to tell him about the signs. And then she would find out. She had been alone in the House of Mystery.

Doorways that led to nothing, windows that opened onto walls, stairways that went nowhere. The Historical Society tour had ended in a building that had grown like a cancer. It was the Winchester House, an architectural obsession. Lourdes, somewhere in the nucleus of the thing, was in a subgroup guided by a female university student who was built like a human tongue depressor. She explained that when Sarah Winchester had purchased the house in 1884, it had been a pleasant Victorian mansion with eighteen rooms. When Sarah died thirty-eight years later, the house had one hundred and sixty rooms, through which the owner had flitted in a dark veil. Sarah's husband, the son of the rifle magnate, and her daughter had died suddenly: the mother in her grief sought the advice of spiritualists. She became convinced that the thousands of Indians killed by Winchester weapons had risen up from the dead and taken her loved ones.

"She found out what she had to do," the student said. "The California soothsayers told her that the ghosts were clever, and they would take her too. They said she had to build a house with endless rooms. As long as she added rooms, corridors and stairs the spirits would be puzzled and wouldn't be able to find her. But if the house was ever completed, then she too would vanish into the world beyond. Instead," she said solemnly, fixing them with a hollow eye, "she vanished into the house. She was like a ghost herself. Some of the house staff never saw her, and the Japanese gardeners didn't either—they were hired to plant these towering hedges to veil the house itself.

"But the carpenters knew her. There were fifty of them. They worked in shifts, carrying out her instructions. You can see—they built room after room, belltowers, cupolas. And in each room there was a trick—a dead end or a false door, something to bewilder the ghosts. For thirty-eight years construction never stopped."

An observation tower was built, she said, but it became useless, embedded in the mass as the rooms spilled out first to the boundaries of the six-acre estate, and then piled high, one on top of the other.

"In 1922," the guide said with relish, "Sarah Winchester died. The ghosts got her. The movers had a time taking out the furniture—they carried heavy tables down stairs that ended in blank walls. . ." The hedges withered, and the house could be seen from the Los Gatos road. It rotted. Now it had become a museum.

Sadistically the guide led her party through the house, deceiving them over and over again, opening doors that led onto balconies no wider than ledges, helping them try to open spurious windows. The Society ladies squealed with tense laughter; occasionally an ominous shriek echoed through the walls as other small groups stumbled in the maze.

Lourdes passed through dark rooms where she clutched at door jambs, reeling with vertigo. Perhaps lunch had not agreed with her; maybe she had food poisoning. It was late afternoon; little light could come from windows that looked out on walls. The guide never seemed to tire of the joke. Like sheep they walked through doors that locked behind them. The dust caught in Lourdes' throat, caused her breath to rattle in her chest, darkened the pink silk of her summer suit. The air was cursed.

The tourists smiled in relief when they reached the gift shop. They laid coins on the counter for picture postcards as if they were paying for the ferry ride out of Hades. Lourdes leaned against the wall. On display behind her were blue-and-yellow Mystery House pennants. Their tips pointed toward her.

At last she got out into the waning sunlight. Knots of Society ladies pushed ahead in the bus queue, complaining about their aching feet. Lourdes hung back, breathing the fresh air. She would not look back at the cursed house.

The hippie, the astrologer, crossed in front of her and winked, on his way to the other bus.

Half in a swoon, Lourdes fell into the seat beside the Society intern. The diesel engine roared and the bus pulled onto the road, fleeing from the place of damnation. Lourdes opened her compact with shaking fingers and saw that powder and foundation had been eaten away, leaving the face of an Argentinian Indian.

The bus merged into the traffic of the Bayshore Freeway, and night fell as the Historical Society travelled back to San Francisco under the north star.

Chuck was startled, the next morning, by her behavior. Alternately she cajoled and wailed at him. She wrung her hands and begged and wept, and occasionally she flailed at his chest with her small hard fists. He tried for a few days to avoid her, but she was intractable. He tried to put her off with inanities. But she was beginning to make him nervous. Finally, after a week, the cat tired of this obsessed mouse, particularly since it wanted the mouse to run away anyway.

A few hours later, Bernie Axelrod tooled down his driveway in the Porsche Targa 911, feeling debonair but at the same time wondering whether the clutch had lost some free play and needed repair. He swung his legs from the ecru leather upholstery and gasped as he saw something detach itself from the shadows of the garage and move toward him. It was a small female figure, indistinct, like a genie emerging from the oil spot on the garage floor.

"You haf a sister which is name Moor-yel?" uttered the wraith.

# Twenty-two

Muriel—or Gloria, as she was beginning to think of herself—had grown careless in Zacatecas. She stopped leaving her rooming house early in the morning to sit on a curb and sketch the cathedral. It didn't seem to matter, because she no longer seemed to need a pretext to stay in Zacatecas. This city without tourists now accepted her as a tourist. When the friendly Mexican student at the boarding house dinner table asked her about her drawing, she smiled and said that it had begun drizzling every morning and she had been going on daytrips in the afternoon.

And it did drizzle almost every morning. By ten a.m. each day the landlady hurried back from the market to yank down the wet clothes of her seven children from the clothes-line where she had optimistically hung them a few hours earlier. It was a Sisyphusian method of housekeeping.

I would be just as foolish as the landlady, Muriel thought, if I trudged up the Calle de Cornejo every morning and tried to take another roll of photos. It would only start raining. She managed to convince herself of this, although she had an increasingly uneasy feeling that the first roll of film would come back from Mexico City completely out of focus and useless.

During the clear, dry early mornings Muriel ate breakfast and chatted with the students and bachelor workers who comprised Mrs Villafane's clientele, while just a few blocks away the covert machining operations were being carried on. Caffeine and lactic acid fought for supremacy in Mrs Villafane's very light *cafe con leche* in its thin ceramic mug. The sleep-inducing warm milk was usually victorious. After breakfast Muriel felt weighted down with beans. And then it would begin to drizzle.

The afternoon brought clearer skies and daytrips. Steve and Diane liked her, and invited her to go sightseeing. She had never been so much the tourist as in this out-of-the-way province and Zacatecas was the only place she had been in Mexico where the sun was not strong enough to give her a burn. She wondered if she had perhaps really metamorphosed into a brunette.

By night Steve Sullivan was the dedicated Jesuit, caring for his flock of soot-stained miners. But by day he was an obliging chauffeur, poking his aged Ford up mountainous roads and smiling a benign, drugged smile as the two women gasped at the splendor of the view and the peril of the hairpin curves.

They visited the ruined city of La Quemada, where the fountains still flowed with eerie water. They saw the mosaic factories of Guadalupe and the colonial sites in Jerez de Garcia Salinas. Time after time they drove up the bladder-like mountain which rose on the northeast edge of Zacatecas: El Cerro de la Bufa, with its funny dromedary humps, was a staple of Zacatecan conversation. "Trying to dry these clothes is as hard as climbing the Bufa," Mrs Villafane cried, plucking clothespins and underwear from the damp line. And after eating his fill at the Villafane groaning board, a diner beat his chest and declared that he "felt so strong he could run up the Bufa."

Days passed. The photographs did not come back from the processing shop in Mexico City. It was really time for Muriel to move on. A letter came from Elba saying that the Foundation had received all her correspondence, and now felt that the story was ripe to be broken. Muriel was expected in Washington. She really ought to get on a bus and go to Mexico City; it wasn't safe to wait around in Zacatecas. She should take some more photographs and have them developed in Washington. Some of them would probably come out all right. And she needed to see a doctor. Her eyes were still blurry.

But any day the photographs might arrive. It wouldn't make sense not to wait a little longer. Everything took a long time in Mexico. The blurring eased when she used eye-drops, and she was not in a big hurry to start wearing her first pair of glasses. It was rather pleasant there in that boardinghouse on the floor of the ravine. Awaiting her in her own country would be press conferences, questions, demands for details. And there was Lovell and its corporate anger. Pagano and Baziotis would know that she had betrayed them.

It was all hard, as hard as—well, as climbing the Bufa.

\* \* \*

Not far from Mrs Villafane's boarding house was Zacateca's faded beauty of a hotel: La Reina Cristina, once a proud aristocrat, now shed plaster tears onto her iron banisters. Her location was of course still good—on the

Avenida Hidalgo, near the town square and the cathedral.

One of the fifty-odd guests of La Reina Cristina returned from the very spot where Muriel, sketchpad in hand, had sat. This guest, a short, dark deep chested man with a rather pendulous mouth, paused at the desk to ask for messages. He spoke in Spanish, his native tongue, like all the guests of the hotel, who were either Mexican businessmen or former Zacatecans. The clerk noted absently that this guest had a Caribbean accent. Told that there were no messages, the guest walked away to his room. Shortly afterward another guest rose, a veiled woman who had sat for a long time, apparently waiting for someone, on the worn leather couch in the lobby.

* * *

It was a clear Thursday afternoon and for once Muriel had nothing to do. Diane Adkins had had a new class foisted upon her by the management of her school, and Steve did not answer his door. Of course there was the evening to look forward to, with the Cine Supremo and tea afterwards at El Cisne.

Muriel wandered to the market, feeling aimless and a little guilty because the Minolta was lying idle in her bag in the boarding house. But of course she really could not leave Zacatecas without picking up a few gifts. She had pesos in her wallet. It would be nice if she could bring back some souvenirs of an indigenous craft, but there did not seem to be any craft in evidence in the old stone arcade. She passed stall after stall. The vendors called after her, *"Que va a llevar?. . .* What are you going to buy?" The air was redolent with plants; sawdust matted on the damp cement floor.

Muriel walked slowly past the fruit and vegetable stands, where stooped women in rebozos had their purchases weighed on little brass scales. She paused, tempted, at a *licuado* stand, where bizarre combinations of fruits were blended into frothy drinks. But she was still weighted down by lunch, and she moved on.

At the back wall of the market was a small selection of toys. There were the crude little wooden household objects for girls: diminutive folding ironing boards, miniature cabinets, pestles for blending good Mexican chocolate. Chocolate. They were selling it in the first stalls she had passed, near the arches of the arcade facing the Reina Cristina Hotel.

But she noticed candle-powered tin putt-putt boats near the girls' toys. She picked one up. It reminded her of Omar. He had run the boat in her bathtub in Salinas. It was probably a good idea to forget about Omar. Then, next to a spinning magnetized top, she saw the cobra: a curved two-dimensional piece of tin about two inches long that weaved back and forth, back and forth, flicking its tongue at her. The vendor, a teenaged boy, noticed Muriel's interest, and called *"Tres pesos"* to her. At his elbow a middleaged man solemnly blew soap bubbles in the air, stopping now and then to encourage buyers.

The toy was ingeniously displayed on a marble slab. The cobra responded to the magnet in the top, which whirled like a dervish, by darting quickly back and forth. Muriel looked from the cobra trainer to the dour bubble-blower. These serious merchants of foolish objects toiled from dawn to dusk for a few pesos; in some ways Muriel found them harder to take than the beggars. She wanted to avert her eyes and leave, but she found herself enchanted by the cobra and its engine, the top, which flew over the marble slab like a hydroplane.

At the moment that the snake was hypnotizing its quarry, the shot rang out. There was a sharp report, followed by shrieks and invocations of Jesus, Jose and Maria bounding off the cavernous walls. Pyramids of fruit toppled over; the candles powering the putt-putt boats blew out. Bubbles dissolved unheeded on the vendor's wild hair, and the top lost its momentum and fell from the marble slab. The tin cobra flipped over to reveal its unpainted belly, and a man lay dead on the sawdust-covered floor.

A nervous crowd eddied around him, falling back when they saw the pistol clutched in his hand. Shouts arose— *"ella, ella"*—and fingers were pointed at Muriel, who shrank back as if every finger were a gun. A delicate stream of blood seeped out from the back of the dead man's head, to the delight of some of the onlookers. The flies arrived long before the police did.

* * *

Her features drawn and sharp over the sweetheart neckline of her dark blue dress, Lourdes Pagano folded her hands in her lap over the paperback novel and waited for the bus to pull out of the terminal. Her overnight case was tucked securely into the overhead rack; she had found the reading light and was ready to turn it on when the long ride began. Everything about her was neat, done to perfection. The gloves she was wearing were not the ones she had worn an hour ago; her dark veil lay stinking in a public trashcan; the gun had been left in the market, placed carefully in a bunch of small fat bananas which encircled it like a hand.

She had remembered everything: foot powder, shampoo, maps and the target lessons she had been given by her father, the arms dealer.

It was night when the bus stopped. The sky in Mexico City was bright with lighted signs. Lourdes took a cab to the depot. In the dining car, heading for the Guatemalan border, she spoke now and then to other travellers and their children, saying, in her Argentinian way, *vos, che, chau,* and uttering the *zha, zha* sounds indigenous to the region of the River Plate. Nobody noticed. They had no ear, she thought contemptuously. She thought about the inquest which would be held in Zacatecas. Would anyone remember his Caribbean accent—the way he used the *-illo* ending for diminutives? Like a Cuban. Would they recall his behavior in the hotel dining room? He had put five teaspoons of sugar in his coffee, as one would if one came from an island where sugar cane was the major crop. Would the desk clerk remember that he had said *parquear?*

Lourdes travelled on. She met and talked briefly with simple people. She showed her passport and crossed borders. Her lipstick wore flat in its tube, but still she travelled on. On a railroad platform in El Salvador someone asked her how to operate a coin telephone. In Nicaragua a leper begged from her. She buttoned her gloves in the stifling heat.

In Panama the tracks ran out. It was time she took her chance. She alighted from the train and reserved a seat on an airplane. Then, near the public phone, she counted the money she had left. Bernie Axelrod had been generous: there was enough for a night in a first-class hotel. She steamed out wrinkles and took a long restful bath. The next day, when she went to the airport to take the plane for Buenos Aires, she expected the police to come there.

Nothing happened. The door of the jet plane was closed, the attendants took their seats, and they soared into the sky. The pilot used his radio, pulled levers and checked instruments. Inside its drum of fluid, his compass rolled like an eyeball, searching for the north. And Lourdes stared out her window, toward the south.

As the jet hurtled over the equator, sandwiches were served. Lourdes ate nothing. She was sustained by her intention, nourished by her unswerving purpose. Night fell and hid the cone of the continent far below her. The Big Dipper slipped below the horizon, yielding its place to the proper occupants of the southern sky: to the huge Centaur and the busy Fly, to the dull Octant and the trotting Wolf, and to the Cross, the smallest of all constellations, which, radiant and delicate, pointed its long bar to the unmarked pole of the heavens.

\* \* \*

When she thought of Lourdes Pagano, Muriel felt wispy and insubstantial, like the dim patterns of light and dark she saw before she put on her cataract glasses in the mornings. Someone had turned up a fierce photograph of Lourdes, and it ran often next to Muriel's picture in the newspapers. The first news stories invariably included a line drawing of the world, with curving arrows pointing to Austria, Mexico and South Africa—the Lovell arms route. Some papers printed photographs of carbine parts, and before-and-after mechanical modifications. Always somewhere there would be Lourdes, her features dark and distinctive. Muriel looked pale in every photograph. She was always described as "unwell" or "recovering".

There was must wild speculation about Lourdes' whereabouts. She was dubbed "the missing corporate wife".

Muriel was "convalescent"; Elba was "the spokesperson". Elba, surprisingly, turned out to have apple cheeks and dimpled hands. Muriel had been sent flying home by the doctor in Washington, to a good eye man at the UC Med Center. Plump Elba, armed by her steel-trap mind and Muriel's photocopies, talked to reporters while Muriel went under the knife. If she didn't shut up soon the story would be all talked out, and there would be no money for interviews with Muriel.

She couldn't help thinking about the money. She was already preparing a shift in her buying habits, circling items in the Brownstone Studio catalogue. Her eye, its clouded lens cut out and discarded, was almost healed. She could move her head normally, and Dennis was trying to help her get used to the infernal contact lens.

"Because I let Hank Blundon darken our door," he said, when Muriel reacted with surprise to his decision to re-enroll in engineering school. He was doing penance.

It was common knowledge now how the microwaves in the video display terminal had zapped Muriel's eye and caused her cataract. "You're lucky you don't have balls," Bernie had said several times, referring to the medical explanations in the newspapers. Everyone seemed to be talking about it. Through the glass windows of restaurants Muriel thought the men inside were talking to their dates and pointing animatedly to eyes and crotches. A malfunctioning cathode ray tube could superheat the body. Blood vessels would expand to compensate for the heat—everywhere except around the lens of the eye and the male testes, those two areas being poor in blood vessels. Sales of microwave ovens were down. "Everyone is obsessed with microwaves," Elba complained over the phone. "Soweto is burning, but they forget about the arms trans-shipments and the State Department complicity. It's always microwaves, microwaves."

Dennis was consumed with guilt. He had brought Blundon in, and he had sawed up Muriel's hairbrushes while she was away to make high grass for his model railroad. Muriel glanced at him over the sticky kitchen table; he sat, remote, brooding.

Bernie was even worse. He chauffeured Muriel from doctor to doctor, and kept talking about Lourdes. He came to watch *Four Feathers* on television, and during the commercial he said, "Don't tell the reporters anything more about the inquest in Mexico. They have some cockamamie legal system down there, but who can be sure they won't try extradition? Maybe they have an agreement with Argentina."

"I don't tell anyone anything. The reporters talk to Elba."

"Well, whoever. Someone's shooting a mouth off. Have you seen those articles about her in the *Chronicle?* What was that one last Sunday. . . 'Alleged Killer Was Stylish Dresser.' They had an interview with her goddam hairdresser, for God's sake. She ought to sue them, wherever she is."

"Nobody knows where she is. Believe me, Reuters is looking."

"She ought to sue them. I'm sure people see American newspapers down in Argentina. This is irresponsible journalism, it's libel. I'll handle the case."

But it wasn't true. There was no case to handle, because Bernie and Muriel both knew that Lourdes had fired the fatal shot. She had gone to Zacatecas on Bernie's money, and fired the fatal shot. They thought about this as the movie flickered.

"There's nothing to feel bad about," Muriel said. "You believed her. You gave her the money. She saved my life."

"I know," Bernie said, sucking on a lifesaver. His mouth was dry. He should have gone to Mexico himself.

*Four Feathers* ended. It had been one of their favorite

movies, but now the theme of blindness left them depressed. Muriel switched the set off. "I'm not like Ralph Richardson in the movie," she said. "I can see okay now. I'm getting used to the contact lens." Bernie didn't answer.

Everyone was strange, full of regrets. Muriel sometimes regretted that she had not been shot. I was meant to be the corpse in the market, she thought, but somehow everything was displaced. Dead from a bullet. At least it would have been definite. Better than being toasted, like a frozen waffle.

But such ideas went through Muriel's head only in her most morbid moments. As she regained her strength, her outlook improved. For the first time in her life, everyone seemed to know how to spell her last name. Omar arrived in San Francisco on one of his mysterious missions and phoned her. A State Department official made a foolish comment and the papers revelled in it. Later there would be a speaking tour.

She was lionized by COCOA and other office worker groups throughout the country. They wrote articles about her in their cheap offset newsletters, the headlines crookedly laid out in PressType. These articles were Muriel's favorites. She put them into her scrapbook and flipped through them with pleasure, reading them over and over. They were the only articles written about the Lovell arms smuggling case that made no mention of Lourdes.

In the years following her breaking of the Lovell story, Muriel was quoted and given awards. Doctors checked her body for radiation effects. There were indictments and trials, and executives went to minimum-security prisons. Muriel attended COCOA meetings and was treated with respect. She learned how to leaflet bank employees, how to call committee meetings. She drifted into labor activism.

But rationality poisoned it. Decisions were made democratically; there were conferences and caucuses. And through all of it, Muriel thought about champion divers, movie stars, secretive Chicanos, fugitives on the lam. "You were so courageous," everyone said, but she knew that her courage had been diffused through many people. She had been told where to stand, where to sit, what to steal, where to run. She was supposed to get shot, but somebody else did. She was supposed to be brave, but somebody else was.

"We're fighting for rights and respect on the job," Barbara Coffey always told prospective COCOA recruits as they stood in the doorway of the office, twisting their handbag handles, vacillating. "We're a support group," Barbara would say. And Muriel would nod at them from her field organizer's desk, longing for intrigue, yearning for betrayal.